Frances Elliot

The red Cardinal. A Romance

Frances Elliot

The red Cardinal. A Romance

ISBN/EAN: 9783743338555

Manufactured in Europe, USA, Canada, Australia, Japa

Cover: Foto ©Andreas Hilbeck / pixelio.de

Manufactured and distributed by brebook publishing software
(www.brebook.com)

Frances Elliot

The red Cardinal. A Romance

THE RED CARDINAL.

PROLOGUE.

I.

ALLOW me to introduce myself to the reader.

My name is Lucius Anstruther, a Catholic gentleman, of middle age, and of an ancient lineage in the north of England.

My tastes are æsthetic, my judgment sound, my manners courteous, I am even given to understand, somewhat imposing. As I was never handsome, age has naturally not improved my appearance. I value myself (if I may be allowed to express an opinion on my own character) specially on the qualities of the *heart*.

You will judge if I am right in the course of this narrative—commenced when I was travelling in the north of Italy, accompanied by my nephew, Frederick Stanley, my only sister's son, seventeen years old, an Etonian, who spends his holidays with me.

*   *   *   *   *

We crossed the Alps by the Mont Cenis road, and arriving in Florence on the morning of the 20th August,

187-, spent a few days in revisiting the galleries, specially the Pitti—not at all, I regret to say, appreciated by Frederick.

Then we started for my destination, Siena.

Siena—spite of steam, electricity and the nineteenth century—still in the middle ages. Nothing more modern than St. Catherine, its patron saint, and Charles V. and the Spaniards. The frowning walls and Gothic palaces, the sculptured piazzas, cavernous streets and mediæval churches, pictures and carvings, domes, turrets and campanili—of a much earlier date.

True there is a railway to Siena from Florence—continuing on to Rome—but the city itself altogether ignores it. The mediæval gates refuse to give it entrance; the lofty walls look down on it with scorn. Under which circumstances it is fortunate that it approaches the city by a long tunnel, and is so folded up and enveloped among the deep scoring of valleys among the hills as to be, save for an occasional puff of smoke, altogether invisible.

The length of time that we were kept waiting for our luggage at the station, a subterranean vault that chilled our very bones, caused Frederick to use language that shocked me in a youth. I am a patient man, because I am a polite one; therefore I was silent. In Frederick's excuse I must say that in no continental city, Madrid excepted, has my temper been so tried.

At length, a gaudily-painted omnibus (another concession to modern times) received us and our portmanteaus, and we drove slowly, through gloomy streets, to the "Grand Hotel."

Here we are received by Mr. Batty, announced in the bills as English, standing, his legs far apart, on a

door-mat, inscribed with the word "Welcome." The
mat, together with Mr. Batty's ostentatiously British
attire, close-cut hair, long whiskers, tight-fitting cut-
away coat, narrow trousers and laced boots, causing
in me grave doubts as to his nationality; an impression
confirmed by his slightly foreign accent and the number and profoundness of the bows with which he
greets us.

Mr. Batty's wife, who has placed herself behind
him, is unmistakably of our nation.

Those red cheeks, keen eyes, and that hungry
mouth, the rows of systematic ringlets, ill-fitting dress,
and slovenly shoes are imported, not native. (At sight
of Mrs. Batty, I mentally resolve to avoid a bargain
with her.)

Mrs. Batty curtseys low, Mr. Batty bows profoundly.
In this manner we are ushered up many flights of
steep stairs. Practice has given the Battys a facility
of standing at certain angles, and bowing—regardless
of consequences.

Being, as I said, personally polite, I try to imitate
them—and narrowly escape falling headlong. So I am
forced—spite of my natural instinct to return a lady's
salutation — to abstain and follow, Frederick at my
heels, muttering scraps of Eton vocabulary I do not desire to hear, certainly not favourable to the establishment.

At last we reach a landing-place on the second
floor, and before I can speak, Mr. and Mrs. Batty—I
don't know which, they act so simultaneously—amid a
profusion of bows, open a door, before which hangs
an embroidered curtain.

Inside is a spacious and handsome salon, looking

south. Several large windows stand open, admitting
an agreeable perfume of flowers, rising in the evening
air—also a charming perspective of valleys and mountains. Certainly not a bad place, this Grand Hotel!

Once safely landed in the salon, I endeavour to
return the courtesies these good people have accumulated on me in the perilous passage of the stairs.

I explain to them that my nephew, Mr. Stanley,
and myself——As I mention his name, I look round.
Frederick, a cigar in one hand, a match in the other,
is in the act of lighting it against the embossed gold
paper on the wall. After which, he flings the match
down, still burning, on the spotless carpet.

Mrs. Batty rushes forward to extinguish it. I also
rush forward. We run against each other.

"My dear Madam—a thousand pardons! Are you
hurt?"

"Oh, sir! What would that matter, in comparison
with an accident to you?"

Again bows all round. Again curtsies and apolo-
gies. Frederick meanwhile placidly smoking, as he
leans out of the window, drumming one of those odious
negro melodies now in vogue upon the sill.

"My nephew, Mr. Stanley, and myself," I continue
—(I should like to give Fred a hint that he is not at
his tutor's)—"only require accommodation for one
night."

"For *one* night!" ejaculate Mr. and Mrs. Batty in
unison. "One night!" As they repeat my words, their
countenances fall. They are still respectful, but profoundly depressed. Then, as ever, the female voice
first finds utterance.

"We had hoped," Mrs. Batty begins, "that the

gentlemen intended to make trial of this establishment for some weeks. Many weeks are not too long to visit the various attractions of Siena.

"Nature and art are both so well represented," Mrs. Batty speaks in a voice and manner which convince me she has learned these phrases out of a guide-book. "Our lions are," she continues with a heightened colour, and a satisfied gleam in her eyes, as of a school-girl glibly repeating her task, "The Cathedral, undoubtedly the finest Gothic monument in the north of Italy—the Church of San Domenico, with reliques of Saint Catherine and frescoes of the thirteenth century; the municipal palace in the great square, mentioned by Dante—the house of Santa Caterina, the tutelary saint of Siena. Outside the city," continues Mrs. Batty — with a slight drawl, but evidently delighted with herself—and delighting also Mr. Batty, who draws back a step or two, his hands in his capacious pockets, listening to her.

("Bravo, Mrs. Batty! Pray go on," say I.)

"Outside the gates there are many charming drives. Six miles to the mediæval fortress of Belcaro; one mile to the villa of Vico Bello; four miles to the Benedictine monastery of Pontignano." So elated is Mrs. Batty with the effect she is producing (I was mentally wondering who could have thought it worth while to teach her all this), that she paused to reckon the various places on the tips of her long, cruel-looking fingers.

Taking advantage of this interval, I again explain that my stay must be limited to one night only. I am on my way to Sant' Agata. Is the villa far from Siena?

At the name of Sant' Agata, a furtive glance passes between the spouses. Then their eyes drop on the carpet.

"No, Sant' Agata is not far as regards distance." It was the male Batty who spoke. "Oh no! but the road is for the last part bad—very—stony and mountainous. When you reach the forest—"

Here Mr. Batty pauses to take breath, and to glance under his eyelids towards his better-half.

"When you reach the ilex-forest, the mountains in fact of the Montagnola—Sant' Agata is visible. The woods run down towards the Tuscan Maremma to Grosseto and the sea."

Evidently Mr. Batty is losing the thread of his discourse, and continues feebly—

"Evergreen oak is called ilex here. The woods are—a-hem——"

Again Mr. Batty stops. The difficulty of an adjective evidently presents itself. His wife's keen eyes are watching him. As he proceeds, she frowns. He is not looking at her at the time, but at me; nevertheless, an electric affinity makes him conscious of her frown. Perhaps Mr. Batty is too polite to stigmatise the forest and the road by which I am to reach my friend's abode, by an offensive term. He shrugs his shoulders.

(To shrug his shoulders is invariably an Italian's way out of all manner of difficulties.)

"I have no personal experience, sir," he adds, as I stare at him. "The road is said to be bad; in some parts, indeed, almost impassable."

"Strange, very strange," I answer. "Do you mean to tell me that a man of the high rank and vast fortune of my friend, the Marquis Gonzago, lives in a house to which there is no suitable road?"

Mr. Batty's countenance now undergoes various changes. He spreads out his hands apologetically.

"I may have been misinformed, honoured sir. I have been told so."

(At this point Mrs. Batty comes to the front, serene and smiling—"Misinformed," she murmurs, "certainly misinformed.")

"But it is also said that the habits of the Marquis Gonzago are peculiar."

Here I can plainly see Mrs. Batty—whose black eyes follow every word her husband utters—touch his elbow, at which Mr. Batty starts, and from hesitating, falls into a stutter. "He believes—he has been told on good authority—that my lord the Marquis prefers solitude. Indeed, a good road might possibly——"

Here he utterly flounders, by reason of the reproving contraction of his wife's well-defined eyebrows.

"Do you mean to say the Marquis receives no visitors?"

"None whatever," is the prompt reply. "He lives alone with his younger brother, the Marquis Sigismund. You, sir, are the first gentleman, as far as we know, who has ever gone there."

"Strange, very strange!" I repeat, musing. "Is the road to Sant' Agata passable?"

"Oh yes, passable!" It is Mrs. Batty who now replies. "But the woods are dark and thick; and as to size, boundless! Boundless!" she repeats as if she enjoyed the sonorous intonation of the word.

Mrs. Batty further opines that a moderately early start is essential, so as not to be overtaken by night.

"No, no; not by night!" echoes Mr. Batty, impulsively.

"Is the forest safe?" I ask.

At this question I indubitably detect mysterious glances between the host and hostess. Neither is in a hurry to reply. Even Mrs. Batty colours and hesitates.

"Safe?" she repeats, as if to stave off a difficulty.

"Yes—safe? Do you not understand English, Mrs. Batty?"

"Oh, sir," with a smile and a curtsey. "You are pleased to be jocular!"

"Not at all, madam," I answer. "Pray reply to my question."

"The forest is perfectly safe from robbers, sir, if you mean that," Mr. Batty replies, advancing to the support of his wife.

Mr. Batty especially emphasises the word "robbers."

"That is enough for me," I answer. Still, as I look at him there is a strange expression about the man's face I cannot understand. He is certainly keeping back something which he, individually, might be inclined to tell, but which the will of his wife forces him to conceal.

At this instant, the valiant partner of his heart and home is in full retreat towards the door, with the intention—judging by her looks—of carrying her too communicative spouse along with her.

"You will be good enough," I say, "to order me a carriage and pair of strong horses, to be in readiness for to-morrow. I will fix the time of starting in the morning."

"I will take care that the best carriage in Siena awaits your pleasure, sir."

Mr. Batty's tone is quite hilarious; he feels himself on safe ground.

"Does the Marquis never come to Siena?" I ask, much puzzled by the obvious reluctance of Mr. and Mrs. Batty to answer plain questions.

"Never, sir! The palace is shut up. It contains a gallery of pictures and of objects of art almost unrivalled. I have lived many years in Siena, sir," continues Mr. Batty, "but I have never once had the honour of beholding his Excellency, the Marquis——"

Here I interrupt him by stating that I should like to dine. At this announcement their countenances brighten.

"Everything is ready,"—(they speak together, like a chorus)—"everything always is in readiness on the arrival of the Florence train. The butler shall be sent up with the bill of fare—or there is the *table d'hôte*—either an English, or an Italian *menu*——"

Then, in a coruscation of bows and curtsies, they leave the room.

*　　　*　　　*　　　*　　　*

The impression made upon me by Mr. and Mrs. Batty is decidedly unpleasant. Little has been said, but much has been implied.

"Impudent creatures!" I exclaim, my clenched fist descending heavily on the dining-table, by which I am seated an hour afterwards. "What do they mean to insinuate? How dare they speak as they do of my old friend?"

Frederick, sitting opposite, looks at me and laughs.

"What sort of diggings are you taking me to, uncle?"

Vexed and worn as I am, I administer a severe reprimand upon the use of slang.

"Dear old governor," is his reply, "I never pretended to be 'taut up' for company."

Worse and worse! Frederick is amiable and good, and spite of a rough outside, sensitive and impressionable, but a hopeless schoolboy!

"The Villa Sant' Agata," I say with dignity, "is one of the grandest and most celebrated abodes in Northern Italy. It—er—er—was built by a cardinal, my friend's uncle. It is mentioned in all the guidebooks," I add, by way of a clincher.

Fred does not seem in the least impressed, but opens that wide mouth of his with something I must call a grin.

I am getting ruffled. I feel it. I am perhaps unreasonably out of temper, but I speak in a calm, judicial tone.

"Remember, young gentleman, when I obtained leave for you to accompany me to Italy, instead of spending your vacation in reading with a tutor, it was understood that you were to accept my plans implicitly. Bear this in mind when you refer to my old friend and schoolfellow, the Marquis Gonzago, head of one of the oldest families in Italy."

"I am quite ready to appreciate all you say, uncle," Fred answers, with another provoking smile, "quite ready. Still I must say that your illustrious friend seems to be, by all accounts, rather a rum card."

I gasp with indignation, but I am fully aware that no protests can stop the boy.

"Don't get riled, uncle," adds good-tempered Fred, coming over to me and kissing me; "to-morrow we will invade the ogre in his inaccessible castle—brave the terrors of the forest and the outlandish trees old Boniface here talks about—and scramble up the road which is impassable. By Jove! it's just like Beauty and the Beast! Your friend is the Beast—but the Beauty! Ha, ha! Good night, Uncle Lucius. I'm dead with sleep."

II.

The Marquis Anzano Gonzago was my old chum and schoolfellow. We had never met since boyhood, but a romantic halo had ever surrounded his name. When I made up my mind to pay him a visit at Sant' Agata, a kind of juvenile ecstasy possessed me.

"Ah, why have you not come before, my Lucius?" was the first phrase in the letter he wrote in reply to my proposal for a meeting. "Better for me had we never parted," was the last sentence.

This letter, received at Florence, was a well-deserved reproof.

I had often been in Italy, but something had always intervened to prevent my going to Siena. Now, every mile that drew me nearer to him made me feel younger, gayer, more expansive. I longed for the morning to come, I pined to hear his familiar voice, to touch his hand, to see his handsome face. To meet him again would be to live once more in the sunshine of my youth, to feel the throb of eager pulses. Oh, boyhood! sweet are thy days! Why—oh, why are they delusive?

Anzano and I had first met, at the respective ages of ten and fourteen, at a preparatory school in Lancashire, kept by a Mr. Stitchome, a tutor. The number of pupils was limited to twelve, "which number no entreaty, however urgent, no bribe, however magnificent, on the part of parents, would induce him to exceed. For," continued Mr. Septimus Stitchome, in the doubtful grammar which characterised his illuminated prospectus, freely distributed among the Catholic families of the United Kingdom, "as a man of honour, he was well aware that the resources of his limited establishment could not suitably accommodate more, with justice to himself and a due regard to his patrons' interests; his constant and daily endeavour being to bestow on each pupil, not only a high class instruction, but a due share in the advantages of a home containing all the luxuries of a well-furnished residence, the incalculable blessings arising from the motherly affection and wholesome cooking of his wife, Mrs. Stitchome, and the fatherly eye of the principal himself, whose life's labour and supremest happiness it was to inculcate habits of devotion to the one true Church in a land of heretics, and to advance his pupils in the classical curriculum."

In a few words, we twelve boys were all Roman Catholics, preparing under his guidance for admittance into the college of Stonyhurst.

Thinking of Anzano, I recalled the dilapidated old manor house, once our home. Built of grey stone, the walls eaten into by moss and lichen of every hue from yellow to black, and from black to grey and sad-coloured white; tufts of fern and wallflower sprouting from the cracks and crevices after years of undisturbed growth; and dormer windows peeping out over the parapet, like living witnesses of misdeeds.

How plainly it all rises before me! The old walls, the low roof, the heavy sculptured cornice and ancient carvings, initials and arabesques, incongruously imbedded in the front, the whole trellised with vines trained upwards in a net-work of branches, which tapped ominously on our window-panes on windy nights.

Behind the house lay a quaint convent garden, shut in by lofty walls, pierced on one side by a range of Norman arches; the garden divided into formal gravel-walks, edged with box, and backed by espaliered apple-trees; the space between the box and the espaliers dedicated to flowers, cultivated by Mrs. Stitchome, a fierce-looking dame, with a pallid countenance, long, red nose, and black front of curls, arranged under a battered man's hat—attired in a smock-frock, which descended to her heels. The flowers, I say, cultivated by Mrs. Stitchome, with much more motherly care—spite the assertion in the illuminated prospectus—than she bestowed on us pupils, whom she cuffed and spoiled by turns, on a system of her own, founded, as far as I could observe, upon the strength of the potations of which she partook at our early dinner; beer inclining her to sleep and good-humour, gin-and-water to fury and blows.

Of our studies I remember little, except that the fatherly eyes of our tutor dwelt often on a birch-rod, hung over a carved cupboard beside the wide aperture of a fire-place in the school-room—once the hall

2*

of the manor-house—which birch-rod I, on one occasion—after having suffered repeated thrashings—in
fair fight, and carrying with me the silent applause of
the whole school, wrested from Stitchome's hands and
broke, dashing the fragments in his face.

For this feat the tutor threatened expulsion, but
subsequently relented. "For," as Mrs. Stitchome feel-
ingly observed in one of her dulcet moods, while I
was helping her to plant crocuses in her flower
borders, "Stitchome was that good, he could never
be brought to punish his enemies, much less a dear
little Catholic boy like you, Anstruther—let alone the
pay, and the time I have waited to have a new black
silk dress to go to the college chapel."

Chapel! How I wonder any human being could
ever enter that chapel except on compulsion! Oh!
the torture of early mass on frosty mornings! placed
as we were in a remote corner far from the stove,
under a Gothic window, with careful openings for
ventilation, gazing helplessly on our own breath curling in a bluish vapour round our bare heads, as we
tottered on our numbed feet, holding on by the pew
ledges.

The cold of these northern winters nearly killed
my friend, the poor little foreigner, who went to hospital
for some weeks, after one specially frosty Sunday, to
emerge at last, wrapped up by Mrs. Stitchome in wool
and flannels, like a sick canary.

My friend, known in the school as "Saunders,"
his real name being Count Anzano Gonzago (he had
not then inherited the title of marquis from his
father, nor the vast estates of his uncle, the Cardinal
Flavio), was much petted by Mrs. Stitchome, not from

the slightest consideration for his rank, which she was far too hazy to appreciate, but from the fact which she did arrive at understanding, that as the son of a great Italian nobleman and the nephew of a cardinal, he might serve as a useful bait by which to catch foreign pupils.

She would take the aristocratic little Anzano on her voluminous lap after dinner—spite of his desperate struggles to get free—and cry over him, calling him in a thick voice: "A blessed little gentleman, sent to comfort her, who ate but little, and never wore holes in his socks. You are all vulgar beasts by the side of him—vulgar, common beasts!" she cried, gazing vaguely round, and menacing us with her fists. After which outbreak, a copious flood of tears would roll down her cheeks, to be followed by a long sleep, during which her equanimity was restored.

On warm summer days, after dinner, Mrs. Stitchome reposed on a stone bench, in front of the manor house, under the shadow of a looping-on stone.

Here she would doze, while the ducks and hens gathered round her feet, pecking at her draggled skirts and old shoes. If any one passed, she would open her heavy eyes for a moment, address some remark to them more forcible than polite, then doze off again. But if she caught sight of "Saunders," she would call him to her peremptorily, and overwhelm him with kisses.

I fear neither "Saunders" nor myself distinguished ourselves by the rapid acquisition of knowledge, inculcated by our tutor's birch-rod. Stitchome was a homely man, but he was a scholar, and did his duty by us as far as we would let him.

Anzano, gifted with a fine memory and lively fancy, loved study, but unfortunately he loved my company more.

I was attracted to him by the irresistible force of contrast. He, gentle, tender, poetical—I, active, boisterous, and ready for any mischief—it was I who made him idle. I hated the Latin grammars, also the Delectus, and every other book of the kind, and avenged myself on them by kicking them round the room instead of learning my lessons.

When I did apply myself, it was the events of actual life which interested me. I did make real efforts to construe the stirring pages of Cæsar—easy Latin, too—over which I ambled without encountering too many pitfalls. Later, the battles of Homer, and such little bits of Xenophon as I could understand, attracted me vastly. I, too, took my place at the siege of Troy—I heard the shrill cries of Cassandra, beheld Hector at the wheel of Achilles' chariot dragged round the walls, Andromache's despair, and the flames of the doomed city mount upwards blazing to the skies.

Then the scene changed. I was carrying my spear in the ranks of that heroic little band of the "Ten Thousand," gallantly retreating over the Eastern plains in the teeth of their foes. With them I suffered hunger and thirst, the prick of the Persian darts, and the wounds their flying javelins inflicted. All this I could understand and appreciate.

My friend's more passionate nature dwelt rather on the weird and the poetic. The tragic woes of Dido described in the long hexameters of Virgil drew tears from his eyes, spite of the jeers of our tutor and the scorn of the older boys. He, dear fellow, sympathised, but understood not; and once, amid the titter of the whole school, asked Stitchome, "Why Dido was so unhappy after she came out of the cave?"

The sparkling wit and suppressed irony of Horace found no response in Anzano's tender soul, while I, as far as my ignorance could compass it, revelled in it.

But it was at a later period, when we were promoted into Greek tragedy, that the difference in our tastes became most apparent. Anzano's mystery-loving nature developed into a passionate delight in the study of Euripides and Sophocles, while I, on the contrary, shirked what I stoutly maintained "could never have happened," mocked at the theories of inexorable fate, and derided the great goddess Nemesis with her train of black-winged Erinnys.

As to Anzano he surrendered himself blindfold to the terrible spell, he grew pale and trembled; and with his large dark eyes riveted on the page, devoured every detail of those monstrous crimes and nameless horrors which the system of modern tuition opens to the mind of the *ingenuus puer*.

"What have you to do with an avenging deity, old boy?" I used to ask him, laughing at his awe-struck face. "You will never commit a crime."

"Who knows?" he would gravely reply, looking steadfastly at me. "Who knows what may happen to me before I die? I may not commit a crime myself, but I may fall under the power of fate by another, as Orestes did through his mother, Clytemnestra. If you would work up your Greek, Lucius, you would understand that the punishments of Nemesis often fall upon the most innocent people. Why, even Herodotus believed in Nemesis, and he was not a poet."

I often found Anzano in summer time, stretched on the grass under a tree, poring over the ghastly story of Œdipus Tyrannus, in a daze of rapturous horror, muttering to himself the words of that terrible soliloquy:

"*Be quick, in the name of heaven! Hide me! Or slay me! Or cast me into the sea that you may never see me more! Hear me, and fear not! For there is no living man can bear such suffering as I!*"

"Go away, Lucius!" he would shriek out, when he saw me approaching. "I am Œdipus! I have married my mother, and murdered my father, and the gods have cursed me!"

*   *   *   *   *

But oh! the ecstasy of hanging up our gowns and caps on the pegs in the schoolroom, and running out, bare-headed, into the fresh free air!

From the walled garden I have mentioned, with the straight gravel walks bordered by espaliered apple trees, we passed through the Norman arches into what had once been a fine old shrubbery and orchard, now run wild, the green sward serving as pasture for a few sheep ("muttons" Anzano always called them), to be slaughtered for the benefit of the school. As the grass was useful, the shrubbery was also utilised as a run for pigs and calves, the calves not roaming at will like the pigs, but fastened disconsolately to the apple trees.

Overhead spread a delicious tangle of laburnums, syringas, lilacs, and guelder-roses, broken by a larger growth of elms and horse-chestnuts. Cherry-trees came later—shrouded in a white pall, as though snow had fallen — also sloes and hawthorns; the yellow laburnums twisted their golden ringlets, and the pure syringa strewed the ground with petals.

Exquisite old wilderness! How I loved it! Especially in the spring-time, when the soft winds showered down flowers in our faces, and the pollen of the grasses covered our feet!

How sweetly the birds sang too, the rooks perched high up in the elm-trees, cawing sagaciously; on fine days, the old ones gravely circling round the tree-tops like senators, then returning sedately to the same branch from which they had started, chattering low to the young ones, hurriedly fluttering up and down!

"Saunders" never delighted in the outward face of nature as I did; he was too much engrossed in Greek fatalism. But he walked serenely in and out among the shrubs, with a calm, pensive countenance, or aided me in my daily endeavours to drive off the abominable sheep from nibbling the tree-trunks: "a labour," as he observed, "as endless at that of Sisyphus."

What treasures to us boys, too, lay hidden beneath the quick-set hedges framing the flat green fields, warm and dry under a range of hills, pale in the distance. On these hills our eyes rested dreamily, as on the outskirts of an enchanted world, too remote and mysterious to be trodden by foot of mortal man.

Autumn was very grand at Stitchome's, the scarlet haws wreathing the hawthorns, side by side with the flame-coloured hips of the hedge-rose; and luxuriant blackberries to be plucked from among sharp brambles. It is true we often streaked our hands with blood as well as with juice; but the blackberries tasted none the less sweet. The deadly nightshade twined in dangerous proximity to the blackberries and trails of bryony and white-bearded clematis besides,—the brown fibres of the hop, as strong as whip-cord, binding the whole together in a woodland knot.

Later on, coveys of young partridges came, whirring over the ground to nestle among the furrows, and now and then we caught sight of a majestic pheasant —while, well to the south-west, the pale yellow sunsets cast gleams of coming frosts, and sombre mists gathered under the hills.

"But," as I often told Anzano, "Give me May and June when I am king! Then the earth is large, the days long, the very nights are full of light, and glorious with stars. Sweet smells come up from the earth after rain-showers, and plums and gooseberries are ripe."

To which the dear boy, looking up from his book, would respond sweetly, as he always did, in his rich, musical voice, that "I was quite right, only he was happy with me, whatever was the season."

It would have been very jolly in the long frosts to catch birds in brick-traps; but alas! concerning these traps, Anzano and I ceased to be of one mind. He, with his southern blood a-flame, vociferating, and furious at what he called my "cruelty," would seize the captive bird in his soft-skinned hands, kiss its frightened beady eyes, then fling it upwards triumphantly into the air.

Alas! for *"cruel me"!* Was there ever such a place as these hedge-rows for nests? But, with Anzano by my side, the nests were as impossible as the bird-traps. I dared not so much as trust myself to

look at them. He would have left me for ever (he
said so) had I meddled with the eggs, or worse still,
had I handled the young ones. I could only walk
along beside him with my eyes fixed on the ground.

Any school-boy will understand what I suffered.
There birds by hundreds—cuckoos and jays, thrushes
and blackbirds, and wrens and robins—all hopping
about, pecking at the rose-berries and bryony, and
laughing at me!

I speak of my sacrifices to friendship in the matter of brick-traps and birds'-nests. This was not all.
To please Anzano, I gave up cricket, foot-ball, and
leap-frog. For this I was jeered at—even threatened
—by the rest of the school, as if I had been a criminal.
Anzano himself would not speak to the other boys, so
they were forced to leave him alone. But I, more am-
bitious, desired to stand well with both parties.

Need I say I failed, as signally as does the Christian who tries to serve God and Mammon!

When the distant shouts of our comrades reached
us from the cricket-field, Anzano and I were often
lounging, side by side, on the banks of a sluggish
river, bordered by alders, forming the assigned limit
to our playground; the heavy scent of the meadow-
sweet and pink willow-wand wafted to us as we lay,
and beds of white water-lilies calmly sleeping before
us on the stream.

Once, I remember, he wrote an ode to a water-
lily. After much hesitation as to which metre he
should select, he chose the Alexandrine. The ode (it
was in Italian, of course), began: "White Mermaid
Queen!" which when I heard, I burst into a fit of
laughter. It seemed so odd a lily should have a scaly

tail like a fish! He, dear fellow, much mortified, tore up the paper and shed tears.

He was sensitive and superstitious to excess. He believed in the evil eye and in witchcraft, and made "horns" whenever he passed a squinting old labourer who assisted Mrs. Stitchome in the cultivation of her borders. Also he believed firmly in an actual, present devil, who would attack him with horns and hoofs, if he were not guarded by a medallion of the Virgin, sewn up in a little satin bag that hung round his neck.

As to ghosts and spirits, he was an unconscious polytheist, so thickly had he peopled every spot with supernatural presences. Wherever four roads met must be haunted ground, with certainly a corpse buried there. Damp, dark corners made him shiver and cling closer to me; the baying of a dog at night was the cry of a passing spirit, and a peculiar sighing of the wind before rain the flutter of angels' wings, hovering about to catch good children and carry them away.

As he grew older, I ridiculed him out of many of these fancies, but to the last, a narrow staircase at the old manor-house, leading to a dormitory in the roof, where we two slept alone, in two white dimity-curtained beds, no power on earth would induce him to pass alone at night.

Trembling like a leaf, he often woke me to declare he heard footsteps stopping at our door (I am free to confess my knees shook under me as I rose in bed to listen), and once he nearly terrified me to death by whispering in my ear that a white face was peering at him through a chink in the wall; but as I could see nothing, and the door was locked when our as-

sistant tutor came at the usual hour next morning to
call us, I tried to forget all about the white face putting it down to Anzano's fancy.

At length the time came for us to enter the college at Stonyhurst—a melancholy occasion, on which
Mrs. Stitchome's feelings so far overcame her that she
was carried off to bed, hopelessly drunk.

At Stonyhurst we lived necessarily much less in
each other's company. Our mutual affection remained
undiminished, but the expression of it was curtailed.

Social distinction had gone for nothing at Stitchome's.
Not so at college. My friend, as the nephew of Cardinal Gonzago—known to stand high in papal favour
—was the object of general attention. Our priestly
professors allowed no occasion to pass without marking
the immeasurable difference between Gonzago and
myself. I was but the son of a Catholic gentleman of
good descent and average fortune. Anzano came of
an historic line, boasting the names of great prince's,
popes, ambassadors and generals.

If anything could have drawn him out of the
dreamy existence he had hitherto led, it would have
been the homage of which he now involuntarily became the object. But his nature was too steadfast, his
heart too true, to allow the subtle poison of flattery
seriously to affect him. Never was he so happy as
when he could break away from these attentions and
wander about with me in his old aimless way—flinging himself down on the grass under an overspreading
oak, or in the sheltered hollow of a mound, one of
those very hills we had sighed after in the pale distance, as enchanted ground.

While I smoked, he would take a volume of his

favourite Euripides from his pocket, and forget all,
except that we were together.

"Dear old Lucius!" he would say, suddenly recalling my presence, and lifting up those speaking
eyes of his to mine. "Dear old Lucius, keep near me
—it does me good!"

I cannot say that my feeling towards him was
entirely free from some suspicion of envy. Until we
became students at college I had been his superior,
his adviser, his protector. Now the tables were turned.
"Saunders" was everything—I nothing. The highest
place at table, the most prominent position on all occasions of ceremony, was assigned to him. All his
exhibitions were applauded—his health, his comfort,
the subject of anxious solicitude—while I, his elder,
came up in the ruck of the college. No professor was
moved to praise my bad Latin verses, and I might
have lain in hospital a year before one of the authorities
would have taken any heed of me.

Reflecting on these supposed wrongs in private,
my heart grew big; but when I came under the spell
of Anzano's generous nature, all was forgotten. To
him I never dared hint a consciousness of my too
evident social inferiority. He could not help it, and
the fact would only have distressed him beyond
words.

There are certain natures so absolutely simple in
their perfect loyalty—so essentially modest under all
vicissitudes of life—that the grosser passions are unknown to them. Of such a nature was Anzano!

Called upon to take his place, on grand occasions,
with men of the highest rank—Catholic magnates and
celebrated professors—he acquitted himself with grace

and self-possession. Never, for an instant, did he encroach on the fortuitous accident of his birth, but was ready, in a moment, to fall back, a unit amongst the multitude.

At length the time for our examination grew near. In power of concentrated thought on special subjects, I beat Anzano hollow. My health was more robust, my cast of mind firmer and more masculine. His studies wanted precision. He had read too long and too much only to satisfy the cravings of his peculiar fancy. I, on the contrary, had come later, to grasp knowledge for its own sake.

Once more my old superiority asserted itself. I took a high place. Anzano would have failed utterly, but for the manifest favour shown him by the examiners, anxious to exhibit his name and rank to the observation of the public.

I feel now, as I write, though such long years have passed, the pressure of his arms round my neck, after the result of the examinations were announced. Tears dimmed his dark eyes.

"I am heart-broken, Lucius!" he said, "humiliated! Your success only reconciles me to life. Else I think I should drown myself."

Then came the parting!—the vows of eternal friendship—the promises of a constant correspondence. The vows of friendship—on my side at least—are still unbroken; but the letters! Not a line ever passed between us, until I wrote the other day from Florence, offering to pay him a visit. It was then that he replied with the reproachful words I have already mentioned:

"It would have been better for us both, Lucius, had you never left me!"

*   *   *   *   *

From time to time, up and down in the world, I had heard of him. His father died soon after he left Stonyhurst. Many years later, his uncle, Cardinal Flavio Gonzago, died also, and Anzano inherited his vast estates. I heard of his brilliant career, not only in the great centres of Italy, but at Paris and Vienna. England he never re-visited, and by some fatality I invariably missed him elsewhere.

And now, after a separation of nearly five-and-twenty years—actually arrived within nine miles of his residence—a discord had been struck in the harmony of our meeting, by the vulgar gossip of the landlord of the Grand Hotel!

All sorts of doubts and surmises kept rising in my mind. How should I find him? Would he be greatly changed? Would the presence of his younger brother chill our intercourse? Would the contrast between the powerful noble and the poetic youth be too much for me? Was he really glad to see me? After his letter, I felt this was a foolish doubt; but I was in a mood to doubt everything.

Should I find him, as these people had insinuated, prematurely aged and saddened? What motive could he have for becoming such an absolute recluse? What could have altered the current of his life, which I knew had, for many years, been such as befitted his rank and fortune?

I felt agitated and disturbed. At last, I actually came to the point of doubting whether I had done right to come at all, after the lapse of so many years.

Might it not be an intrusion on the habits he had adopted? How was it possible—if he led the life described to me—that I should be welcome?

Pursued by these distressing thoughts, I finally took refuge in bed. Even there they pursued me. After tossing about for some time, I heard a church clock strike twelve. The stroke sounded to me like a funeral knell. The funeral of whom——?

At length I fell into an uneasy sleep, and dreamed that I was wandering in a dense wood of black, unearthly trees. Before me rose the outline of a statue, battered and worn. It stood aloft on a pedestal. An indescribable horror seized me as I gazed at the empty, cavernous eyes, grinning, toothless mouth, and shattered, moss-grown limbs. Under the statue, huddled in a heap, lay what looked like a human form. The face was turned to me. In the dim light I beheld the emaciated features of Anzano.

I awoke in terror. So distinct was the scene—so life-like—it seemed less a dream than a vision—the place, the pale moonlight, and my poor friend's distorted countenance!

Then I slept again—a long and tranquil sleep—until the brilliance of the autumnal sun beaming into my room, forcibly chased from my mind every feeling but that of enjoyment.

END OF PROLOGUE.

THE STORY.

CHAPTER I.

On the afternoon of the next day, Fred and I took leave of Mr. and Mrs. Batty and drove out of Siena by the San Marco gate.

It was very hot.

We had been tempted by the splendid Cathedral, which moved even Frederick to admiration, and the many churches and galleries, to make our start later in the day than we intended. The grand old city, throned, like Rome, on many hills, its domes and pinnacles clasped together by a zone of Cyclopean walls, lay behind. In front a perfect sea of mountains, the summits wrapped in a hot haze; but loftier and grander than all the rest the double crown of Monte Amiata rose clear in the brazen sky, and the dark scoring of unnumbered valleys and defiles, marked the incessant heaving of the land.

So far the road was excellent, but steep and tortuous. The distance from Siena to Sant' Agata is nine miles. That does not look much on paper, but it is necessary to know what nine miles means on a mountain road in Italy. Five hours' driving at the

very least! There is no twilight; evening is coming
on, and we have barely reached half the distance.

At this moment we are climbing a steep ascent,
two miles long. The horses are streaming; Frederick
and I more than agreeably warm; the sun is scorching, and there are myriads of flies, quite impartial as
to which they bite—us or the horses.

Now a broad flat stretch of land lies before us,
dividing a richly cultivated plain. Here, too, there
are mountains—"The Montagnola," mentioned by Mrs.
Batty—extending to Grosseto in the Tuscan Maremma
and the seaboard at Piombino.

Dear Italy! Find me an outlook from Ivrea to
Taranto without mountains.

As we pass, we note the vines, festooned from tree
to tree, laden with juicy grapes blackening for the
harvest. The corn is yellow in the husk, the pointed
leaves of the maize already fallen back withered from
the stalk. There are the blue flowers of the hemp,
the red blossoms of the saintfoin, and peach and fig-
trees growing in between.

Now the road takes a turn to the right, up an in-
cline, towards a circular chapel, of yellow, unbaked
bricks, with a flat roof and stone portico; a group of
dark pine trees overhead. The yellow walls glisten
(they would burn the hand, I am sure, if it touched
them). A little bell rings from the belfry, and a woman with gold pins in her hair, and a lace handkerchief folded over her red stays, looks out of a door
adjoining, probably the presbytery.

As we slowly ascend the rise, a brown-skinned
clerk—a shock of matted hair falling over his eyes,
and wearing a dirty shirt—rushes forward.

"Gentlemen—honoured gentlemen!" he cries in a shrill voice. "Stop! listen!"
andWe who are in the carriage—I, who am speaking, Fred—listen, but cannot stop, for the simple reason that we have no control over our driver.

Filippo, a stalwart youth, whom we engaged in the Piazza at Siena, where we with difficulty escaped skin whole from other drivers seeking a job—Filippo, I say, his reins well in hand, his brigand hat jauntily set on one side, a red carnation in his ear, has no intention either of listening or drawing rein.

We see this in the erectness of his back and the squareness of his shoulders. We see that he despises the ragged clerk, the little roadside church of unburnt bricks, and the tinkling bell. Does he not dwell in a city where there is a cathedral of white marble, challenging all others, beautiful as a dream, and so vast that it covers an acre of land? A cathedral with a roof whereon stands an army of sculptured saints and martyrs, facing the blue sky, among minarets and domes, arches and pilasters?

"Gentlemen—good gentlemen! Stop, for the love of heaven!" again shouts the clerk, addressing us inside. And as he shouts, he digs his tawny hands into his hair, then endeavours to seize the bridles.

Before I can speak, Filippo lashes his horses forward.

"*Canaglia!* — pig!" he shrieks, springing on the splashboard, and whirling his whip aloft. "Loose my horses, or I will slay thee!"

"Gentlemen—oh, pious gentlemen!" cries the clerk, as he wrestles with the animals, who plunge and rear "By the sacred God of the world, what would you do?"

I am going to speak, when Fred interrupts me.

"Uncle Lucius!" he cries, in the wildest excitement, "why do you interfere? Let them fight it out, the cripples! My stars! What a lark!"

In a quiet way I am almost as much excited as Fred. I want to see who will get the best of it.

Resolutely, and despite of Filippo's whip whistling round his head, and of the horses' hoofs rattling about him, the clerk grasps the reins.

"Listen! Do you not know? It is the day of St. John! The procession! The body of the Lord! See, yonder it comes!"

Now it is my turn to spring to my feet.

"If you do not stop," I cry out to Filippo, "I will summon you before the Questura at Siena."

CHAPTER II.

A PAUSE ensues. Frederick, also on his feet, urges on Filippo by his gestures. But he drops the reins, and shakes his head in silence.

I pull Frederick back on the seat, giving him my opinion of his interference in one or two forcible words.

The clerk has withdrawn his hand; the horses quiet themselves. Only the little bell overhead rings out louder than before, swinging wildly on its cord, and overbalancing itself in its zeal.

Softly, out of the delicate blue-green of the olives, a low chant arises—a muffled chant as of a swarm of bees. Louder and louder it comes, rising on the still air. At length a long black trail appears upon the dusty road—a procession bristling with lighted torches and tapers carried by some fifty peasants, walking two and two. Every eye is cast down, every mouth open, intoning the sing-song litanies.

One man in front, wrinkled by the labour of some seventy years, bears a white staff which he brandishes aloft; a gold star cut out in paper pinned, like an order, on his breast.

"Here's a go!" cries Frederick, staring with all his eyes. "I say, uncle——"

Alas! nothing impresses that boy. As a Catholic, I am deeply affected. The devotion of these poor people is most touching.

On they come, slowly, slowly. A crucifix, some eight feet high, gaudily gilt, the sponge, hammer, nails and spear conspicuous; at the top a crown of thorns. More peasants, two and two, a deeper drone in their voices. A faded tabernacle, red and yellow, suspended on four gilt poles, and under the tabernacle the parish priest, in his hands the Host, raised high above his head.

I soon came to know that priest better.

His name is Don Antonio Perletti, and the name of his little church San Martino al Monte.

Don Antonio presents the aspect of a man not old, but prematurely shrivelled. He does not work in the fields like the peasants, but he looks almost as much a countryman as they.

The effect of all this on our driver is amazing. Not only has he ranged his horses reverently on one side, but he himself is kneeling—his hat beside him —in the road. If either of the horses, stung by an especially aggravating fly, kicks, he mutters under his breath:

"A thousand curses! Have you no religion, Bestia, when you see the Santissimo?"

Then he crosses himself, stoops down and kisses the earth.

"What a brick that fellow is!" exclaims Fred, in a burst of genuine admiration. I am glad to say he also has taken off his hat, and is behaving with unusual propriety.

Meanwhile, the procession passes into the church, the peasants crowd in after, and all kneel at the altar.

Filippo is on his feet again, seizes the reins, vaults

upon the box, cocks his hat, gives a twitch to the carnation behind his ear, cracks his whip and starts off at a rapid trot.

Sharp to the right we turn.

"Is this a road?" I exclaim audibly.

"No, uncle," responds Frederick. "A sheep-track. You were forewarned. We are approaching the enchanted castle. Remember Mr. Batty."

I *do* think of him and sigh.

Red-soiled, rocky and as steep as a house-side—a pretty road indeed! On either hand, the outskirts of an immense ilex-wood, covering the heights which rise above our heads; low, stunted trees with dark shining leaves; here and there a cypress or a juniper—the roots clinging to mossy boulders, and thyme and heather growing between.

As we mount higher and higher, into the mystery of the great wood, a magnificence of trunk and limb, a splendour of ever-green foliage, enshrouds us in a fantastic gloom. Not a plant or tree of lively green. The rays of the setting sun strike through the branches in horizontal lines; below, open out deep ravines and precipitous dingles, where copper-coloured rocks protrude, and stony avalanches mark the site of winter torrents.

Filippo allows the reins to drop on the necks of his wiry little horses. They pant; their sides are streaming—the flies stick to them in shoals. Vainly does he pass his whip over them—they return again instantly.

"'This road is of Satan," he mutters. "His work when he fought with the angels. Why does a Christian Marquis live in such a hole?"

Then to his horses:

"Patience, my children! Patience! In the shade the flies will vanish. We shall soon be at the statue of the Satyr. There it is cool!"

As we are crawling upwards, Frederick and I get out and walk, a proceeding which offends our driver not a little, until I manage to make him understand that Englishmen are always on their feet.

Meanwhile, the sun has set, the shadows deepen, the great wood thickens. Twisted branches glisten like serpents' eyes, and veils of white moss stand out like old men's beards. Low rocks upheave the ground, black and uncertain. There is no underwood to soften the eerie lines; nothing but weeds, grown rank in the shade, wafting a strange narcotic perfume. But few leaves strew the ground.

These ilex-woods change but little with the season. They bear within their bosoms no flowers to charm the eye, nor do they shelter any birds in their thickness, nor insects on the ground. Death is in their shadow—death to all that grows; so that the very serpents loathe them, and the worms curl themselves up and die!

The landlord's words come to me with a start. Frederick remembers them likewise. If he, like myself, were not overcome by the strangeness of our position, I know he would chaff me unmercifully. But, for the first time in his life, I find Frederick incapable of fight of any kind.

At this moment a dense cluster of impenetrable ilex trunks gather in front. In other places there have been breaks, rough, rocky spaces of broken ground, with stunted timber, where recent cuttings had somewhat thinned the wood. But here I can distinguish but a dim whiteness between the boles. In spite of my reassuring words to Frederick, a feeling of distrust is creeping over me.

"How far are we from the Villa?" I ask our driver.

"Excellencies, we are close under the statue of the Satiro. It is just a mile to the Villa."

"Is that the statue of the Satiro?" I ask, picking my way carefully towards a large white mass which looms before me.

"Precisely, Excellency. We call it the 'Satiro' for short. The woods are very thick and very dark hereabouts."

His voice is low, his manner embarrassed.

I would not tell Frederick for the world—I hardly like to confess it to myself—but *that is the statue I saw in my dream* last night, a muffled figure lying under it.

Something warns me that I am entering on some mysterious phase of life. The black trees—the pale moonlight—the weird shadows. All are the same!

"What is the Satyr?" asks Frederick, grown very grave.

"I don't know," Filippo answers, in an odd, suppressed tone. Then, placing his face close to mine, he whispers into my ear: "They say it is the devil. The peasants have destroyed it with stones."

Cautiously advancing, I behold the outline of a colossal figure, some twenty feet high, raised on a lofty pedestal. It is without form, and void, save in the lower extremities, where folds, as of drapery, can be distinguished. The surface, indented with holes and cracks innumerable, is filled with moss and earth; the trunk surmounted by what once had been a head, with stony hair and horns, now flattened into a hollow disk, bearing a faint resemblance to humanity; eyes, nose and mouth battered into blankness by volleys of stones (they lay in heaps upon the ground, silent witnesses of the superstitious fury of the passers-by); a satyr's legs and hoofs, faintly discernible, are crumpled up under the body in a sitting posture.

A grassy circle opens in front, bordered by giant trees. Under the trees a solitary marble bench, blackened by rain and time.

"She sat there," whispers Filippo, who has silently followed me, pointing to the bench, "when she was taken. Now, they say, another sits there, as like her as self to self."

I turn round, utterly confounded.

"What do you mean?" I ask. I am speaking in the same hushed tone. For a moment an inexpressible dread possesses me. I soon shake it off, but for a few instants I am literally paralysed. "Either tell me, or drive on. What have you got to say?"

"Yes—what?" puts in Frederick, who has followed me, pale as death.

"If your Excellencies will move on a little, I will tell you what you please," says Filippo. As he speaks, he contemplates the statue with dilated eyes, as if expecting to see it move.

"I can say nothing here," he whispers, leading the way back into the road. "I feel safe beside my horses; with them I care not for spirits."

"Spirits!" I exclaim.

"Spirits!" echoes Fred, backing a pace or two.

"Do you mean to say the ilex wood is haunted?"

At first he does not answer. Then, leading his horses past the circle, where the moonlight gathers, he casts a hasty look around.

"It is not good to speak of such things here" (another searching glance), "although no one has ever seen her so late as this. It is always near the Ave Maria. She was taken then."

"Seen! Taken! Who was taken? Out with it, man!"

Filippo shakes his head.

"Come, come!" I continue coaxingly; my curiosity has now mastered my nervousness, and I am quite calm. The ludicrous aspect of our position also strikes me. In the middle of a strange wood, listening to a ghost-story. "We will remember *her*, whoever she may be, in the *buonamano*."

At this rather ill-timed jest, Frederick lays his hand on my shoulder, and scowls at me reproachfully.

"The story and the *buonamano*, or no story and no *buonamano*."

"Gentlemen!" says Filippo loftily, "I answer for nothing. It may be all true, or all false—I cannot say. I will tell you what I know. Your Excellencies will be liberal?" with a whine. "A poor man must live."

"Yes, yes," I replied impatiently. "Go on!"

CHAPTER III.

"Long, long ago," begins Filippo, "these mountains were all forest for hundreds and hundreds of miles. Not a church, not a house, from San Martino down to the sea. The lands have always belonged to the great Gonzago family.

"Next before the marquis, a cardinal—Cardinal Flavio—came here in his villeggiatura to visit the hermitage of Sant' Agata, and took a fancy to the ilex-woods, and built a fine villa, with walks and gardens, all set with marble statues that overtop the trees.

"A cardinal! Dominedio! Priests are all alike; only this one was rich and powerful, a grand gentleman, neither young nor old, with a red face, they say, and a long nose. What they did up here, *chi lo sa?* They say that in the Thebaide, named after the deserts in Egypt and the monks, there were twelve chapels, one for every month in the year.

"Besides the chapels, the cardinal placed big statues, carved in marble, all round the house; mostly of pagans, who did not believe in God. Besides the Satyr here, there is the Hercules, sixty feet high. Per Bacco! You will see him in the morning, Signori, and gods and goddesses, saints and sinners—dozens of them.

"Why the cardinal put up the statue of the Satyr,

I cannot say; nor why it should quake and groan in the high winds. No one will pass after dusk where its shadow falls; no grass grows—no flowers—and why? I will tell."

At this moment a faint moonbeam strikes through the trees, and an owl hoots out of the ilex within the mystic circle, then flies away with a screech, its wings flapping against the boughs.

"Down in the valley there is a torrent," he points to a precipitous descent below, "dry in summer, and an old bridge; also the walls of what was once a hut. An old peasant lived there, called Giacomo, and with him his little granddaughter, Gigia. She had no mother, no father, no brother, no uncle—all were dead.

"The grandfather was a scholar, he had been a sort of secretary up at the villa. He could read and write—*via!* like a priest, without the Latin! And he taught Gigia.

"She was so small people called her the '*donnina*,' fair-skinned, with golden hair and blue eyes, like a little Jesus. You might know her anywhere, they say, by a droop she had in one of her eyelids, also by her black brows and eyelashes, which gave her a strange look. She had small hands and feet, and was not browned by the sun as other peasants, but white all over, like cream.

"The grandfather would not let her go out when it was hot, but made her sit in the terrace under the sloping roof, where the maize-tops hung in bunches to dry, her little fingers twisting the thread on the distaff, as she sang love-songs about '*amo*,' and '*adoro*,' and '*caro*,' and '*amaro*.' People called her the '*donnina*,' because she was so small—neither woman nor girl, as the folks said.

"When the shadows gathered, Gigia drove her grandfather's pigs into the ilex-woods to feed on the acorns. Mostly she loved to go towards the statue of the Satyr—that ugly monster there, with a mouth full of black earth and his hairy limbs curled under him.

"The stone bench in the circle of trees was her favourite seat. There she would weave garlands of wild flowers, singing her songs, while the pigs spread themselves all about, turning over the red earth. The old boar with a bell always let Gigia know where they were. If they wandered too far off, Gigia sounded a whistle, and the pigs came running back to her, as tame as dogs.

"One afternoon, as she was sitting under the shadow of the Satyr—an evil shadow, gentlemen, as everybody knows—there came a sound of harness-bells and wheels, and suddenly turning the corner, before she could run away, two carriages passed. In the last, a big, painted chariot, driving very leisurely, so as not to shake him, sat the Cardinal Flavio, all in red, with a broad hat on his head—red too.

"The Cardinal stared hard at Gigia, standing among the flowers which had fallen from her lap, and Gigia stared back at him. He made a sudden motion with his hand to stop the carriage. Then, seeming to think better of it, fixed his eyes on her still more steadfastly, nodded and smiled, and stroked his cheek with his fat white hand, on which were many glittering rings, Gigia, on her side, opening her blue eyes, and putting back her hair, the better to observe him.

"The Cardinal, still smiling, leaned forward and

spoke eagerly to his secretary, sitting opposite, a young priest with a white face and a look of terror in his eyes, who bowed low and said something, pointing towards Giacomo's hut.

"Then, casting a strange look at Gigia, the Cardinal took from his finger a ring, with a wonderful big diamond in it, and dropped it at her feet. As long as he could see her, he turned his head.

"When the ilex trees closed in and hid him and his red chariot, Gigia stooped down and picked up the ring. She had never seen a jewel before, and this lay in her hand like fire, without burning. Laughing to herself, she kissed it and wondered at it. Then, putting her two little fingers inside, she ran in among the ilex trees—the pigs after her—to show it to her grandfather, and tell him about the Cardinal.

"Old Giacomo listened in silence, and crossed himself several times. When she had done he laid his wrinkled hand upon her head.

"'May the blessed saints guard thee, Gigia, when I am gone. Don't wear the ring, child, it is unlucky. Go no more to the Satyr, my child!'

"Next day Gigia went out as usual with her pigs, the old boar with the bell trotting on in front. She promised her grandfather to go no more to the Satyr. If she kept her word, who can say?

"The sun set over the western hills towards Cajetano; the moon rose, but Gigia did not return. Giacomo listened for every sound. At last he heard the tinkling of a bell, and he knew it was the old boar running down the hill. With the boar would come Gigia.

"Not a bit! The old boar, as if he had a Christian

heart, stood opposite to Giacomo, and grunted violently —and the other pigs grunted too. It was clear they had a great deal to tell, poor beasts, if they could only have spoken. They were covered with mud, and panting as though they had been driven very hard, and so hungry that they gnawed the boards on the stair leading up to the door until the old man came down and fed them.

"'Though the pigs came back, Gigia never returned.

"Next day Giacomo was like a man mad. He wandered up and down the ilex-woods, calling out: 'Gigia! Gigia! *Donnina mia!'* mostly in the neighbourhood of the Satyr, standing there for hours, calling on her name. Other words too, he spoke, but no one cared to repeat them. He tore his hair, and groaned and wept, then threw himself upon the ground. The neighbours picked him up insensible, and carried him home in their arms, for he was too weak to walk.

"'That night, as he lay in his bed, looking at the moon and thinking of his little Gigia, there came to him a sound that formed itself into the song that Gigia used to sing, floating, as it were, out of the trees from the side of the Satyr, very faint and low like a moan, rising and falling with the sighing of the wind.

"Giacomo sat up in bed and listened. Could it be Gigia coming home at last? At that time of night!

"No—impossible! Vague and horrible presentiments came over him. Terror at her probable fate froze his very soul. While he was debating with himself what he should do, he heard quite plainly a faint knock at the door, and Gigia's voice calling to him from the terrace outside:

"'Granny! Granny!'

"In an instant he was up, and opened the door. There was only the moon shining brightly on the terrace. But, as true as Santa Caterina will save Siena by her prayers, Giacomo felt a cold little hand placed on his—a hand so small and slender, he knew at once it was Gigia's, and no other's, and a voice said to him: 'Dear Granny!' It was Gigia's voice, but he had never heard it with that tone before.

"As he stood there quite bewildered, the song sounded again very low among the trees, then fainter and fainter, up the hill towards the Satyr.

"Giacomo felt no fear, but he knew that he should never see the child again, and that, dead or alive, she had come to tell him so.

"All this was known among the peasants.

"Whether the Cardinal was told that Giacomo went up and down the woods, crying for Gigia, and speaking words that no one cared to repeat, or whether he had reasons of his own for getting the old man out of his way, who knows? That is a mystery. But sure it is that Giacomo was found one morning soon afterwards, lying under a tree, a dagger with a gold handle (such as no peasant owned) thrust into his throat.

"Where Gigia had gone, who could tell? It was said by some charcoal-burners, that on the evening of the day she had disappeared, they had seen two men, wearing the Cardinal's livery, along with a young priest, hiding among the ilex-trees at the back of the

Satyr; that they (the charcoal-burners) heard screams, and then a noise of pigs grunting and running violently, as if Satan himself were after them, quite in an opposite direction from Giacomo's cottage.

"Next morning the men looked about, and saw the marks of many feet in the red earth. Dead flowers lay on the ground, and some threads of long yellow hair were trodden into the earth.

"No one dared speak, or ask questions, for fear of the Cardinal. But the peasants, when they had the chance, pelted the Satyr with bits of rock and big stones, until before a month was over from the time Gigia disappeared, the ugly grinning monster, who knew all about her, lost shape and form. It was never taken down, however, and there it stands, gentlemen, before you, to prove I speak the truth."

With startling rapidity Filippo raised his arm, and pointed to the white outline. My eyes involuntarily followed his outstretched hand. Had it grown larger since I looked before? I stare in mute astonishment. Just as I saw it in my dream—that blackened round where the face ought to be. Surely—or do my eyes deceive me?—twice as large! Heavens, too! it moves!

The very breath leaves me. I have presence of mind, however, to hold my tongue. I take another look. The moonlight must deceive me! No—there it is again!—a movement, a swaying forwards of the head, almost imperceptible, it is true, but—a motion! I see a minute streak of moonlight through the trees. I am sure that was not there before. When the head moves, I plainly see it. Then I lose it.

If I were alone, I would at once go up to the

4*

statue and examine it thoroughly. I am not a nervous man, and my curiosity is keenly excited. I am sure some weird influence is gathering round me. But there is Fred—one word to him, and, in his schoolboy way, he is quite capable of getting frightened, and setting off on foot back to Siena.

As all this flashes through my brain, I sigh. What trouble awaits me?

The echo of that sigh comes back to me distinctly from the statue! This time there can be no doubt of it. Frederick, too, has heard it. He turns a bewildered face towards me. We stare at each other. Then at Filippo.

"Don't be alarmed, gentlemen," he says in a mysterious voice. "The Satyr does make strange noises at night. Lots of people have heard it."

I mentally decide that I will closely question the Marquis about this mysterious statue. But what, in the name of common sense, can induce my old friend to live in a haunted ilex-wood? A recollection of the Batty's—husband and wife—becomes painfully vivid.

All this passes quicker than I can write. Again I turn to our driver. Can he be imposing on me?

"Listen!" I say. "I will not go forward until you have told me *all* you know."

A queer look passes over Filippo's face. I can see he respects me for my acuteness.

"Genistreto of Genistrello, did say once, your Excellency—I mean Genistreto who lives on the hill opposite St. Agata, near the statue of the Hercules—Genistreto did say something about his wife having been, the day before, in the ilex-wood, leading her lambs home about the Ave Maria, and that near the Satyr, she saw Gigia——"

"Saw Gigia?" exclaims Fred out loud, forgetting any fear of hearing his own voice. "Why, I thought that she was dead!"

"No, not dead!" answers Filippo, pressing up very close, and speaking under his breath. "Assuredly she was gone, and we may hope, buried; but she was seen all the same.

"Gentlemen," he continues: "If I must, I must; but I am white with fear. It is not well to speak of such things at night, in the middle of the wood."

"Go on!" I repeat imperiously. "Make haste!"

"Yes, Excellency. It was Gigia—the *donnina*—but oh! so changed! A pale, haggard little face, with streaming eyes, that never winked, and hair hanging to her heels. She waved her hand for Genistreto's wife to come to her—waved her hand and pointed to her mouth, as if she would speak! Holy Virgin! I hope we shall not see her now! Gentlemen! Is there anything about? I dare not look round."

For Filippo keeps his back religiously towards the statue.

"There is nothing!" I reply.

I am fain to confess I also found it convenient at this moment to turn my back. Frederick was in such deep shadow I could only see the outline of his figure, but his breathing betrayed his excitement.

"Three times Genistreto's wife heard her name called out—Orsola! Orsola! Orsola! very plainly. Then, as she turned to fly, there was the sound of the fluttering of wings in the air—passing away rapidly towards the south.

"One night, Ettore and Balduccio, coming from Siena late after market, by this road, saw what they thought was a child sitting under the trees, wringing her hands. Knowing nothing about the story, they stopped, and Ettore went forward, and there, sure enough, sat a figure, glistening all over with jewels, in a long, white robe, draggled in the mud, and turning a livid little face towards them—like nothing human, they said, for they both saw it plainly—beckoning to them to follow it into the wood (but they were too frightened). Then it glided away among the trees, and was seen no more.

"These things, Excellencies, got spoken about, as you may think, and Zaidee, an old, old woman, people called a witch—she is dead now—laughed and crowed to herself, and pointing with her thumb up to the villa, muttered that '*Gigia would always haunt the head of the house until a life was taken for a life! Then she would rest.*'"

I confess that these words, vague as they were, and foolish, perhaps, made a profound impression on me. They pointed directly to the marquis, my friend. He was the head of the house—the heir of his uncle. Was he under the ban of one of those mysterious prophecies which so often, spite of reason and science, work out their own fulfilment? Had I been called in to witness the realisation of some horrible curse? A vision of the Satyr, as I had seen it in my dream—a muffled figure lying at the base—rose before me. I shivered to the very marrow of my bones.

Then Filippo's voice came to me as from a long way off, and I listen.

"A *vetturino*, 'Tista by name, my friend, who stands his carriage alongside of mine in the Piazza at Siena, drove some timber merchants here two years ago. It was late when they arrived, so the steward gave them all a bed and stable-room, that they might start early the next morning.

"'Tista was put to sleep in a room in the old factory, that stands by the chapel, on one side of the villa. It is called the *old* factory because a new one is now built, but the old one served in the time of the Cardinal, and there were rooms over it for the household.

"Just as daylight broke, 'Tista was awoke by a scream so shrill it made his flesh creep. He sat bolt upright in bed, and, as I live, saw in a corner of the room the figure of a girl, grey and shadowy, with hair like gold hanging about her back, crouched down before an altar, set out white, as for a marriage. Before 'Tista had time to turn, the door of the room flew open of itself, and the dark outline of a priest, tall and stately—all in red—filled up the doorway, behind him the dim forms of other figures, bearing lights.

"'Tista, the *vetturino*, stopped to see no more, but then and there leapt out of the window, which he had left open, for it was summer, and the night was hot. This, gentlemen, is as true as that Paradise is for the saints.

"Now, I believe," adds Filippo, with a mysterious air, "that Gigia was entrapped down here at the Satyr, and murdered in the self-same room, where the Cardinal pretended to marry her, and that he still walks with the four servants bearing lights as he did that night; and that Gigia's soul cannot rest in peace until *some one belonging to the Cardinal gives his life for hers.* Old Zaidee said so—*she* knew!"

As he repeats the ominous phrase, I tremble and turn cold. A weird sense of evil comes to me in the very air. I feel the unseen hand of fate in the presence of the Satyr, so closely connected with Anzano's destiny. I try to shake off the feeling, specially before Fred, but I cannot.

CHAPTER IV.

Now we are rattling along a good road in the moonlight.

The Satyr, with its ghostly memories, retires into the night. Filippo whistles gaily; the smacking of his whip, and the jingling of the harness-bells, sound like the voices of cheerful companions.

Frederick, whose nerves, I like to think are weaker than my own, and whose composure has been more shaken, cannot help now and then casting furtive glances behind him. All at once I see his eyes fix themselves on a dense mass of foliage in front. He utters a wild cry, signs to me, and points.

Flickering lights are dancing among the dark leaves.

"Uncle—uncle!" he gasps, catching his breath.

Fred's grip is so tight, I call out.

"Uncle Lucius. It is coming—look out!"

Before I can answer, the lights grow larger and more distinct, obliterating the leaves. A murmur of voices is wafted towards us. Filippo stops. He, too, listens, and looks anxiously ahead.

"Bravo!" he cries at last, after a pause, "Bravo! *Cara Madonna!* They are come at last. They have taken their time, these Excellencies!"

"Hola!" he shouts, at the top of his voice. "Hola! Who goes?"

"Friends," is the answer from voices coming from the lights, which I now perceive to be torches, carried by tall men, who, as they pass along, illuminate the inmost recesses of the woods, until the ilex trunks stand out like the dark pillars of a temple.

"Friends! Friends!" cries Filippo, cracking his whip. "*Evviva!* How sweet are these voices in this desolate place!"

By a rapid movement of his arm, I know that Filippo has crossed himself. He would have denied it, but I know he did. Fred breaks into a nervous laugh.

In another moment our carriage is surrounded by tall figures, armed with torches. The sudden blaze dazzles and blinds me. I can make out the dark figure of a man, muffled in a cloak, standing out from the rest, who fall back respectfully as he approaches the carriage, on the side where I am seated. A hand is stretched out.

"Welcome, a thousand times welcome, my dear Lucius!" says a penetrating voice, in which the old music still lingers.

"I have been very uneasy about you," the deep voice goes on to say. "I feared you had met with some accident."

In a moment, grasping the thin bony hand extended to me, I am out of the carriage and standing beside the Marquis (for it is he) on the road. Frederick follows me. Still holding my hand, Gonzaga draws me towards him and kisses me on both cheeks. As he does so I glance upwards, and see a pale, haggard countenance, shaded by a broad felt hat, in which I

vainly seek for the recognition which came to me with
the sound of his voice.

"My dear Marquis, how glad I am to see you once
more!" I wring his hand as I speak.

"Once more! You may well say that, Lucius,
after so many years."

"Well, I have no excuse! I feel, however, that I
am forgiven, for you have come to meet me. Allow
me to present my nephew, Frederick Stanley. I trust
that your friendship for me may descend to him."

The Marquis responds by a dignified salute; raises
his hat and extends his hand to Frederick. This
gives me time to observe my old friend. I should
certainly not have known him. I forget the alteration
in myself, to gaze amazed at him. His raven hair,
once the object of my intensest envy—(I am myself
what is called sandy)—streaming back from his brow
like a natural diadem—is now thin and sprinkled
with grey; his forehead is bald and prematurely
wrinkled; his clear olive complexion—the very perfection of a healthful paleness—turned sallow, and his
whole face, as I recall it, beaming and responsive to
my own, clouded and worn. His well-defined eyebrows alone, have not, like his hair, changed colour
or diminished; but full and dark as ever, become, in
the general alteration of the features, an anomaly;
producing an unpleasant effect, increased by the
hollow cavities round the deep-set eyes.

Yet, altogether, this rigid countenance is noble. If
it bears the marks of suffering—it is suffering borne
with dignity. Nobler perhaps than the beaming face
I remember, flushed with the trivialities of youth, and
shifting with the play of every passing emotion—

nobler and more intellectual; and that look of gravity becomes it well.

"My brother, Sigismund," says the Marquis, as a towering form steps forward out of the gloom.

Sigismund is much younger than Anzano, and somewhat lighter complexioned, knit altogether in a more manly frame.

I did not at once, in the uncertain light, appreciate the full effect of the almost faultless beauty of his chiselled features; his dark, lustrous eyes; the haughty carriage of his superb head and marble-like throat; his well-cut mouth, characteristically haughty, but with yielding lines about the lips and chin, readily gliding into as fascinating a smile as ever lit up the face of man.

But I did note the natural stateliness of manner, into which neither pride nor presumption entered, which struck me at once as the very perfection of manhood—just what my dear friend ought to have possessed, had he fulfilled the promise of his early youth.

Upon the appearance of the Marquis Sigismund upon the scene, mutual salutations were again exchanged and hats lifted.

Once more I had to present Frederick, literally drawing him forth from the shadows into which he had retreated.

While the introductions were taking place, the torch-bearers, sturdy, sun-tanned, shaggy-haired fellows—very scanty as to raiment, with large, bead-like eyes—turned wide open on us as if strangers from another planet, formed themselves into an illuminated circle, within the centre of which we stand.

I observe that Filippo has already fraternized with them, and is lighting a cigar at one of their torches.

While we are talking, the smoke forms a lurid canopy over our heads; again the earth turns of a bloody hue; again the over-arching trees rustle with a moan, and the desolate cry of a night-bird roused from its roost comes to me, as the palpable voice of the language of this strange wood.

Involuntarily I shiver.

"Come, Lucius," says the Marquis, whose eyes have, even in this brief interval, wandered off absently among the trees, but now settle themselves in an earnest gaze on me; "you are cold; the damp of the night air among these ilex-trees is unhealthy. We are still some way from the villa, a quick walk up the hill will stimulate your blood."

He passes his arm familiarly through mine, and we pass out of the blood-red circle of the torch-light, into the pale track of the moonbeams scantily streaking the road, beside which the ilex-trees rise up like mis-shapen giants.

"I hope you do not feel ill," Gonzago added, breaking an awkward silence.

(God knows it was not want of matter which kept me silent. A whirl of thoughts, past and present, bewildered my brain.)

"No, not ill, but greatly excited and fatigued. It is a fearful road. We have been for some hours in the dark woods."

"Hours!" and he caught up my words impatiently, almost as if displeased. "How so? You ought to have passed through in less than one hour at furthest. What has delayed you?"

His sudden curiosity alarmed me. I seemed to be in possession of a guilty secret. Down at the Satyr I had decided to question him as to the truth of Filippo's story. Now, I could say nothing.

"The horses were tired," I answered, hesitating. "We had to wait to rest them. Not knowing the way, I could not venture on alone."

This explanation seemed to satisfy him.

"I am really relieved that nothing has occurred," he observes, returning to the subject persistently.

"What did you expect to happen?" I ask, my voice involuntarily sinking almost to a whisper. Why I say this I know not. I suppose I cannot dispel some outward evidence of the sinister impression made upon me by the mysterious statue. Before the words are out of my mouth I am aware I have made a mistake. My friend's face darkened, and, from his deep-set eyes he cast a strangely suspicious glance.

"Happen!" with a forced laugh. "Happen! Why should anything special happen? I alluded to the ordinary accidents of a mountain road, rocky ground and a dark night. You must have started too late from Siena. It was my earnest desire" (he emphasised these words with what appeared a needless vehemence) "that you should have arrived here by daylight."

"Daylight or moonlight—what matter? I was coming to you, Anzano! That was enough for me."

My words turn the current of the conversation, which had been painfully drifting into an unmerited reproach. Now he linked his arm closer in mine, and turned towards me.

"Thank God *you* are not changed, Lucius," he murmured, with a deep sigh.

That sigh, and a certain melancholy intonation, implies that all else has changed. He fell into a muse, then, rousing himself:

"Be frank with me, Lucius. You met with no adventure in the wood? Nothing unusual? You are so very late, remember—so much after the time."

His questions are asked hurriedly; again he fixes his deep-set eyes on me, as if to read my very soul. Is it an intense anxiety to know whether anything unusual has occurred, or has he forgotten what he has already said? In either case, what shall I answer? I cannot begin my visit with the confession, that a ghastly relation connected with his uncle, the Cardinal, has been disclosed to me. The only course open to me is to ignore Filippo's story altogether. Am I wrong in this? I have no time to consider.

"An adventure, my dear Anzano! What makes you think so?" (At this I feel his arm wince.) "Nothing of the kind. Only a garrulous driver and bad horses."

I try to laugh. How can I or anyone else laugh, among these awful trees, crowding round like dusky listeners? My very voice seems to be transformed into a strange sound.

We are now walking fast, the rapidity of my friend's pace exceeding my own. In an agitated voice he exclaims:

"Garrulous driver! Wretch! I should like to shoot those chattering apes from Siena. What did the driver say? I beg of you to tell me. Repeat every word, Lucius, I implore you."

He speaks imperiously, as if impelled by an irresistible impulse. An instant afterwards, he adds quickly:

"I beg your pardon. Don't mind me. I would not for the world trouble you about the fellow."

This sudden change—a protest against his own question—this apprehension lest I shall satisfy his own desire; his evident preoccupation—for his eyes are continually roving round in an abstracted stare—appear to me most extraordinary.

All that I had heard at the hotel at Siena of his eccentricity was far, very far, from reaching the truth. Ever since we met I have been passing from wonder to amazement, from amazement to sorrow. My poor friend! What ails him?

Conscious, I suppose, in some degree, of the painful impression he is creating in me, he adds, as if apologetically, at the same time moderating the extreme rapidity of his pace:

"You cannot think, Lucius, what devils the Sienese are. How their curiosity torments me! A city of liars! That is why I never go there. Liars! All liars to the core. They pass their lives in slandering me. No wonder! They would slander the mother who bore them. Never let them address you, Lucius. But you are a stranger. I daresay you listened to the fellow? Perhaps you questioned him. If so, tell me frankly."

I feel an inward pang. Perhaps his overwrought sensibility noted it.

"Is it so? Was it about the woods—the statues? Probably the Satyr?" (Here his voice quivers.) "You passed the Satyr. People don't like it at night. Was it about the Satyr?"

A deep glow comes into his eyes. I feel forced to dissemble.

"Not I," I reply, being determined to give him no present clue until I am enabled to judge what foundation exists for the story. Later it will, I hope, be possible to relate to him all, and to learn from himself how much of actual truth there is in the statement.

Hitherto the Marquis had been so entirely absorbed by his desire to know what revelations had taken place in the wood, that he had no time to make any allusion to the past. Certainly this was not the kind of welcome I had expected. I feel hurt and chagrined. A somewhat sulky silence on my part followed.

"Pardon me, my dear Lucius, if I appear preoccupied"—he had evidently guessed my feelings, which, after all, were only natural—"pardon me and bear with me. You do not know me now. Am I not greatly changed?"

"Why, yes, you are changed," I answer; "but not more, I daresay, than I appear to you, since the days we sat by the river at Stitchome's."

"But we parted at Stonyhurst," he puts in, sharply. "Do not confuse me; I am changed in mind as well as in body. We have not been ten minutes together, Lucius, yet I can assure myself that it is only your outward man that is altered; your mind is still fresh. You are as warm-hearted and affectionate as ever. While I"—he pauses and sighs profoundly—"I am a mere wreck. Dead to all feeling—tortured—distressed —harassed, with faith in nothing, least of all in myself."

"Have you lost your faith in me, Anzano?"

"No, no—not in you! that faith still remains as vividly as if we had only parted yesterday. How many years is it?" he asks abruptly.

"Five-and-twenty last June," I answer. "I have always kept, carefully noted in my tablets, the day of our first meeting at Stitchome's, and our parting at Stonyhurst. What tears we shed! We were to write to each other every week!"

"It is true!" he exclaims, "yet we never exchanged a line. How ill these boyish promises are kept. My tears were not soon dried, however. I was desolate without you. I never made another friend. I swear that through all the vicissitudes of my life— and I have been so fearfully tried—that my attachment to you has never varied. To me you were always my hero—my Achilles!—Achilles, who loved and protected his poor Patroclus. When that red-haired bully at school (I quite forget his name—*then* it was written in fire on my brain—I wanted to stab him!) struck me down and kicked me in the playground; how you hit him, though he was as big again as you! Both his eyes were blackened and his face a jelly. You were merciless—you fought like a Trojan! How it all comes back to me! I have forgotten nothing."

"Not forgotten your Greek, either," I observe. "I judge so by your classic allusion. Do you still believe in the decrees of an avenging fate? How about Nemesis and the black-haired Erinnys? Do you fancy yourself still under a curse? An Œdipus or an Orestes?"

At these unhappy words the Marquis started back, as if the earth had opened before him, and a sigh so profound—it was more like a groan—broke from him.

"Hush, hush, Lucius! I implore you!" in whispered tones—"The awful decrees of fate are no subject for idle jesting."

"I did not jest," I hasten to reply, greatly annoyed at having pained him. "I only recalled what you must well remember."

"I dare not play with life now," is his answer. "Mine has been too tragic."

Here is cause for fresh wonder: "Tragic!" What does he mean? Always some new mystery.

"Let us talk of yourself," he continued, as if desiring to plunge into a fresh subject. "From time to time, I heard of you, Lucius, travelling in Italy. But, as you never proposed a meeting, I concluded you had ceased to care for your old friend—after the lapse of so many years. What could be more natural? I had so little pleasant to offer. However, when, a week ago, your letter arrived, proposing to visit me, I felt happy! Yes, *I*—Anzano Gonzago—felt happy!"

A bitter laugh followed these words, as if in mockery of himself.

"I thanked God that at least one faithful friend remained to me." His face brightens as he says this.

"You cannot feel greater happiness than I do, dear Anzano," I reply, wringing his hand.

"Speak that name again, Lucius!" he exclaims passionately—"Anzano! No one has called me Anzano for years. When last I heard that name, it was uttered by a voice I loved—a voice that breathed

5*

peace into my troubled soul. Now it is mute in death.
Had she lived, Lucius, all might have been well."

Again he sighs. The light wind ruffling the ilex-
leaves, catches up the sound and repeats it—bearing
it far into the woods—with strange distinctness.

We both stop involuntarily. My friend slowly
turns his head and gazes into the trees, as if dreading
—yet expecting something upon which his eyes may
rest.

Infected with the same nervous dread, I also turn.
I see only Sigismund and Frederick walking side by
side, their figures in shadow, backed by the blazing
torches. As they move, lurid circles follow them—
turning the speckled mosses on the ilex-trees into the
semblance of gigantic monsters coiling round the
trunks.

A word now and then dropped from Frederick in
answer to Sigismund, whose voice, deep and penetrating like his brother's, comes to me more distinctly.

"You regret, then, having come to Italy for your
vacation, Mr. Stanley?"

"Yes," Frederick answers, in execrable Italian (he
understands the language, but speaks it badly). "I
feel such an unutterable muff at being able to say
nothing. Wear out my hat, you know, bowing to
fellows."

Sigismund laughs.

"Oh, don't laugh, or you will extinguish me. I am
going to Oxford next term, and shall study modern
languages. My uncle—a good old fellow, but crotchety
—*will* send me to Oxford. I chose the army."

I am somewhat taken aback by the terms in which my nephew alludes to me. However, if he only has the sense to keep silence about Filippo and the "donnina," what matter?

The first moment I am alone with him I will warn him to be absolutely silent.

———

CHAPTER V.

Now the Marquis is speaking.

"It is a poor welcome, Lucius, to entertain you with the sorrows of my life; but I have nothing else to tell. I grow more and more of a recluse. Now I never leave Sant' Agata. And you?—you live in your own home? You have never married?"

"Not I. I never could make up my mind whom to choose. Women are all so charming. I admire the sex immensely, but *en masse*. It seems to me invidious to particularise."

"Oh, Lucius! Still taking life as merrily as of old. Would that I could do so. Perhaps if you had protected me by "*le Box*," as you did at school, I might have done better. I was born to a heritage of sorrow. A time came when this was revealed to me."

"You have had, then, another grief, besides the death of the lady you loved?"

My question, though growing naturally out of his own remarks, appeared to embarrass him.

"Crises occur in all lives," he replies, with a sudden reserve. "My life must not be judged by that of others. I am here to fulfil a purpose. A certain time is needed to comprehend this. Exceptional responsibilities have been thrown upon me."

"Well, Anzano, at any rate, with the responsibilities, you have succeeded to the inheritance. I hear you are one of the wealthiest men in Northern Italy. How little you seem to appreciate your blessings."

"Oh, you speak of the blessings of mere riches. But if these rob you of your peace of mind, is it not much better to be poor? Take from me all I have and give me peace, Lucius—give me peace," he adds dreamily, fixing his eyes vaguely into the night.

With an obvious effort he recalled himself, and continues:

"The loss of the woman I loved was a great sorrow. She died within a week of the day fixed for our marriage."

Almost involuntarily I utter a sympathetic sigh.

"Yes," he continued, "a terrible mystery was connected with her death."

"Tell me what you can. I am profoundly interested."

"Yes; what I can."

It is just that. I was convinced that he was trying to avoid what Filippo had revealed as the real mystery of his life.

"The name of my affianced bride was Gemma, the youngest daughter of an ancient Sienese family. I will not describe her; it would be too painful. Ask me to show you her miniature some day. *Events* I can relate, personal details seem to me irrelevant.

"At that time Gemma was living at her father's estate of Rosea, midway between Sant' Agata and Siena. A week before I was to call her mine, a girl, a stranger begged to be permitted to speak to her alone. The pretext was charity, some tale of misfortune to be confided to her ear. Gemma was an angel to the distressed.

"No one specially noted the stranger's appearance. The servant who admitted her, only remembered afterwards, that she was slight in stature; and that, under the folds of a thick black veil, a quantity of fair hair fell about her neck.

"So long an interval elapsed after she was admitted, the servant knocked at the door. No answer was given. She opened it. Gemma was leaning back in her chair dead. Purple marks like the impress of small fingers were on her throat. With her own hands the stranger had strangled her."

"How horrible! Was there no investigation?"

"Investigation?" He catches up my words bitterly, and gives a laugh—so bitter it shocks me. "What investigation was possible when there was no evidence? Lucius," and his voice sinks into a whisper, "there *is* one who answers to the description of the murderess— I know her but too well—a prescience—a horrible prescience points to her, and her only. Yes, yes," he continues, as though speaking to himself, "I brought this fate on my poor Gemma. The evil destiny which haunts me clung to her. All that I have ever attempted ends with a catastrophe!"

"Nonsense! How could you, my dear friend, be answerable for a death so mysterious—aneurism of the heart, a fit—any sudden malady might have caused it. Without an inquest, which, I presume, was not permitted, no one could venture on an opinion."

Again there is that low laugh, as if in mockery of himself; again his deep-set eyes wander off with a stricken gaze into the darkness, then turn themselves with a pathetic intensity on me. (What I say seems rather to irritate than to console him.)

"A great sorrow weaned me from the world. Then a fatal knowledge—my uncle the Cardinal"—at this name a nervous quiver runs through my frame. He relapses into silence. Whatever revelation he is about to make concerning the Cardinal, dies upon his lips.

If I did not feel a guilty consciousness of having unfairly come to the knowledge of the crime the Cardinal committed, I should certainly, even at the risk of offending him, have insisted on an explanation. But that consciousness, and the almost stern repulse with which all my inquiries are met, effectually silences me.

After this we fall into an awkward pause, broken only by the sound of our own footsteps, and the hum of voices in the rear. The wheels of Filippo's carriage also creak faintly. My friend's mysterious allusions agitate and alarm me. A glassy stare that habitually comes into his eyes entirely changes the character of his face, and gives it a sinister expression. Hardly a phrase falls from his lips that has not some hidden meaning. His manner is so strange it is impossible to feel at ease in his company.

The stifling closeness of the wood, the oppressive gloom of the trees, the total absence of that interchange of thought that I had so ardently anticipated, added to bodily fatigue, at last quite overcame me.

"Is this road never going to end?" I ask impatiently. "You spoke of a hill—where is it? We have all this time been walking on the same terraced road which began at the statue of the Satyr."

"The Satyr!" he cries. "Then it was pointed out to you? What do you know about the Satyr?"

All my friend's former suspicions are again aroused.
I feel in no mood to indulge them.

"Do you think, Marquis, we did not use our eyes?
If you don't want people to notice the Satyr, you
should knock it down."

My rough reply rouses him.

"Bear up a little," he says. "We are not far from
the villa. You will soon see the avenue of statues."
He speaks with the utmost courtesy. "I fear you are
much fatigued, Lucius. I ought not to have allowed
you to walk. Your dinner will certainly be cold.
But you are changed indeed if you mind such trifles."

"Not I. My nephew is much more interested in
it than I. The rising generation is very epicurean."

"Your nephew, Mr. Stanley? I hope he and my
brother, Sigismund, will be friends."

(I do not like to say how little chance I see of
this happy result.) Frederick's boyish pride and shyness are so great, they would only yield to a friendly
siege partaking so much of the nature of an assault,
that I can hardly imagine the stately Sigismund taking
the trouble to attempt it.

"You really must overlook the unfitness of the
place, Lucius. I have lived here so long alone, that
I have got accustomed to it. Now it strikes me all at
once I ought to have received you in Siena."

"Your palace there is splendid. I admired it from
the Piazza."

"An old barrack," he answers, "with some pictures and artistic collections. But I do not care for
these things now. God and nature alone occupy my
mind. Of man I have had too much! Here the
past obliterates the present. Under the shadow of

immemorial woods the world recedes. Forms—
visions——"

Again he casts a hasty glance around.

"No, no, Anzano," I answer, "not visions. These
are fancies bred of solitude. What does your handsome brother say to your vapours?"

He shakes his head and frowns; my light tone
evidently displeases him.

"Sigismund dislikes Sant' Agata. Like you, he
says it encourages my natural melancholy. Heaven
be praised, Sigismund speaks in ignorance. Melancholy! Why not? What have I to make me joyful?
The advance of life is full of sadness—a chronicle of
crime," he adds, lowering his voice. "Whole families
—circles of friends—die out; shadows fill their places.
The world becomes haunted by memories. A little
space, and the busy brain that reasons will be food
for worms also. And then? And then? The sacrifice will be accomplished!"

CHAPTER VI.

AT last our feet touch the rising ground. We draw breath audibly up a steep ascent. Already a freer air fans my brow. I can see the stars overhead, shining in the purple vault of heaven; the moon rising behind walls overtopped by gigantic clipped hedges. In the broad road on which we are walking I can discern an avenue of statues niched within their green recesses—statues so high that, in the half light, they grow quite dim about the head and shoulders.

Before us is the Villa. In front, lofty iron gates, attached to a delicately-sculptured balustrade, breast high, enclose a forecourt, or garden. Within, more white statues, also vases and fountains, placed symmetrically, the water shooting up in thin columns, to fall back in sprays of silvery refulgence under the moon.

I can see the outline of palm and orange trees, spiky aloes and luxuriant pampas grass, the feathery fronds delicate and glittering.

From this garden, lying so softly poetic in the moonlight, a broad flight of steps leads to a colonnade or portico, extending along the entire front of the house, and on either side, but detached from it, spacious wings, which, with the iron gates and carved balustrade, constitute the four sides of a forecourt.

"There is my house, Lucius," says the Marquis, halting just within the gates; "my house, which is now your own."

Could a welcome be more touching? I press his hand; I cannot speak; something rises in my throat which stops me; tears moisten my eyes. Before his house stands my friend, with his grave, care-worn face, master, not only here, but of many other houses, and of boundless acres, as helpless, as it seems to me, and dependent, as a child.

Without being able to define what moves me, his wan look and weary attitude raise my infinite compassion. I experience the same feeling as at Stitchome's, when the big Irish bully tried to kick him, and I instantly pommelled the wretch to the bone, then walked triumphantly round the play-ground, my arm on "Saunders'" shoulder. Boyhood has gone, youth has followed, now middle-age has settled on us both, our hair is whitening for the harvest of eternity; but his love for me, and my love for him, is still as vivid as in those early days, when we both revelled in the vague delusions of untried life.

Alas! for the awakening!

Now and then real bursts of natural feeling make amends to me for much that is painful and depressing about him—bursts bringing refreshing glimpses of the youth I loved so well. To the other man, known as the Marquis Gonzago—impenetrable, suspicious, dominated by some weird agencies, that contract all natural expansion into what seems a tyranny of secret dread—I feel a stranger.

Had I been aware how much he was changed, should I have come? I think not. But, being here,

I shall endeavour to forget his strangeness, and the strangeness of his environments.

Does he want help—and it seems to me that of all men he needs it most grievously—I will give it. Let me only discover the direction in which I can aid him, and all I can do would be too little. I swear it! After this mental oath I feel calmer.

To whom else could he turn? To Sigismund? Sigismund is much younger. Of another type, with other sympathies and other views, Sigismund, even as I have briefly seen him, lives in another world. No special sympathy seems to unite the brothers; and from some chance words my friend let drop, it appears to me he desires altogether to exclude him from the fatal spell under which he considers himself to have fallen.

Does he divine my thoughts? The flush upon his pale face, the warm pressure of his thin hand and the glances of deep affection he casts upon me, as we stand, linked arm-in-arm, reveal to me that he does.

The sound of approaching footsteps, and the murmur of voices, rudely break the spell. Not only does our mood change, but all the aspect of nature changes with it. The pallid moonbeams vanish before the lurid glare of the torches, flashing fiercely on path and statue—mounting upward even to the roof, and dashing the fountains as with sparks of flame.

Frederick now comes up with Sigismund. Both are smoking.

"That house don't fetch me at all, Uncle Lucius. I'll take my oath it's haunted like that beastly wood," whispers Frederick into my ear.

"Foolish boy," I reply under my breath. "Think

what you like, but, for Heaven's sake hold your tongue."

Frederick shrinks back astounded at my unusual sternness; he only knows me as a good-natured, convenient old uncle. But I can be hasty when I am provoked. Take exceeding care, Master Fred. I can tell you you are on ticklish ground.

"Luigi." The Marquis is addressing one of the torch-bearers. "Go and light up the great hall, and order supper to be served immediately."

As Luigi and the other torch-bearers fall apart to obey this order, our dusty carriage and the tired little horses, with heads and tails depressed, Filippo enthroned on the box—are disclosed to view. In an instant Filippo has leapt to the ground, dashed away his pipe and posed himself, hat in hand, in an appropriate attitude.

"Most illustrious Marquis——" he begins.

"Take that fellow away to the steward's house," cries my friend angrily, turning quickly on his heel:

"On no account allow him to enter the house."

Poor Filippo! The last I see of him is an appealing glance of mingled rage and mortification, addressed to me, as he rams down his hat defiantly on his head.

"What an exquisite night!" the Marquis remarks, as if awakened to a sudden consciousness of the necessity of speech. "The air is full of perfume. You have nothing like this in England, Lucius. Your sickly moon is always in a haze, and your everlasting fogs envelope everything."

We are standing on the central gravel path conducting to the portico, under a shadowy roof of tropical foliage, the moon over us, the centre of an expanse of silvery radiance, and a few stars, dimmed by her lustre, gathering on the dark fringe of the mountain horizon.

Luigi and the others are rushing hither and thither within the house. Their blazing torches displaying in fiery patterns, every delicate curve and minute detail of the external colonnade; and from the colonnade itself the reflex of the flames dashed upwards, wakening every window-pane into a vivid splendour.

Little by little, the illumination grows fainter and fainter, dying away at last altogether, as the last man disappears. Then the silver moon resumes her sway, bathing every object in the whiteness of her rays.

"A pretty effect!" Sigismund remarks, as he stands watching these alterations of light, the moonbeams framing his majestic figure as in a mystic background—the living image, as I think, of the fairy prince.

"These improvised scenes are always the most happy. If one had tried to produce that effect of changing lights, it would certainly have been a failure."

As he spoke, I see that Sigismund's eyes are earnestly fixed on a particular window in the upper story, just over one of the balls of a huge stone coronet, forming the central decoration of the richly sculptured façade.

The Marquis, who had turned to listen to his brother's remark, also detects the direction of his eyes, and his eyebrows contract into a spasm of sudden pain. Then, with a movement, passionate in its abruptness, he turns away, and draws me under the shadow of the tufted shrubs. I think he is about to communicate to me the cause of his sudden displeasure; but minutes pass by, and he continues in the same attitude, frowning and gazing vacantly into my face. At last the frown dies away, and the same helpless, pleading expression comes into his eyes, that before, in the wood, touched me so deeply.

"Your house is really magnificent, Anzano," I say at last, not wishing to appear to notice this silent episode between the brothers, and the distress it has evidently caused him. "I do not know what blemishes daylight may reveal; but, in the moonlight, it has the air of an enchanted palace. So immense too! You must need a whole retinue of servants."

"Ah!" he replies, speaking more naturally. "Servants!—that would not be much. But you forget that in this solitary place, so far from other habitations, we have also to lodge and feed a whole tribe of outside dependants, shepherds, game-keepers, poultry-men, gardeners, peasants, grooms and helpers; also the land-steward and his family, who have their own rooms in the new factory, to the right, forming one side of the square. Servants there are too, inside, at least a score, and many aged pensioners, a burden entailed by possession. Sant' Agata is a little territory of itself. Nor is the next world forgotten," he adds, trying to call up a feeble smile. "That is our chapel," pointing to the left, as we stand with our backs turned to the house, towards a Grecian-fronted façade, with a sculptured doorway, standing close to the main building.

"—Only opened on great occasions or when Don Antonio comes up from San Martino to say mass for

us on *festas*. Soon, however, I hope the doors will
unclose for a propitious ceremony, such as rarely
takes place in our family."

"What, a marriage?" I ask eagerly. My friend
silently indicates Sigismund, just visible through the
orange leaves, standing exactly on the same spot; his
back towards us, his head raised to a light, shining
through the outer shutters of the same window in the
upper story.

Sigismund is either too much engrossed to hear
my question, or affects to be. At this moment the
light disappears; and with an uneasy start, as of a
man recalled suddenly to himself, he crosses the garden, and disappears into the house.

As the Marquis watches his movements, he shakes
his head mournfully. It is clear that something is
amiss between the brothers. Sigismund is perfectly
courteous in his manner to his elder; while the Marquis, on his side, pointedly refers to him on every
possible occasion, yet I observe that his absence evidently relieves him, and that he then speaks with
greater freedom.

"What is that ugly low building with an over-
hanging roof," I ask, "between the chapel and the
marble balustrade? It seems out of place there. You
should pull it down."

Pale as my friend habitually is, the moonlight
shows him to me, at this instant, almost deathlike.

He draws a long breath—then presses one of his
hands over his eyes, as if to shut out some distressful
image.

"That house is the old factory," he replies, trying

to render his voice steady, and succeeding but ill. "It is shut up now; we have no further use for it."

Breathlessly I fix my eyes upon it, Filippo's words about the apparition seen by 'Tista rushing into my mind. I long to ask the Marquis why it is shut up, and what really took place there—if the story of the murder is an invention, or only some accident giving a semblance of truth to a hideous fiction? After what passed in the ilex-wood, I dare not—I can only gaze in silence at the heavy shadow of the overlapping roof, deepened into an ominous blackness; a single pane of glass in one of the windows turned by the moonlight into the semblance of a narrow eye, malignantly watchful.

Was she crouching there now, in the corner, that fair-haired girl—the basilisk gaze of the Red Cardinal upon her? Here I feel a clammy chill creep over me. The Marquis, with those uneasy eyes of his, observes it.

"Has this old house any special interest for you, Lucius, that you survey it so intently?" (His voice has the same suspicious tone, as when he questioned me about the Satyr.)

Before I can decide what to answer, I hear Frederick's footstep on the gravel.

"Heaven keep him silent!" is my mental ejaculation. My prayer is heard. Frederick appears, bursting with mystery, but only communicating to me in a whisper that, if supper is not ready soon, he shall eat the Marquis.

Getting no answer, the Marquis repeats his question.

"Surely, Anzano," I say; "you forget that I am here for the first time."

"Excuse my impatience, Lucius. I live so much alone, I fear that my abruptness degenerates into rudeness."

Then, taking in the whole scene with a sorrowful glance, as if weary of himself and of all around, he passes his arm within mine and we pass under the portico, Frederick following us with a loud and hungry yawn.

———

CHAPTER VII.

As we cross the threshold the Marquis again embraces me.

"Dear Lucius!" he exclaims with a fervour the occasion hardly warrants; "would that you had come before! Who knows whether the fates might not have been more propitious!"

In the hall he addresses himself to Frederick, but, so absorbed is that young gentleman in staring about him, that I actually have to administer a sharp rap upon his shoulder to make him attend.

"You, too, Mr. Stanley, are welcome to my house. Now, it is for your uncle's sake—soon I doubt not it will be for your own." With a winning smile he extends his hand.

"Thanks; you are very kind," replies Fred, his eyes round with wonder at the vaulted walls, illuminated by clusters of wax lights fixed in golden sconces. "But it is all so awfully grand, it quite bewilders me."

"Certainly, Anzano," I say, endeavouring to qualify Frederick's *gaucherie*, "you are lodged like an emperor."

"Oh, believe me, if you had travelled more out of the beaten track in Italy, you would think little of this mountain retreat."

"Mountain retreat! What, the bijou residence of

a rich Cardinal? We know the depth of ecclesiastical pockets too well to believe that. Even by night, and with the cursory view I have had of it, I can see what enormous sums must have been lavished here."

As if anxious to drop a distasteful subject, the Marquis made no reply, while I, knowing what I do about the Cardinal, repent that I have again alluded to him. My friend not only shrinks from all mention of his uncle's name, but invariably tries to suppress all allusion to his wealth or any praise called forth by its possession.

But for this peculiarity, under his own roof he becomes quite another man, and performs the part of host with an alacrity and graciousness I could not have given him credit for. Now he is stepping from side to side, anxious to explain everything to me.

The hall is supported by pilasters of giallo-antico and deep red porphyry, the intervening spaces lined with panels of Siena marble, white, relieved by a bold design in black and yellow. Opposite the lofty entrance appear the Gonzago arms, coronet and supporters, emblazoned on gold, and at the extreme end, backed by a canopy of purple velvet, a cardinal's red hat, with pendant cords and tassels.

Semi-colossal busts on carved pedestals line the shining walls.

"The twelve Cæsars," says the Marquis. "Antiques, brought from Rome. We live here, inside and out, in a world of sculpture. The statue of Victory to the right, and that of Plenty opposite," he is pointing to the portico, "are from the gardens of Antinous. The fresco on the ceiling is by Raphael Mengs, the apo-

theosis of an ancestral Pope into Olympus—rather a
pagan treatment for the Vicar of Christ."

"Oh, but," I answer, "they have never shorn the
Papacy of the honours of the Pontifex Maximus. The
power of the keys locks up almost as much pagan fiction as Christian forgery."

"Ah, Lucius, still unorthodox. We must send for
our chaplain, Don Antonio, to exorcise you into filial
obedience. These different rooms," as he speaks, he
indicates four marble portals at the four corners of
the hall, "lead to the library, my own study, and the
domestic apartments, including the cellar—an important item in a house where so much wine is made.
The principal saloons are on the first floor. This is
the dining-room, which concerns us most at present."

"I care not how soon that concern is made apparent," say I. "I confess to a very hearty appetite."

We turn to the left through the first of the pillared
doorways into a well-lighted room, glowing with rich
tapestry. A well-furnished table, set with fruit and
flowers, and resplendent with ancestral plate, occupies
the centre.

"This is but a small room," observes the Marquis,
following my eye as it sweeps round, "compared with
the size of the house; but Italians are not diners-out
like the English. We rarely or ever entertain at dinner, except in great cities, or on official occasions.
The dining-room is, therefore, constructed with regard
to the family circle. It is usually the smallest of the
living-rooms."

I had missed Fred while we were inspecting the
hall. Now, to my horror, I behold him, seated at the
table in company with Sigismund. The sight of food

has apparently thawed his shyness and enlarged his
vocabulary. He is talking volubly. His boyish gestures, unformed features, and absurd effort at a mous-
tache contrasting painfully with the statuesque outline
of head and neck, the lightly-curling black locks, and
full, silky beard of the stately Sigismund.

Truly my poor Fred is but a schoolboy, but one
feels that the other's clear black eyes, with much of
the veiled fire of his brother's glance—without the
restless, far-off look—could never have been different.

Sigismund, leaning back carelessly in his chair, is
scrutinising his companion with an amused stare.
Though seated at the table, he has not touched anything. He is incapable of eating in the absence of
the master, a refinement quite lost on Master Frederick.

Gliding noiselessly about on the soft carpet, an
elderly major-domo in black receives the dishes from
an opening in the wall.

As we enter, he bows his head with an air distress-
fully apologetic to the Marquis, as for having presumed
to serve the table in his absence. By an expressive,
not-to-be-described pantomime, the major-domo signi-
fies that he has been forced to do so against his will;
then, drawing a particularly imposing arm-chair from
the wall, he places it at the head of the table. Frederick and Sigismund both rise—Fred with his mouth
full and very red in the face.

"Do not move, I beg," says the Marquis, taking in
the whole scene, and smiling. For Sigismund's empty
plate, and the deprecatory action of his hands, indicate
that it is the visitor's fault, not his own, that impli-
cates him in an action so wanting in respect to his
elder.

"Why such ceremony, Sigismund?" says the
Marquis. "Why apologise? I am delighted my young
friend, Mr. Stanley, has already begun. We have
loitered unduly in the hall."

I give Frederick a glance that he perfectly understands, and colours to the roots of his hair. Such a
want of *savoir faire* is intolerable!

"What will Frederick attempt next?" I ask myself
with dismay, and, not for the first time, I silently ana-
thematize my folly in having brought him.

Once seated, the excellence of the cuisine causes
me to forget his misdemeanors. The numerous dishes
have just that relish of the forest and the field, so
attractive to an appetite jaded with the routine of *table
d'hôte* dinners.

First came wild boar, stewed in a delicious condi-
ment called "sour-sweet" sauce, composed of almonds,
pistaccio nuts and plums, as impossible for any but
Italian fingers to concoct, as for Christians to manufacture sherbet. Then quails, with a mountain twang
of aromatic herbs, vainly to be looked for in the well-
fed birds that fatten in our woods, thick with soft
roots and tender sprouting underwood; the course of
game followed by a cunning combination of maccaroni
flavoured with spiced livers, cock's-combs and unborn
eggs, called "risotto," interchanged with interludes of
golden "fritto," cooked in the first pure *cru* of olive
oil, and "gnocchi," exquisite cakes of newly-ground
Indian corn, with a pure clean taste quite indescribable,
save "in action" between the teeth, something related
in its purest element to almonds, with a delicate
souvenir of cocoa-nut superadded.

There is the inevitable roast and salad; only the

roast is a lordly peacock, its brilliant tail extending across the entire table, its head erect, with glistening glass eyes bent upon us reproachfully for the barbarity we are perpetrating towards the majesty of fowl, as slice after slice is withdrawn from its roomy chest until the breast-bone shines out sepulchral.

As to the sweets—vain were my pen. Oh, muse, inspire me! Nothing but alexandrines of longest and loftiest metre could set forth the triumphs of the *dolci*.

I sit opposite ·to a Grecian temple of pastry, glittering with pillars, capitals, cornices and vaultings of various coloured fruits, with a frothy roof of whipt cream, high-crested and rolling, strewed, as by a beneficent hurricane, with bon-bons. The Grecian temple is followed by ices, coloured and shaped into the semblance of peaches, pomegranates, grapes, melons and oranges, piled up amid leaves and stalks; equally deceptive to the taste, as to the sight—for each ice bears a resemblance, not only in form and colour but in flavour, to its prototype.

A cake, there is too, most marvellous to behold, fashioned into the outline of a mountain landscape adorned with rocky cliffs and precipitous defiles of sweet and bitter almonds; the snow-capped mountains —sugar, with every variety of coloured preserves, cut into trees, shrubs and flowers. Even the groups of shepherds and shepherdesses à *la* Watteau, in the foreground, clothed in red cherry and greengage, the ribbons cut from the rinds of oranges; the flags and pennants from the speckled skins of summer melons and red cactus fruit.

From extolling the dishes, the conversation naturally turns upon the wine. Here the Marquis becomes really interested. He has listened with polite indifference to my eulogies of his cook—Frederick backing me up in all I utter; somewhat in the style of a rough Greek Chorus, untutored to the proper note of intonation.

Our eulogies of the wine touch my friend's feelings. He insists on my trying various qualities; more or less of the "Broglio" or "Chianti" vintages—all red wine about Siena partakes of the general qualities of Baron Ricasoli's lordly brews of Chianti at his mediæval castle of Broglio, frowning from the Apennine Casentino over the undulating hills that hem in Siena.

My friend's home-made champagne is detestable, and perilously sour; but a certain kind of Malaga, as frankly luscious as the first juice of the summer grape can make it, rests on my palate as an excellent specimen of native manufacture.

"That wine," it is the Marquis who is speaking, "was improvised to serve for sacramental purposes at the Vatican, at the time of the Gonzago Pope, and was deemed a success. It is called 'Vino Santo' (holy wine), and is used on all high festive and religious occasions by every one of our name, here at Siena and also at Mantua. For I must tell you, Lucius, that the ancient Gonzago palace which came to me from my father, is at Mantua, not at Siena.

"It is so long since we have had a birth or a marriage, the custom has almost been forgotten; but when Sigismund brings home a bride——"

At these words, Sigismund changes colour, leans back in his chair, and raises a pair of flashing eyes, full on his brother.

Not heeding Sigismund's movement, nor the agitation that works silently upon his features, the Marquis repeats the same words a second time, louder and more emphatically, casting at the same time a defiant glance round the table.

"I repeat, when Sigismund, *my heir*——"

As the words "*my heir*" pass his lips, his voice thrills into the corners of the ebony-furnitured room, a threat and a menace.

"Gonzago!" cries Sigismund, starting to his feet. A moment after he re-seats himself, but his indignant eyes are still riveted on the Marquis, who not by the smallest glance deigns to heed him.

"When Sigismund brings home a bride," he repeats, in the same defiant tone, looking straight before him, "it is in that sacramental wine that I shall drink her health, and prosperity to the ancient house of the Gonzagos."

Before this passage of arms between the brothers, we had been talking almost gaily between the courses. Now we all fall back into solemn silence. Sigismund drops his eyes upon his plate, and the Marquis sits frowning and impenetrable.

Why did my friend continually revert to the subject of Sigismund's marriage? This was the second time he had done so, in words almost identical. And why was that marriage a prohibited subject? Ever since I first knew him, the Marquis had invariably shown himself just, generous and self-sacrificing. Even now, greatly as he was changed, he had said much that had called forth my respect and my admiration.

But at this moment, I could not help thinking that he was both tyrannical and insolent, except on the supposition of some gross misconduct on the part of his brother; which, looking at Sigismund's noble countenance (as refined in expression as perfect in beauty), sitting immovable, in a kind of dignified protest against the Marquis, I could not believe possible. Even if Sigismund did become his heir, by his brother's voluntary abstention from marriage, what right had he to force on him an alliance evidently abhorrent to his feelings?

I confess I found myself distinctly taking Sigismund's part against my friend. There was a fierce determination about the Marquis absolutely offensive. His very voice changed to a harsh metallic ring. Altogether a new revelation to me of his character, and one to which the past could afford me no analogy.

During the awkward pause that ensued, I began to cast my eyes around the room.

On entering it had been too dark to distinguish anything plainly. Now I see that the walls are hung with some brocaded material—stamped leather, I think —with much dark gold about it, and that heavily carved ebony cabinets, marble tables and pictures in splendid frames, break the surface of the walls.

I am sitting on the right hand of the Marquis; on his left is an empty chair.

From the moment I perceive that chair, a sort of fascination seizes me. For whom is it placed? Why is it vacant? The Marquis has mentioned no other member of his family besides his brother. Gradually the sinister air of the place seems to gather round me. There is mystery in the woods—in the old factory. Is there mystery in the house also? That chair! Is it placed there for an earthly occupant, or is it designed to receive the impalpable impress of some spirit of the dead?

The Marquis arrested my glance in the very act as it were of inquiry. A faint tinge of colour rises on his cheeks.

"You are observing that chair, Lucius? It ought not to be there. Our party is complete."

He speaks hurriedly. Sigismund, who has been sitting with his face shaded by one hand, whilst with the other he has carried glass after glass of red wine to his lips, as though unconscious of what he was doing, now drops his hand upon the table with a force that makes it tremble; then leaning forward, rivets his eyes upon his brother.

To my amazement, the Marquis quails under his gaze. A visible tremor passes through his frame. Without offering one word of explanation, he turns abruptly to the major-domo, who is standing behind his chair.

"Remove that chair, Antonio," pointing to the empty seat. "Place it no more at table."

Antonio, too well-drilled to offer any observation, simply bows, but the expression of his face shows his astonishment.

"The most Illustrious shall be obeyed in all things," he murmurs, as with evident reluctance he places the chair against the wall.

"No, no; not there—not there!" says the Marquis. "Remove it altogether from the room! Take it away! You know its place——"

There is neither anger nor passion in his manner. It is rather the firm, but sorrowful bearing of one called upon to perform a painful duty.

This seems more than Sigismund can bear. With a furious gesture he rises.

"You cannot—you dare not—banish" (I did not catch the name). "Her right is equal to your own! Never while I live shall you avail yourself of her weakness! If she goes, I go also!"

He stops, arrested by the death-like pallor of the Marquis, who sits, pressing one hand against his heart, and panting for breath. Then, as if all at once realising my presence, Sigismund bows to me hastily, and strides out of the room.

For once in his life Frederick has the sense to understand he is not wanted, and, as he can eat no more, he rises also, and disappears.

CHAPTER VIII.

ANZANO and I were now alone. He was leaning back in his chair, too much overcome to notice anything. His chest heaved, and the muscles of his throat were swollen to bursting.

What could possibly be the cause of such intense excitement? Sigismund? His marriage? Some feud between the brothers?

I dared not ask my friend. I dared not even express compassion for his condition, so cold and impenetrable was his aspect, as he sat apart, battling with his emotion. Gradually his laboured breathing became more regular, the rigid attitude relaxed. I perceived that I had judged rightly in leaving him to recover himself in silence, for no sooner was he somewhat restored, than I could see he was endeavouring so to control his features as to make it appear that he attached no importance to Sigismund's reproaches.

Raising himself with an effort, he slowly took out his cigar-case, offered it to me, who declined with a silent bow, selected one for himself, and began to smoke.

In the brief space occupied by these moments of suffering, I came to realise what a lifetime had passed since we had met. What did I know of the secrets those years contained? That he had secrets was clear. To say nothing of Filippo's story, he himself had confessed as much to me. Would he now disclose more?

"Lucius," he said at last, gazing appealingly into my face and clasping one of my hands—his thin, bony fingers lingering among mine, as if the contact was grateful to him—"Lucius, when you proposed to visit me, my first movement was one of joy. I had not known such joy for years. I seized a pen, and in a kind of *furore*, indited a letter entreating you to come. Before that letter was finished reflection followed. I doubted whether I ought to receive you. Never did I feel—no, never"—again he pressed my hand—"more profoundly how much I loved you. But there are circumstances in our family over which I have no control—Would to Heaven I had!" he ejaculated in a parenthesis, "—upon which I must be absolutely silent. Dear Lucius, I warn you of this beforehand. Do not let it vex you."

His manner was as tender as a woman's. A mournful, yearning expression was in his eyes as he turned them on me—a kind of physical clinging in his attitude more felt than expressed, that lent conviction to his words.

Quick as lightning, a flash of thought revealed him to me as a man predestined to some fatal doom; what I could only guess, but doomed irrevocably.

"Anzano,"—my voice was trembling, and tears were in my eyes—"we have ever been as brothers."

"More than brothers," he murmured, glancing with knitted brows at the seat lately occupied by Sigismund.

"Tell me frankly, by the confidence between us,

shall I return to-morrow morning to Siena? Our carriage is still here. Believe me, I would go, never doubting your affection."

"No, no!" he cried, almost wildly. "No!"

His deep-toned voice woke the echoes of the room, darkened by the sombre reflex of the deep red hangings and the funereal hue of the antique furniture.

"Shall it be said that Anzano Gonzago is sunk so low that he dare not receive his friend?"

Here he was forced to stop; his voice shook so violently. Had he uttered another syllable, he would have sobbed aloud. What he said was wrung from his innermost heart. He did not want to speak—he would have preferred heroically to suffer in silence; but his strong attachment to me overmastered his pride, and drove him to expression. How I pitied his struggles—the struggles of a noble nature, vanquished by a relentless fate.

The tears brimming in my eyes now rolled down my cheeks.

"I will do what you like," I answered, as soon as I could speak. "I place myself at your disposal. Command me. If you wish me to stay, I stay; if you wish me to go, I go. I will do anything to serve you."

"I know you will, Lucius," he replied, clasping my hand warmly; then added, when we were more composed: "If you want to comfort me, stay. Your departure would wound me beyond expression. Stay, Lucius, and help me to bear what lies before me. Brain, reason, life even——"

A profound sigh broke his words. Then, as if

determined to change the subject, he made a feeble effort to re-light his cigar.

"You do not smoke?" he asked, trying hard to resume his usual manner.

"Rarely," I replied. "Not now," and I put aside the cigar he offered me. "But, my dear Anzano, how can I help you, if you do not trust me? You confided to me the loss of your betrothed. Go on further."

"True, true," he replied, "whatever relates to myself. But you do not know—you cannot comprehend the difficulties of my position. It involves others besides myself. Both the dead and the living. The dead vicariously, the living as the condition of my birth. Besides, I am convinced you would not believe me. You would treat all I said as the hallucination of an over-excited brain. You English are so different; you live in the light of the sun; all your actions are open. There is nothing, in fact, to hide about you or your families. But we, born of the old Latin races, crime-stained and historic, are otherwise.

"Within the mouldering halls of our feudal palaces, lurks many a dark tale of treachery and murder. Our ancestral strongholds have been too often the scene of conspiracy and bloodshed. Son has risen against father, brother against brother, the vassal against his lord. The gloomy traditions of the past cling to our walls. Even among the wild fastnesses of our mountains, in the solitude of our pre-historic woods——"

Here his voice failed him for a moment. Would

7*

he seek to map out thus in measured language his
own history?

"The fair face of Nature blackened by shadowy
forms, called up from another world to cry vengeance
against the living! Such is often our life, Lucius—a
life burdened, not always by our own misdeeds, but
by those bequeathed to us from our fathers. Inherited with our lands—stained with the blood they
shed, the sacrilege they committed."

"In a word, your old enemy, the Greek Nemesis,
Anzano, of classic drama, brought into modern life!—
eh, my friend?"

But he gave no heed to me. His face had grown
dark, his voice sounded hollow, and those wild eyes
of his moving restless in their orbits, seemed un-
ceasingly to follow something which horrified while it
fascinated him. I had noted this in the ilex-wood.
Now I trembled for his reason.

It was this feeling which made me endeavour to
give a lighter turn to the conversation.

"You are very mysterious," I continued in the
same tone. "The Italy you describe is not the beautiful, cheerful land I delight in—full of happy, pleasure-
seeking multitudes. I cannot venture to dispute with
you on your own ground," I added, "neither can I
pretend to understand you."

He shook his head mournfully.

"Thank God, it is not with you as it is with me,
Lucius! Seek to know nothing here beneath the surface. When knowledge brings sorrow, happy are the
ignorant! I, too, was once ignorant! Would that I
had died before that changed!"

He stopped and shuddered, then dropped his head on his breast, and sat like one entranced.

I felt utterly at a loss. This atmosphere of mystery, this sombre pre-occupation, oppressed me. Always on the point of telling me some terrible secret, he always drew back just as the words trembled on his lips.

Bodily fatigue too increased my perturbation. I moved uneasily in my chair. The bronze clock on the carved chimney-piece pointed to eleven. I had been astir since five.

"I will say thus much, Lucius," said the Marquis suddenly, evidently following out some line of thought that had risen in his brain. "Let nothing that my brother, Sigismund, says or does, surprise you. Sigismund has many noble qualities. His physical beauty is his least merit. He is brave, constant and loyal; until lately, I should have added, deeply attached to myself. For many years we have lived together as true brothers, spite of the external difference of age and of habits.

"But the time has come when I have been called upon to control him. He resents this as a deadly injury. He is acting under the influence of passion. He hates me!—Soon he will curse me! Nor will that move me; time and circumstances must be my justification."

What a weary sigh heaved his breast! And how far away his wild eyes wandered!

"This is not the moment," he continued, trying hard to assume a more equable tone, "to speak of myself—the moment of your arrival. I had hoped Sigismund would have exercised more control in your

presence, but he forgot himself. Under that gracious
exterior he is capable of desperate resolves. Again I
say, be surprised at nothing he does or says. Pass it
over, my friend—Do not observe it."

I was utterly staggered at this extraordinary language. The marriage! The empty chair! Was it
about that empty chair the brothers had quarrelled?
That chair, or rather the person that should have
filled it? Why should Anzano not tell me?

As we sat on, my eyes following the slowly revolv-
ing minute-hand of the clock, and wondering within
myself when he would propose a move, I heard footsteps outside in the hall. The stillness of the night
was so intense, that the sound quite startled me. Immediately after, Sigismund and Frederick entered together. Every cloud had vanished from Sigismund's
brow. He too, like his brother, evidently desired to
make me forget what had passed. Avoiding the side
of the table on which Anzano sat, he placed himself,
with studied courtesy, on my other side.

"I have just met Mr. Stanley in the colonnade," he
said. "We have been talking; I am glad to find he is
fond of sport. He affects to laugh at our Italian game;
but I tell him that the wild-boar in these ilex-woods
and the deer on the tops of the mountains will afford
him quite as much excitement as fox-hunting."

"Ah! but it is the sport—the riding! Not the
little miserable fox!" I replied, smiling both at
Frederick's pretensions and Sigismund's determination
to make the most of what he could offer.

"I propose," continued Sigismund, "to spend a
quiet day to-morrow showing Mr. Stanley our woods.
You must not be prejudiced against them by first im-

pressions taken at night. By daylight, I assure you,
you will think the ilex trees magnificent."

An audible yawn from Frederick, who had thrown
himself upon a distant couch, broke in upon our conversation—a yawn so audible that even the Marquis
was aware of it.

He first looked at me, then at Frederick.

"I see you are tired, Lucius. As for my young
friend there, I need not ask if bed will be agreeable
to him. His unsophisticated frankness delights me,"
he added, as he rose from the table.

Sigismund, keeping well out of the range of his
brother's eye, rose also, and taking a hasty leave of
me, retired before we left the dining-room.

The candles were burning low in their sockets
when we returned to the hall. A strong current of
outer air from the entrance—(the door was still wide
open; indeed, I may here remark that I never saw that
door closed at any hour)—was blowing them about
wildly, the light glancing fantastically on the busts;
there catching a lock of marble hair—there the stony
eyebrow of an imperial personage; playing on the tip
of an august nose, or on a pupil-less eye, formed to
command; the cardinal's hat assuming colossal proportions as it swayed in mid-air, and a central giran-
dole scintillating fitfully.

Frederick and I trod uncertainly upon shafts of
yellow light flitting across the marble floor, and
stumbled as we miscalculated our distance in the
gloom.

From a table of rich mosaic, our host took a
lighted *lucerna*, and with a ceremonious bow proceeded
to usher us towards an archway which broke the side

wall to the right, leading to a flight of stairs that lost themselves in darkness.

"Excuse me, Lucius," he said, before setting his foot on the first step, "if I precede you in my own house. The servants have omitted to light up the stairs, and you may find the ascent difficult."

Holding the *lucerna* high above his head, he passed on, his dark figure forming itself into a centre round which the light played.

What stairs! Straight, broad, steep and funereal. Each step answering to the next, as if they never were going to end. I heard Frederick puffing behind me; the Marquis ascended steadily. Now he shifted the *lucerna* a little, and his figure formed itself into the image of a gigantic spectre, engulfing us in its sepulchral gloom.

At length we reached a broad square landing, where marble casings enclosed various lofty doors. Straight before us stretched another flight of stairs, steeper, if possible, than the last.

"Ay Jove!" exclaimed Fred, "this is a winder!"

The Marquis smiled as he noticed our looks of dismay.

"You will get accustomed to this in a week, Lucius. We must have space for our vaulted ceilings, especially in such rooms as these," and he pointed to the closed doors opening from the landing. "They lead into the state apartments. Permit me."

Again he preceded us, and again he assumed the appearance of a gigantic spectre. Some muttered exclamations from behind betrayed the discomfiture of Frederick.

Just as I was giving in, overcome by heat and

fatigue, the stairs ended, and the Marquis, with a bow, led us along a spacious gallery, on one side of which a row of closed windows fronted, as I perceived, the façade of the house, over the stone coronet. One of the windows which, lighted up, had so riveted the gaze of the handsome Sigismund, when we were standing in the garden looking up at the illumination.

Various doors broke the surface of the wall opposite. All were closed. Not a sound of any living creature anywhere, only the low moan of the night wind as it sighed mournfully under the broad eaves of the roof.

"Here, Lucius, is your room," and the Marquis opened a door at the further extremity of the gallery. "It is the most comfortable in the house. I would not consign you to the guest chambers below, which form part of the state apartments. The dark hangings and the enormous bedsteads would probably have spoilt your rest. I am sure they would not have been to your English taste. Here you will be more at home, I hope."

Whilst addressing me, he lighted a pair of massive silver candlesticks upon the toilet.

"You will thank me for the climb in the morning, when you see the view."

I thanked him as well as my short breath allowed, and looked round.

"Nothing can be more homelike," said I. "An iron bed, with white cotton hangings, plain handsome walnut furniture, a soft carpet, mirrors, a clock, an armchair. What can I wish for more? I feel I shall sleep like a top. Good-night, dear Anzano! You judged wisely in not putting me into one of the state bedrooms. Good-night——"

"And now, my young friend,"—the Marquis is addressing Frederick, after shaking my hand affectionately—"follow me to your room."

"Am I to sleep in a state bed with velvet and brocade?" asked Fred, looking at him aghast.

"And if it were so, Signor Stanley, what have you to fear?" he answered haughtily, drawing himself up to his full height. "Do you think I have a band of brigands concealed within my house?"

As he closed my door, I heard him still continue in the same offended tone:

"Youth ought to fear nothing—nothing but sin!" he added hastily.

What reply Frederick made to this sententious remark, I was happily spared from hearing. Probably he was too puzzled to reply at all. Gonzago evidently over-awed him.

Their retiring footsteps came dimly to my ear through the closed door. Then I heard another door bang violently at the extremity of the gallery, the noise ringing through the silence like the report of a pistol, and another door opened and shut.

Surely Frederick had said nothing to offend the Marquis, or were there more persons about than had appeared as we traversed the upper story?

CHAPTER IX.

INSTEAD of going at once to bed, I drew out one of the arm-chairs and sat down.

I was dreadfully tired, but I had reached that stage of fatigue when the action of the brain, concentrating in itself all the energies of the body, produces an intense excitement fatal to sleep.

Left to myself, I forgot my friend, I forgot Sigismund, I forgot everything but the strangeness of the place in which I found myself. Did the sun ever shine on the roof over my head, or did the mountains rise up and cover it? Did men like others, live in this strange abode, or were ghosts, bogies, banshees and spectres let loose to torment the living who dared to intrude here?

Nothing but the reassuring neatness of the white curtains met my eye, but between me and those innocent curtains a fantastic world lay hidden.

How ghastly it must be down in the ilex-wood under the pale glimmer of the moon! The brooding masses of quivering foliage drooping over the red soil! Were the trees, bending their heads and swaying their branches mutely, and were owls, bats and bullfrogs, screeching out their midnight chant in horrible chorus?

The Satyr! As I recalled that faceless monster in the moonlight, its mangled form aloft on its pedestal,

I actually shuddered. Was its wicked head still swaying in the wind, as I saw it? Was it sighing that hollow sigh that echoed mine? Was Gigia watching under
its evil shade, her dazzling hair glittering against the
stars?

Bit by bit, Filippo's story rose up palpable before
me. I saw the Cardinal's red coach turn the angle of
the road, Gigia start from the marble bench, out of
the midst of flowers, the leer he cast upon the child,
his outward-pointed thumb, his whispered command
to his secretary, the jewelled ring sparkling on the
earth, the paid assassins, who carried her off, her
ignorant terror, those monstrous espousals, still celebrated, night after night, by spectres, and that last
dagger-thrust, which ended her innocent life, when
that life was blasted. The young priest, too, with the
look of terror in his eyes, who died so suddenly. Was
he murdered, that he might not sqeak? And the old
man, Giacomo—Gigia's grandfather?—Did the curse
of these iniquities cling to Anzano? The vacant chair
—what did that portend? Was some horrible crisis at
hand, in which I should be implicated?

Here my brain lost itself in wild conjectures. If
it were so, I resolved I would not forsake Anzano. I
had promised to help him—I would keep my word.
This thought calmed me. It was a practical issue out
of bewildering unreality.

Then my train of thought shifted, and I endea-
voured to recall all that I had, from time to time,
heard of my friend's career.

In my present mood, fatigued and exhausted, but
wakeful, my memory ran back, with startling distinct-

ness, over a whole series of years—recalling long-forgotten events and dimly remembered details.

The "*bell' Anzano*," as Gonzaga was called (after all, Sigismund was but a replica of his brother on a grander scale), was, I had heard, a leader among the highest aristocracy at Rome, and rode to hounds on his English hunters as no Italian ever did, before or since.

He was not wanting either in more gentle accomplishments. As a boy, he had played and sung admirably. Later, I was informed, he was esteemed, even in fastidious Italy, a first-rate musician; also an elegant artist in the *genre* style. Some of his works were exhibited at Milan, among other places, where I had recognised them with pleasure, signed by his name.

"His manners were said to be the happiest mixture of sweetness and dignity." A French Diplomatist told me this, and added:—"There was a charm about him which even broke through the *morgue* of the Roman princesses. He arranged fêtes, pic-nics and *petits-diners* of an *entrain* never before permitted in their august circle. All prejudices—envy itself, was silenced by his goodness and talent."

The Pope, I heard, during one of my early autumn visits to Rome—where I had always missed my friend, for that was the time of the Italian villeggiatura, when the world of fashion was absent—had made him a personal request to command his Guardia Nobile. This Gonzago declined, as I understood, as infringing on his independence, political and personal. (There was a report that his devotion to a certain royal princess, then residing at Rome, was the true motive of this refusal.) A coolness with the Vatican—I am now speaking of many years ago, when the Pope was not a "prisoner"—ensued, which caused my friend to leave the City. To Victor Emmanuel he never rallied himself.

Many of these details I had completely forgotten, but in my excited condition they all came back to me. Every little word recalled as clearly as if told me but yesterday.

Then I heard of the Marquis, years after, at Siena, keeping open house in his ancestral palace, with a magnificence quite mediæval. I had at that time made up my mind to pay him a visit, but the death of Frederick's mother, my favourite sister, called me back unexpectedly to England.

During a hasty trip to the Italian lakes, a rumour of his approaching marriage reached me. The lady's name escaped my memory. Indeed, as I had not heard that the marriage was broken off by the tragical death of his betrothed, the particulars of which he had just related to me—I was under the impression, when I proposed visiting him, that he was already married. But his reply undeceived me. The loss of this lady, however severely felt—and the strange circumstances attending her death, were such as would shock in no common degree a nature as sensitive and superstitious as Anzano's—could scarcely have sufficed to sever him so utterly from his former life.

No! The cause must be sought in some mysterious connection between his uncle, the Cardinal, and himself. His own half-dropped words led to this conclusion. These dark hints pointed manifestly to some cause out of the ordinary course of nature.

The morbid workings of his brain, the abrupt

transition from ordinary conversation to lugubrious abstraction, his brooding looks and the weird atmosphere in which he lived, alarmed me for his reason.

My poor friend! How he must have suffered! At this point my thoughts suddenly drifted into a new current. Was it possible that, after all, he was an incurable hypochondriac? He looked thin and ill. Could disease have transformed him into what I found him?

A hypochondriac! A new idea! Yes, that might account for his condition—his melancholy aspect and extraordinary prepossessions!

After all, what had I heard? A wild story from a driver of Siena. As the Marquis said, he might be a liar, and his lies might have led me, unconsciously, to imagine a great deal, referring to entirely different causes. The division between the brothers, so tragically impressive from that melodramatic manner natural to Italians, might, in reality, be nothing but a temporary estrangement; some passing fancy of Sigismund's, unsanctioned by his brother. Yes, yes! it must be so. I had allowed myself to be unduly impressioned.

That Gonzago, with his boyish belief in Nemesis and the blind power of fate, might, after a solitary existence among these dreary woods and repellent mountains, be suffering from a monomania dangerous to his sanity, was of course possible; but that I, breathing the wholesome tonic of the outer world, should catch the infection, was a supposition both childish and absurd.

Feeling thoroughly ashamed of myself, I rose from the comfortable chair in which I had ensconced myself, and proceeded to undress.

Some benevolent individual connected with my

friend's household, had unpacked my trunk and
thoughtfully laid my dressing-gown across a chair.
Never before did I so rejoice in the possession of that
loose and commodious garment, in exchange for a
cloth coat, so inappropriate to August in Italy.

I looked round the room.   Could anything be
more cosy?   A happy union of homeliness and luxury.
The wax-lights in the tall, silver candlesticks burned
brightly, doubling themselves in a toilet-glass, more
appropriate, in size and decoration, to a belle preparing for a ball, than to a stout old gentleman with
nothing in the way of personal attractions.

Turning round, I lovingly contemplated the bed,
with its white hangings looped up with pink bows.   A
touch of art, those pink bows, from some amiable
female; the bed-linen, too, as white as snow, and smell-
ing sweetly of lavender, looked most inviting.

Had I been asked at this moment if I had heard
or seen anything extraordinary since I had entered
the ancestral woods of the Gonzagos, I should have
laughed scornfully and answered—"No!"   All thought
was melting into a delicious torpor.   The whole world
loved me, and towards the whole world I felt a sleepy,
comfortable benevolence.

*   *   *   *   *

The promise of the bed was not delusive.   A more
downy combination never yielded to the form of man.
Sufficiently soft to sink into—yet endured with an
elastic resistance that raised it above all suspicions of
the emollient weakness of feathers.   I was in the very
act of obeying literally those expressive words of
Scripture—"Folding my hands to rest, and my eyelids

to slumber," when the door burst open, and Frederick stood before me.

"Uncle Lucius!" he exclaimed in a husky voice, utterly unlike his own. "All that fellow Filippo told us, is true! *I have seen her!*"

"Hey—what?" I answered, out of the bed-clothes.

"*Her!*" he repeated, with a gasp.

"Seen *whom*, Fred? Speak out, boy."

He only shook his head.

"Then, perhaps," said I, waxing wroth at this unseemly interruption, "if you cannot make it convenient to tell me whom you mean, you will go away and leave me to sleep."

"Mean!" ejaculated Fred. "Why, Gigia—the ghost! Oh, uncle, why did you come to this awful hole?"

"Ghost, indeed! Frederick, you are either out of your mind, or drunk! You have been improving the occasion downstairs with Sigismund."

"I'll take any oath I haven't stirred." And, without another word, he sank upon a chair.

"Oh, go to the devil!" I cried, now thoroughly exasperated. "What right have you to come here and waken me out of my first sleep? I don't care to hear about your ghosts. Go away!"

"Uncle, I cannot go away. I—I——" His voice died away in his throat.

"Are you aware you are making yourself a nuisance —a positive nuisance?" I was now sitting up in bed. In that position I could see him better. He was as white as a sheet; his lips, even, colourless.

"As you have woke me up, do prevail upon your-

self to explain as quickly as possible what you mean,
and then—*go!*"

I emphasised the word angrily. A reproachful
glance from Frederick silenced me. Poor boy! there
was a hollow look about his eyes, darkened by black
circles, and he shivered so violently that his teeth
chattered. As he sat staring straight before him, the
living image of terror, that fold of universal benevolence
which had so lately enshrouded me gradually gave
place to a vivid recollection of the mysterious warnings
I had felt in the presence of the Marquis.

"Be a man, for God's sake, Fred!" I said, prop-
ping myself up with the pillows. "Whatever you have
seen, or think you saw——"

This doubt brought Frederick to himself. He
started up, and the ordinary expression returned to
his face.

"*Thought* I saw, uncle! There was no thinking
about it! I had no time to think. I tell you I have
seen her—she came into my room!"

"Oh, bosh!" I answered. I must confess I did
not want to be persuaded that he had seen anything
supernatural.

"Upon my honour!" he cried; "my *honour*, uncle
Lucius!"

"Oh, you be hanged!" I replied angrily, turning
towards the wall. As soon as I had spoken the words,
I was sorry. It was an unfeeling remark. Fred on
his part was furious.

"What right have you to doubt my word?" he
demanded, with flashing eyes.

"Softly, Fred, softly; don't put yourself in a passion.

Remember we are the guests of the Marquis Gonzago, under his roof and enjoying his hospitality."

"Hospitality be blowed!" answered Fred quickly, standing by my bedside and throwing his arms about like a maniac. "The Marquis has no right to offer hospitality when he knows he has a ghost in his house. Besides, I don't like his looks; he is a bad lot. I warned you when we were standing outside the house! It looked like a whitened sepulchre in the moonlight. There is some beastly mystery about the whole place, and the people that live here. They are not up and down all right. Why on earth you, who are such a brick, came poking after that old party, your school-fellow, I can't conceive! Being here, I will not go away without coming to the bottom of it all. That black-looking Marquis—I'll unearth him! Don't dispute with me, uncle," he added, in answer to a mute expostulation of my hands out of the bed-clothes. "It is no use. The ghost has come to me, and I will know the reason! She——"

"Who is *she?* Will you condescend to explain yourself? Only, for God's sake, don't scream so! You will awake somebody."

"Wake! I wish I could wake the whole house and tell them what I think!"

"When you are calmer, Frederick, perhaps you will kindly enter into some intelligible details. Remember I am in utter ignorance of what has occurred."

I leaned back on my pillows and sighed. Was sleep gone from me for ever? I suppose I looked what I felt—both exhausted and dispirited. Frederick suddenly softened.

"I beg your pardon, uncle. It was your unbelief that nettled me. No fellow has a right to disbelieve what another fellow says, unless he knows him to be a liar."

"Go on, *please*," I said meekly. I was becoming really alarmed at the complications that were closing about me. Now, here was Frederick declaring he would not leave the house, until he had hunted up the family spectre.

"It is to be hoped," I added spitefully, "this apparition will not frighten you so much the next time you meet."

Fred reddened to the roots of his hair.

"I won't be spoken to in that tone," he answered. "It is too bad!"

"My dear Fred, if you want me to listen to you, try to be calmer. I am ready to give credit to all the marvels you may have to relate; and further, I am willing, if you can obtain the Marquis's permission, to remain indefinitely in his house, in order, as you say, to unravel a mystery involving himself and his family. Pray observe I make no objection."

Gradually it seemed to strike Frederick that I was in complete ignorance of what had happened.

"Listen, uncle! When the Marquis—I am sure he is an old villain——"

At this I waved my hands, determined to avoid needless discussion.

"When we left you in this room, he led me to the other end of the gallery. When I passed with you, I did not notice a thick curtain covering an archway in the wall opposite the range of windows. This curtain was now drawn aside, and a dim lamp, fixed in the wall, shewed another gallery, much longer and narrower, leading to an entirely different part of the house. The Marquis passed very quickly by, giving me an ugly look as if to see what I had noticed; then stretched out his hand to close the curtain, but, thinking better of it apparently, went on, without doing so. Opposite your room there are two doors. He tried the one nearest to the stairs. It was fastened.

"This seemed to upset him terribly. He turned the key in the lock several times, and shook the handle violently; then fell back, and with the light examined the panels all over. Again he tried the handle; it was no good—the door was fast. Saying something about 'malediction' in Italian, he went on to the next door, the one nearest to the window. The handle of this turned easily enough.

"I took notice of all this, because there was something so peculiar in his manner, and he seemed so angry about the locked door. He never said a single word except that oath in Italian, but he kept twisting round his head as if he expected to see something behind him. Once he stopped short, and listened. I heard nothing, nor did he, I think, for after a moment, he seemed satisfied.

"The room we got into was small—much smaller than this. There was no bed in it. A fire was smouldering on the hearth, a sofa drawn out beside it, and some flowers in a vase smelt very sweet and homelike. The chairs were all pulled about, as if they had been lately sat on. A black lace veil hung on one, a shawl on another; and a broad blue ribbon lay, just as it had dropped, upon the floor.

All this put the Marquis out more and more, par-

ticularly when going on into a second room, opening
from this one (the same, I conclude, as that of which
he could not undo the lock), he tripped over an open
box. The lid he rammed down with a bang, and
kicked the box into a corner, looking all the time as
black as thunder.

"With a lofty gesture, like the heavy father in a
pantomime, he pointed to the bed in the inner room
(bare enough, I assure you, without a scrap of furniture), made me a grand bow, and went away.

"I was not a bit sleepy; the Marquis's odd ways
had set me thinking. I took up the lace veil and
examined it; the blue ribbon was gone, he must have
bagged it. They must both belong to some pretty
girl, I thought. That rogue, Sigismund—was he concerned? And his old Turk of a brother in a devil of
a rage that I had come on it?"

It will be seen that, as he proceeded, Frederick
has resumed his usual bluff manner. But I must observe that before continuing his very disjointed narrative, he had taken a small travelling-flask of brandy
from his pocket, and apparently emptied it.

"Well, Uncle Lucius, I stretched myself on the sofa,
and fell to thinking about Sigismund, and how he contrived to amuse himself in this old rookery, with that
antique brother, who bows with his heels together like
a dancing-master; until, at last, I laughed outright.
Somehow, my voice did not seem my own, but some
one else's. That gave me a sort of turn, but I got
over it, and began to arrange how I would chaff that
upsetting Sigismund in the morning, about the owner
of the blue ribbon.

"Then all the strange things that coachman said,

came to my mind. The poor little devil of a girl running about in the woods with her pigs, singing her little songs, to be clawed up after all, by that brute of a Cardinal.

"I suppose I dozed off on the sofa. I woke up with a start, and there, Uncle—as I hope to be saved —before me, on the hearth, was something white, crouching! I could make out only the outline. I turned as cold as death. I wanted to call out, but my voice was gone. I broke out into a cold sweat all over. There it sat, all white—holding out its little hands to warm them! Something stirred in the fire, and a long, bright flame shot up the chimney. There she was, plainly, just as the man said—all huddled together. Long, light hair hanging all about. A white face and dark eyebrows!

"All at once I felt her eyes upon me. Lord! How cold they made me! There was a cry. I don't know where it came from. I don't know if I cried, or how it was—but after the cry, there was nothing between me and the fire.

"I rubbed my eyes. It was gone! I wanted to follow it—through the house—into the woods, anywhere; but, hang it all! I had not strength to stand, much less to run! There I sat like an idiot, until I pulled myself together, and rushed off to you. But I will follow her, poor innocent little thing; if I die for it, I will! She came to me. Perhaps she will speak to me. That coachman said she called to people in the woods. Brutes! Why did they not answer? By Jove, I will! If that olive-skinned party, the Marquis, has anything to do with it, I'll—I'll—damn it—I'll horse-whip him before his own servants."

"Frederick, you are a noodle! Just now it was all terror, now it is all revenge. Oblige me by at least respecting the name of my friend, the Marquis, until you have anything definite to accuse him of. Your language is exceedingly painful to me. The Marquis is as honourable and high-minded a man as God ever created. If you have really seen anything supernatural—I don't mean to offend you, but I believe Filippo's story was in your head, and that you dreamed you saw something."

At this a loud and indignant snort from Fred.

"—Never mind, that is my opinion. The girl, Gigia, is said to haunt the woods, not the villa, remember. Whatever you decide to do—and I am sure I have no power to restrain you—avoid remark or observation. That there is some story about, connected with this place, is clear. What foundation there is for it is not at all so. At any rate, it must be a painful subject. Now, pray, go back quietly to your room; or, if you are afraid, lie down beside me on this bed."

"Thank you, Uncle," said Frederick, much mollified. "You are very kind, but I will not disturb you. It was the first fright, and that infernal driver's stories down in the ilex-wood that upset me. Now, I give you my word, I would sacrifice all I possess"—(meaning a tooth-pick and a boot-jack)—"to see her once more."

"Well, Frederick, I am glad you take the ghost so heroically. I daresay it won't come back again. They never do."

"I only wish it would," was his answer.

"Mind, if you cannot sleep, come to me."

"All right, uncle! I don't care to sleep—Good-night."

Again my door closed; again I was left to my own reflections.

Far, very far, were they from taking the light tone I had adopted with Frederick. It was deep into the night before I closed my eyes.

———

CHAPTER X.

I WAS awoke early in the morning by the persistent sunshine. Like a conqueror, deriding all barriers, it forced itself into the room.

I rose and unfastened one of the windows. The fresh morning air pushed both the sashes open, and an odour of countless sweets rushed in, along with the song of birds and the chirrup of insects.

As I leaned out, a more laughing prospect never gladdened the heart of man.

What a contrast to the gloomy picture I had made to myself last night of my friend's abode. Last night! I felt as if it had never been. Surely nothing but a dream—a nightmare—from which I had awakened!

Before me, in the softest tints of blue, shading into lilac, uprose a mighty mountain. Not a speck of mist, not a cloud of vapour shrouded the crystalline outline of its double summits. From the position I knew that it must be Monte Amiata, the highest Apennine between Umbria and Rome.

A vast, undulating plain lay beneath. In the near distance, lines of hills ridged upwards like furrows, dotted with innumerable white homesteads, each with its little cane-brake and group of cypress. Villages there were also, thinly scattered—for it is a mountain region—dyed brown with the sun, and still browner churches, with tall, open campanili and small burghs, half-castle, half-tower, perched on elevated knolls.

Further away to the left, backing the range of the Chianti hills, still wrapped in deep shadows, lay a wild, volcanic region, terminating in lines of defiant-looking mountains, among which I guessed that Perugia and Cortona lay nestled. And behind a certain low ridge of barren hills in the same direction, well to the left, the lake of Thrasymene must be hidden.

Immediately in front, a dark cincture of forest divided the lands of the Marquis from the plain, and shut in the plateau on which the villa stands. A glorious mantle—one sheet of myrtle-green—on which each evergreen leaf glittered resplendent.

Great fleecy clouds hovered over the mountains, and, minutely mapped out, before me lay the symmetrical garden, where we had rested last night in the moonlight; the gravel walks, with their trim border of orange-trees, bristling cacti, and the silvery fronds of pampas-grass—statues and vases marking the angles; the fountains bubbling among the flowers in a music of their own, to the joy of shoals of gold-fish floating underneath.

Little gusts of warm air went and came, bearing fragile petals. Birds twittered under the roofs, and every now and then a hurried rush of wings told that the swallows were departing.

Up to the verge of the lofty iron gates which we had passed last night, and in which I recognised the fine iron-work for which Siena is renowned, the ilex-trees came stealthily creeping.

How sad is a net-work of dark branches against a brilliant sky. Specially in the morning, when the day

is young and all nature gleeful. The dark leaves and
interlacing branches rose up ominous. I knew them
but too well. They came to me as a terror of the
night, dimly remembered—and the avenue by which
I mounted to the house, with its fantastic border of
clipped hedges and lofty statues, leading down to a
steep declivity, to re-appear again on a distant summit,
where a colossal statue of Hercules seemed to touch
the sky.

I was wondering what o'clock it was—for in the
confusion of last night I had forgotten to wind up my
watch—when the sound of voices caught my ear, coming from the right-hand corner of the house. I moved
to another window.

One of the two voices I instantly recognised as
that of Filippo, our driver. He was just under me. I
knew him by the cock of his hat and the shock of
sunburnt yellow hair at the back of his head.

The other voice must belong to the gardener, for
I could make out a figure with a blue apron and
tucked-up sleeves. Beneath, in a kind of court, sacks
of charcoal lay piled up against a wall, and there was
a cart, to which oxen were yoked; at the bottom of a
hill, a black-skinned charcoal-burner, with a red face
and curious eyes peering out under his grimy cap,
passing to and fro.

I could see that he was making little attempts to
attract the attention of the two men under me, wiping
his mouth with his sleeve as a preliminary, but to no
avail.

Filippo and the gardener had settled themselves
with their backs to the wall, and went on talking.

"Is that man a spy, that he hangs about so?"

asked Filippo, pointing with his thumb to the charcoal-burner, slowly descending to his cart.

"*Chi lo sa?*" was the answer. "It is well to be careful here. But I cannot move further off and leave my wine-barrels. The steward thinks I am cleaning them." A grin.

"It is well to do no work, and get paid all the same," Filippo responds. "But if you were to offer me a month's wages, I would not come to this hole of Satan again."

He paused to light a pipe.

The sound of Filippo's voice vividly recalled to me all that had passed last night under the Satyr. Suddenly the fair face of Nature seemed to pale—the great circle of ilex trees to rise up large and dark like a wall—the network of branches to bristle against the sky, bringing to me an undefined sense of misery and suspense.

Again the voices,

"Achilles!" says Filippo, addressing the gardener, in the pauses of his pipe, "you see the last of me here. No money will bring me this way again. I never closed an eye last night, for fear of what I might see."

"I sleep well enough," is Achilles' grave rejoinder.

"So do I," puts in the charcoal-burner, who had returned unperceived, and was handling the pile of sacks on the ground, "when the frost does not bite me on the side off the fire."

The charcoal-burner's remark not being attended to, he strode silently towards the ox-cart, two sacks upon his back.

"Why does that fellow plague us?" asks Filippo,

looking after him with disdain. *"Cospetto!* I tremble as if in an ague! An old gentleman with a fat face and a big stomach" (this was myself, evidently—complimentary!) "and a young lunatic with him, who engaged me in the Square at Siena, made me relate the whole story of the Donnina last night, just under the Satiro. *Per Bacco!* If I am not well paid for that piece of work, my name is not Filippo Sanguerra."

"Speak lower," says Achilles, pointing significantly to the house; "where our master is the very walls have ears."

"Your master!" rejoins Filippo, in a tone of deep disgust; "leave him to his friend, the devil. I wonder he has not fetched him home long ago! A thousand years seem to have passed since I saw his nasty, yellow face in the moonlight! I made horns at him, Achilles, when he turned my way. He has the evil eye, that Marquis, if ever a man had!"

"Ah, our Marquis," replies cautious Achilles, "doubtless his Excellency has his reasons."

"*Altro!* why else should a rich gentleman live here?"

Filippo's hand waved contemptuously towards the villa and its mass of wings and out-buildings, in appearance like a small town.

"If the Marquis believed in God and the saints, he would inhabit his palace at Siena. The dust must be thick on those floors."

"Yes, unless ghosts dance there," hisses out Achilles spitefully.

Again the charcoal-burner approaches to fetch more sacks, hesitates for a moment, facing the two men, then smiles and nods his head, but as neither of them took the smallest notice of him, he turned away, whistling a tune, and slowly proceeded to charge himself with another load.

"Has your wife seen the ghost of Gigia lately?" asks Filippo suddenly.

At the mention of Gigia's name, I listen with all my ears; I cannot, as I have said, see the faces of the men, being directly over them; but I notice a certain intonation in Filippo's voice, as of one who advances cautiously on what he feels to be delicate ground.

Before he answers, Achilles' brown hand is burrowing deeply among his stiff head of hair.

At last, slowly: "My wife! why my wife? Amina is as another."

The stolid Achilles is evidently determined not to compromise himself.

"But the Marquis sees her," he adds hastily, as if conscious of having struck on a safe vein for satisfying his friend's curiosity.

"The Marquis sees her often; then he has his fits. No one dares go near him then but Narcissus. He sees, too, they say, all the spirits of the people murdered here by the Cardinal."

Again Achilles takes counsel by burying his fingers in his matted hair.

"But for the bread and the wine for the children, and our little patch of olives and chestnuts, who would stay? Beppo, the tin-smith, saw Gigia last Tuesday, with his own eyes."

"The devil!" exclaims Filippo suddenly.

"Hush! if you scream so I will tell you nothing," says Achilles resolutely.

The return of the charcoal-burner from the ox-cart

closes his lips. Again he stopped before the two men, again smiled and nodded in vain, then, with a shrug of his square shoulders, proceeded to load his sacks, giving one of Achilles' wine-barrels a vicious kick as he did so. As soon as his back is turned, the voices resume:

"It was about eight o'clock in the evening, when Beppo came along the road. The Marquis was standing in the road covered with a large cloak, and beside him a thin, glistening figure with eyes that burnt into your head. Down by the Satyr it was, and full of black shadows. Beppo, who is a prudent man, and dreads the devil, ran as fast as his legs could carry him down the hill. If the Marquis had seen Beppo he would have cursed him, and he would have dried up like a leaf!"

(My poor noble-hearted Anzano. This is the way the wretches who live on your bounty speak of you. I should dearly have liked to drop a ton or two of lead on the heads of these two scoundrels.)

"What would you expect?" puts in Filippo, "when a man dares not approach the Blessed Sacrament!"

"Ah, amico, I could tell you a great deal about that—the Blessed Sacrament and the Chapel," and the backs of two sun-burnt hands went up into the air.

"Tell me, tell me, my own Achilles!" whines Filippo, in a falsetto voice. "The best bottle of wine I have, and a ride through the town of Siena the next fête-day, for the Sora Amina are yours, if you do."

The gardener, evidently a man of few words, but those to the purpose, hesitated. Perhaps only for lack of that power of language the lowest Italian generally possesses, perhaps feeling he is embarking on a dangerous course.

"Consider the friendship of our families," urges Filippo, hanging on apparently to his neck. "Recount to me about the opening of the chapel. I am dying to know!"

The chapel! Here is a new vein of mystery! The ilex-wood; the old factory; Frederick's room; now the chapel. Whither am I drifting?

No more could be then said, for the charcoal-burner, with the same, wistful look on his face, again stood before them. He has been away longer this time. The more sacks he carries, the more difficult it is to him to load the cart. I had seen him struggling to get each one into its place in rows, and well-balanced, so as not to weigh too heavily upon the necks of the oxen—waiting with closed eyes, the picture of patient toil.

Now he fumbled among his dirty pockets and brings out a black pipe, which he twirls in his grimy fingers, casting an appealing look at the two friends. Evidently he is debating with himself whether he may venture to ask them for a match, but as neither speak nor move, the poor fellow turns on his heel and goes back to his sacks (there are but two or three left), lifts them slowly on his back, and, patient and laborious as his own grey beasts, slowly descends towards his cart.

In a few minutes the wheels are rumbling down the hill—the bells of the oxen sounding in the silent morn. Now he has turned a corner and is gone—but the echo of the bells sound farther and farther off, until—fainter and fainter—they die away among the trees.

"It was the month of May," Achilles begins. "Our Marquis had quarrelled with the rector about some altar furniture, so Don Antonio was to say mass. That Don Antonio!" A pause here, and much combating by Achilles among his hair. "He knows much.

"When the chapel was full and all the peasants kneeling (our Marquis kneeling too, before his seat, with the coronet on the back. He looked, that day, as if all his wholesome blood was turned to gall and poisoning him), and Don Antonio just raising the Host, there came such a clap of thunder, he would have let the Santissimo fall, if little Luigi, Cosimo's child, had not been sharp and caught him by the arm."

"Diamine!" from Filippo. "Is that all?"

"No!" Evidently Achilles cannot get on. He labours with his words, and twists his hands among his hair. Something very like an oath escapes him now. "If you hurry me," he says. "I will not say a word."

A volley of excuses from Filippo and a fresh start.

"When the very reverend Don Antonio had recovered, put away the Santissimo into its box, and was proceeding to repeat the Agnus Dei, the Marquis had gone."

"His evil conscience!" put in Filippo. "Before the Santissimo ·even the devil must confess. I am wise," he adds thoughtfully. "I know many things."

"That night, very late,"—Achilles is now fairly started in his narrative—"Adamo, our *fattore* (steward) looked out of the window before he went to bed, to see what the sky promised for cutting the barley in

the morning, when the figure of a young priest glided
down the steps of the old factory, where they hang
the grapes to dry because no one will sleep there."

"Yes, yes—I know," from Filippo. "Because of
the *donnina!*"

"Adamo said he saw the young priest as plainly
as I see you, Filippo—tall, in a black robe, and very
pale, carrying in his hand something that glistened.

"A ring—a ring!" suggests the irrepressible Filippo.
"Gigia's ring, with a big diamond in it! Her marriage
ring; Perhaps it was forgotten in the old house."

"I don't know," is Achilles' stolid answer. "I
heard nothing of a ring or of a marriage. The figure
crossed the grass among the statues and the orange-
trees, its shadow spreading over miles and miles of
wood, Adamo wondering, for the key was safe in his
pocket, because of the grapes. Then it melted into
the earth, close by the chapel door, and Adamo
dressed himself and went down, but he found nothing.

"Next day, as he was new to the place, he came
to me in the garden, and asked what it all meant."

"Wonderful, my Achilles!" returns Filippo, rubbing
his hands. "Truly, at Sant' Agata the devil does
what he likes."

     *   *   *   *   *

Now the men emerge from the shelter of the wall,
and Filippo takes out a large silver watch and looks
as it.

"Seven o'clock! Per Bacco! Why don't that old
fool of an Englishman get up and give me my money?
Time flies in good company! Come, my Achilles, lend
me a hand to rub down my horses. They must be

looking for me this long time. Horses are much better than men," observes Filippo sententiously. "They don't stab and poison like these Gonzagos, nor do their ghosts appear. *Santa Maria!* How I long to be back at Siena—in the rattle of the streets."

With one arm on Achilles' shoulder, they moved off into the outbuildings, Filippo's voice audible to the last:

"Not a cup of coffee to be had, nor a crust of bread! Infernal abode of Satan! Why did I come?"

———

CHAPTER XI.

THE first thing I did after Filippo and the gardener had disappeared, was to ring the bell.

That anyone should answer it in a house so enormous, or rather that a bell should have the power to vibrate to such a distance, seemed incredible. After a little delay, however, I actually heard footsteps in the far distance. Gradually they sounded along the gallery, and at last a knock at my door introduced an intense-eyed young man, with curly hair and a cheerful countenance, carrying a cup of coffee on a silver tray.

"Do me the favour," I said in Italian, thankfully accepting the coffee, "to find out the driver, Filippo by name, who brought me from Siena last night. Give him this money from me, and tell him to leave Sant' Agata instantly. If he refuses, or makes any difficulty whatever, assure him I shall at once report him and his sayings to the Marquis. Do you understand?"

"Perfectly, signor," replied the young man, becoming more cheerful and intense-eyed—indeed, absolutely beaming with cheerfulness as he saluted me —"The Excellency shall be obeyed. Has the Excellency any further orders for Narcissus? I am Narcissus, at your service."

"None, thanks."

Then the door closed, shutting out Narcissus, who retired with a graceful bow.

I may here mention that after the lapse of a few minutes, I was rejoiced by hearing the sound of wheels, rapidly driving away on the further side of the garden. It was a real relief to me to know that Filippo had departed.

Leisurely continuing my toilet, I felt, on the whole, rather ashamed of having listened to the conversation of this fellow and his friend. Curiosity is my weakness; I do not deny it. I was tempted, and I fell. After all, what had I heard? Nothing substantially more than I knew before, mixed up with absurd stories, and low, scurrilous abuse of my dear friend.

In the meantime, I surrendered myself to the magic of the sunshine, giving even my fat cheeks, as I contemplate myself in the glass, an aureole of brightness.

Sounds of life now rose up from below, telling that the household was astir. Servants cross and recross the gravel paths of the garden, from the colonnades of the portico to the entrance of the fattore's house.

Presently the fattore himself appears, in the person of a well-dressed man, with an air of deputy-mastership not to be mistaken. A large white mastiff follows at his heels, exciting the jealousy of a minute rat-terrier, with half a tail, barking on the threshold. The fattore dispenses his favours impartially between the dogs. The mastiff licks his hands, and makes dashes at him perilous to his equilibrium. The rat-terrier gambols confidingly between his legs.

Adamo—this must be Adamo, of whom I have just heard—takes all in good part; quiets the mastiff, caresses the terrier, and strides off, at last, through the iron gates, the dogs after him.

Then three beggars, a man, an old woman, and a boy, with naked feet, and barely decent as to clothes, come up by the grand entrance, through the iron gates. The old woman, a coarse white cloth upon her grisly hair, boldly leads the way. It is well the dogs are gone. The man, a poor, fever-stricken wretch, on whom death has set his seal, and the poor, hungry-looking lad, with even less clothes than the other two (I can see portions of his skin at *not* rare intervals), are much more shy. But the old woman pushes on, and seats them and herself upon a stone bench under the balustrade, where they remain so motionless, one might take them for statues, until they turn their heads as the door of the factory opens, and a comely matron, evidently the steward's wife, calls out: "Filomena!" when another half-naked person speedily presents herself, in the shape of a girl, very swarthy about the face and neck, with long, lanky legs made for running.

At a sign from her mistress, who really, as I look down on her, is a very enticing dame—although nothing she wears seems to fit her, and only hangs on by pins—Filomena vanishes.

Then, as she stands contemplating the beggars, who never move, she is gradually surrounded by scores of poultry, some flying, some running, some striding in their haste. A flock of peacocks trailing gorgeous tails, the hens meekly pecking as they go, strutting turkeys, speckled guinea-fowl with red ears, and hens and chickens of every form and breed, the bigger ones racing the little ones, who fall upon the ground.

Now Filomena, on her long legs, is back again, bearing a wooden platter with huge slices of coarse bread, and a bulky flask of red wine, which the steward's wife proceeds to divide between the beggars.

The sick man has dozed off on the bench, and is nodding painfully. The old woman wakes him by a rude shake, at which he starts and casts a reproachful glance, while she, for answer, pours a draught of red wine down his throat, bringing a faint flush of colour to his emaciated cheeks. The sick man cannot eat, but the boy and the old woman can, plentifully. The thick slices of bread disappear to the last crumb, and are washed down by wine.

I believe they would be eating still, if, when the dish was cleared and the flask emptied, the steward's wife had not made them a sort of rough curtsey, and driving back the troop of screeching poultry—perseveringly pecking at her shoes—held out her hand to help the sick man—who rises with a groan—gently leading him out of the iron gates (the old woman and the boy following), and with a nod wishing them good day. Upon which all kiss her fat hand, the sick man making a feeble endeavour to raise his cap.

Still engaged with my shaving at the open window, I next perceive a troop of goats descend from the mountains to be milked. They are quite alone, nibbling from side to side, and, as if they know their business, halt before the gates, until the great mastiff, who has returned, engages in a free fight with the he-goat, a hoary patriarch with twisted horns and matted hair; the mastiff getting much the worst of it and backing before the goat, until the steward's arrival decides

any doubt as to the issue of the combat. He igno-
miniously kicks the mastiff, and carefully leads in the
does, to the infinite disgust of the veteran, who, finding himself shut out, paces up and down the road,
butting at imaginary foes.

A flock of lambs next present themselves before
the grand entrance, as honoured guests. Just clipped,
they are as white as the first flakes of snow. A
shepherd-boy, of whose features nothing whatever can
be seen, by reason of his hair, drives them gently forward, waving an olive branch. The docile creatures
cluster round him when he stops, and lick his hands.

As the does vanished inside the gates, so vanish
the lambs. Then loaded waggons come lumbering
down, drawn by soft-eyed, grey oxen; a red fringe
dangling across their eyes; and light carts drawn by
diminutive ponies, carrying men much bigger than
themselves; all in turn to be caught up, and hidden
in the depths of the ilex-wood.

Just as I withdraw my eyes from the window, to
give the finishing touches to a dark blue cravat, and
to brush back such hair as kind nature still entrusts
to my care, a distant clock, the first clock I have yet
heard, strikes nine.

I open my door. The gallery, with its row of windows, and gay, trellised frescoes covering both wall
and ceiling—is bathed in sun. I see the arched door
with curtains, mentioned by Fred, as leading into more
distant corridors, but the curtains are closely drawn,
and I am afraid to meddle with them.

Opposite to me, are the two doors he described,
leading into the two rooms he occupies. One door is
open; perhaps Fred may be there.

I peep in. The room is empty. Never surely was anything more unlike the scene of a ghostly visitation. The walls are hung with pink paper, muslin curtains enshroud the windows, and a gay chintz covers the furniture.

I decide at once, being in a thoroughly lively and hopeful mood, under the influence of the splendid day and the general picturesqueness, that Frederick must have been dreaming.

"One of his fool's tricks!" I say to myself, complacently, as I look round.

Now I address myself, with due caution, to the descent of the perpendicular stairs—a feat requiring much sustained attention on the part of a novice, not desiring to break his neck.

On the landing of the first floor, stands the Marquis. Beside him a black-robed ecclesiastic, middle-aged and thin, whom I instantly recognise as the mahogany-skinned curate who, the day before, carried the Host in the procession of St. John.

As soon as he was aware of my presence, the Marquis dismissed the priest, who, bowing low, descended into the hall, and awaited me on the broad landing. Proceeding cautiously, I had time to note how worn and ill he looks by day-light. Either he has slept badly, or not at all. The dark rings round his eyes might have been painted. He greeted me, however, with his accustomed warmth, and again expressing his delight at seeing me under his roof.

As a rule, I hate any kind of display of feeling between men, but there was a manly tenderness about Gonzago, that was quite irresistible.

Anxiously he informed himself how I had passed

the night—if I had seen Signor Stanley? How he had also slept? All this with an unaccountable earnestness.

Having satisfied himself on these points, he opened one of the four doors on the landing, and, taking my hand, led me—(some reminiscence, I suppose, of the way we wandered about the meadows at school)—into a spacious ante-room, hung with pictures, on a background of red brocade.

I especially noticed four full-length portraits, somewhat in shadow, hanging on opposite walls.

As he was passing on rapidly I detained him.

"Family pictures of the Gonzagos?" I asked.

"Yes, yes," was his hurried rejoinder, endeavouring to lead me on.

But I was obstinate.

"The Gonzago Pope, of course?" and I pointed to a pale, hollow-cheeked pontiff, with a disproportioned nose, robed in white, seated on a throne, behind which rose the dome of St. Peter's.

The Marquis assented, and was proceeding with nervous haste, when I again paused.

"Cardinal Flavio?" I asked, as my eyes rested on the form of a majestic-looking prelate, in the prime of life, standing before the sculptured façade of a palace, his scarlet robes so arranged as to display a faultless foot and ancle.

While I gazed transfixed at the image of the man whose crimes had wrought such bitter wrong on his descendants, a sudden spasm passed over my friend's face; standing with his back towards the picture, his hand grasping the lock of the further door, while he cast an impatient glance at me.

"You appear to be deeply interested, Lucius," he said at last—that ever-ready suspicion getting the better of him. "May I ask what you know of the Cardinal, that you are studying his face so intently?"

"Nothing—nothing," rejoined I, ashamed of my own falsehood.

"Then pray come with me. The other pictures need not detain you," and he opened the door of the adjoining room,

(I really was obliged to force myself from that picture. It was exercising a fascination over me I cannot describe.)

"This is the saloon," said he, taking a long breath, as if evidently relieved. "The first in the suite of the state apartments."

"How superb!" was my involuntary exclamation. "And all this is yours, Anzano?"

His answer was a sigh.

"Well, you *are* a philosopher!" I exclaimed. "A philosopher or a cynic."

"I am not a cynic. I wish to God I were!"

The walls of the saloon—or hall, indeed, so vast were its proportions—were painted in the gaudy school of Raphael Mengs, or Luca Giordano. Historic scenes of groups and figures, as large as life, standing out from a varied background of sea and forest, city and plain. Something more brilliant and striking than tapestry, but with equal vigour of outline and gorgeousness of tone. Mirrors framed in richest arabesques of dead gold, divided the frescoes into panels.

The vaulted ceiling, separated from the walls by a heavy cornice, broken by supporting figures, also in dead gold, was ablaze with gods and goddesses, who,

freed from the restraints of earthly garments, were
joyously ascending into a central glory of saffron and
purple clouds.

The furniture, of the same date as the wall
frescoes, was ponderous with carved work. A long
table of carved ebony ran down the centre, laden with
a display of exquisite specimens of Faenza, Majolica
and Gubbio ware, tazze, Raphael plates and plaques,
fine jewelled chasings of the Bellini school, antique
bronze statuettes, and open cases of gems and coins.

A cool, half-light from the outer green shutters
cast a softened tint on the clashing splendours, also
toned down by a dark parquet floor, heaving door
hangings and window draperies.

The Marquis met my amazed eyes with a weary
smile.

"All this is suitable enough for a villa," he re-
marked carelessly. "You should see my collection at
Siena! That is worth looking at! You would not
care for any of these trifles then."

"And these trifles, as you call them—do they not
delight your eyes? Why, Anzano, I should spend my
life in turning them over."

As I spoke, I took up an amethyst lying in a satin-
lined case, with an exquisite cutting of Hercules and
Omphale. Then I lifted a priceless plate, with lovely
arabesques encircling the medallion of a Cupid. Next,
I lovingly fingered a Gubbio vase, with such an
opaline glaze, that it might have left the oven but
yesterday.

"I cared for these things once," was my friend's
cold reply. "Now the sight of them distresses me."

I looked at Anzano as he leaned over the table on

which my fingers were so busy, to read, if I could,
something on his face that might explain his words.
He was literally emaciated. Always rather tall, and
thin, his clothes now literally hung upon him, as if
nothing but bones remained. And how coarse and
common these clothes were, too! A rustic cut that
would have vulgarised any man less innately distinguished. And he, too, of all people! Such a *petit-
maître* once, no tailor could content him!

I noted also how feeble and languid were his
movements, as he followed me in my rapid dashes at
the wonders spread around. What a weight had
gathered on his brow, from which the poetic locks of
youth had receded! Mental agitation had consumed
vitality too visibly to make his face a pleasant study
for one who loved him.

Having exhausted the saloon, I was in the act of
drawing aside the tapestry which concealed the door
of the next apartment, when I found myself arrested
by his arm.

"Enough, enough, my Lucius! What do all these
baubles signify?"

He gazed into my face with an expression so
mournful, that I felt shocked at my inopportune curiosity. His glance seemed to say: "Knowing what you
do, can you allow mere curiosity to over-master you
when I am by?"

I passed my arm affectionately through his, and
we paced silently up and down, I doing my best to
restrain my vagrant eyes from wandering over the
artistic treasures.

After a while, we paused in our measured walk.
He flung open a lofty window, and I saw extended

before me a broad grass terrace, bordered by marble
statues, higher than the trees, a continuation indeed
of the approach on the further side of the house; and
traversing a perpendicular height, a flight of broad
precipitous steps, cut through the ilex woods.

A more stately *coup d'œil* never met the eye of
man.

"The 'thousand steps' and the Hermitage," said
the Marquis, pointing to a mediæval tower at the
summit, dark against the sky, "where twelve Benedictine monks live, dependent on our bounty. We
must explore these hills together, Lucius, and look at
the view from the top of the mountains. The Hermitage
is of the middle ages," he added, "when these woods
were still unclaimed forest land."

A heavy sigh followed.

"To-day I cannot dwell on such matters. The very
light of the sun offends me."

As quickly as he had unbarred the window, he
now hastened to close it.

"What has happened to-day, dear Anzano?" I ven-
tured to ask.

CHAPTER XII.

"Much," was the reply. "Don Antonio, from whom I parted just before you joined me—you must have seen him on the stairs—has brought me bad news, worse even than I anticipated. My brother"—an intense excitement lighted up his eyes, as he named Sigismund, then passed away, and a grey look spread over his face like a pall.

"I had hoped, Lucius, to have spared you the knowledge of our present disagreement. It lay with Sigismund whether it should be so, or no. I had hoped, after waiting so many years, to enjoy your society in peace. Peace!" he repeated, a bitter smile curling his lips; "what am I saying—peace and I are for ever parted."

I could see how he struggled before he could bring himself to allude to his brother.

"Well, what of Sigismund?" I asked. "I must tell you, however, beforehand, he is so handsome I range myself on the side of Sigismund."

I spoke in jest, but in my friend's excited condition all jest was unpalatable. He drew back from me and his dark eyebrows almost met.

"You are speaking about what you know nothing," he said coldly. "It is not possible that you, my best friend, should support my brother against *me*, the head of our house, the guardian of our honour. Let me tell you at once that Sigismund insists on a marriage to which I will never consent. I would rather see him dead. I would rather die myself. I *will* die," he added, in a lower tone, his eyes gathering themselves steadfastly on some distant object, "if that marriage takes place."

His manner was growing wild, his far-off gaze more and more intense.

The dread of some hidden terror seemed pressing upon his brain. He made an effort to relieve his agitation by hurrying up and down the room. Midway he stopped, trembling violently. Instinctively I stretched out my arms to support him. As instinctively his troubled head sank on my shoulder.

Thus we stood in the centre of the darkened saloon, the gems and the treasures, the rare porcelain, the mirrors, and the gold mocking us.

How I pitied him, the inheritor of this ancestral wealth—a man, in himself pure, unsullied, tender, brave—clinging to me for help!

What secret lay in the shadows of those dark woods that waved so serenely without? What crime? What horror?

Can that be justice which demands from him atonement for others? Why is he to suffer for his uncle's misdeeds?

Even while I asked myself this question, the answer came to me in the knowledge of his too sensitive nature, shrinking from all suspicion of iniquity.

The very existence of guilt was disgusting to him. How much more the reality!

It was enough to uproot the very foundations of

his moral being. No wonder he loathed all that he possessed when he esteemed it stained with the price of blood.

Meanwhile the Marquis, somewhat recovered, gently extricated himself from my arms.

"My reluctance to speak must seem strange to you, Lucius."

"It does, it does, most extraordinary."

"I would tell you anything about myself. Anything. If I believed myself guilty of any sin I would confess it to you. Any sin that involved myself alone. I believe you are the only person in the world who loves me."

The tears were in his eyes. I mutely responded; I could not form an intelligible word. Something rose in my throat to prevent it. I could only wring his hand—He understood me.

"But I cannot reveal even to you secrets that concern the honour of my name. What those secrets entail must be borne in silence. Lucius, ask me nothing. I implore you, ask me nothing. But do not reproach me."

"Reproach you! Oh, my friend, if you knew how I pity you."

"Yes; it has come to that, Anzano Gonzago is an object of pity"—a groan escaped him—"Oh, that I could die! How often have I been tempted to end my miserable life and be at rest. But the cowardice of the act, the confession of defeat, the base want of fortitude to support with dignity my appointed lot, all this has stopped me. No, I will not consent to shorten my life, however loathsome that life may be.

"But this is all beside the mark," he added, noticing the distress depicted in my countenance. "We were speaking of Sigismund."

I shook my head.

"What is Sigismund to me compared with you, Anzano?"

"Do not grieve for me, my Lucius. Think how brief life is—how soon death comes to us. If I die in the struggle, what matter? A Gonzago more or less—a forgotten name—a funeral dirge—a monument——"

"Do not speak so, Anzano, I cannot bear it," I cried, seizing his hands in both of mine.

"But Sigismund will live," he exclaimed, too much excited to notice my distress. "Sigismund is younger—he has never known care. I have guarded him. Sigismund will bear our name with splendour. He is the last of our house, on his marriage the very existence of it depends. Sigismund must be free. No shadow must rest upon his life. No mystery tarnish the fair fame of his consort.

"But he defies me!—he insists on a marriage. Oh, God!" he exclaimed, breaking off, and clasping his hands. "Such a marriage! I cannot think of it —I cannot bear it!"

"Where is Sigismund?" I asked.

"I do not know; I have not seen him since last night. I believe he has left the house. In this he has done well. One roof cannot cover us both until he submits."

"I doubt your brother's submitting to any one in the matter of his marriage. He will strangely falsify my opinion of him if he does."

"He *must!*" rejoined the Marquis, vehemently. "He shall. But at this moment he is outraging all propriety.

Can you believe that he has dared, without my knowledge, to communicate with Don Antonio? Has actually given him legal notice of his intended marriage, and called on him peremptorily to perform the ceremony? Don Antonio came this morning to apprise me. Under the new law, he dare not refuse. The very day is fixed."

"Who is the lady?" I asked.

If a bomb had burst between us, Anzano could not have looked more appalled.

"Yes, Anzano, I ask you, who is the lady? How can I judge of the position in which you are placed, unless I know who and what she is?"

He turned from me with a fever of impatience.

"If I told you her name—what then?"

He had had time to recover from the shock of my sudden question. The hard look on his face, and the nervous twitching of his hands, betrayed to me that he both dreaded to answer and would avoid doing so, if possible.

"I ought not to have mentioned this marriage to you at all, Lucius, but your curiosity overcame me."

I listened to this, and to what followed, feeling that he was only putting me off.

"Your English ideas differ so totally from ours," he went on saying, in a hurried voice, keeping his eyes averted from my gaze.

"In the matter of marriage, Italians are bound by much more conventional rules than govern you. A certain outward decorum must be observed in all things; the measure of that decorum is purely arbitrary. Add to these considerations, the secret history of many

of our noblest families; the hatreds, feuds, rivalries—
some hidden crime, perhaps."

His voice lowered, and for an instant he eyed me
suspiciously.

"Sometimes it is want of revenue to support a
great name. Sometimes the necessity of a special
alliance to obtain political power, or hereditary ag-
grandisement. Marriage with us takes the form of a
compact beneficial to both parties. The enticements
of passion, and the vulgar sensibilities of the common
herd, are alien to our manners; we choose our mis-
tresses for love—our wives to be the mothers of our
children."

"My dear Marquis!" I exclaimed—I felt I had
given him ample time for explanation—"you have not
yet answered my question. The lady's name is still
unknown to me."

Morbid curiosity, bred by all the tales I had heard,
was getting the better of me. I was indignant at the
idea of remaining in my friend's house at such a
crisis, ignorant of what was passing.

"The very servants," I added, "know more than I."

My appeal did at last seem to touch him.

"Would you force me, Lucius, to act contrary to
my judgment?"

The look of nervous tension on his face had
relaxed a little, and he spoke more in the natural
tones of his harmonious voice.

"Remember," I urged, observing this change, "remember I am willing to go away, if you cannot accord
me your confidence."

A deprecatory movement on his part forbade the
possibility of such an idea.

"If I remain you must trust me. It is due to us both. Else——"

"Not go, Lucius. Not in anger."

He pressed my hand, and a gleam of the sweet boyish look lit up his face for an instant.

For an instant only; the shadows returned, but the passing coolness between us had vanished.

"I will tell you what I can," he said, with great hesitation.

He was debating, I believe, in his own mind how little he should reveal to me. I longed to tell him how much I already knew.

A painful conviction was each moment forcing itself upon me that much that I had heard was true.

The gay indifference with which I had thrown off all recollection of last night, with the glorious burst of morning, was again, in its turn, giving place to a settled belief that, in some unfathomable way, the story of the "donnina" Gigia and the Cardinal was at the bottom of all my friend's perplexities.

And if it were so.

An appalling vision of what Frederick (who might at any moment appear) would perhaps disclose, in carrying out his threat of discovering the family mystery, rose before me, and turned me cold from head to foot.

Nothing but an ignominious expulsion from the villa seemed impending.

Meanwhile the Marquis, seated in one of the massive chairs, was passing his fingers nervously up and down the edges of the velvet pile, as if debating with himself what to say.

At last he raised his eyes to mine.

"Remember, Lucius, what I say is wrung from me by your threat of leaving me."

Another pause, and the long, white fingers still working on the velvet. Would he ever speak? At length the words came.

————

CHAPTER XIII.

"THE marriage of Sigismund has occupied me for years, ever since, indeed, I made up my mind that I should remain single.

"My own life has been blasted. I am a barren stock from which no green shoot will ever rise to renew the sap of the Gonzagos.

"Under these circumstances I conceived that *I* had the right to decide who his consort should be. As in any other case the lady would have been my wife, I reserved to myself the right of selection for him."

I shook my head at this argument, but said nothing.

"That was my view. In speaking to Sigismund I never concealed it.

"He raised no objection—quite the reverse. He is, as you see, much younger than I am. From my habits of life and premature gravity of disposition, our relations have hitherto been more those of a father and son than of brother and brother.

"Still there was harmony. Rarely a word of discussion troubled our intercourse.

"How could I imagine that the one act of his life on which the existence of our family depends should be snatched from my control? Nothing had prepared me."

"Had Sigismund any other attachment?" I asked.

"As far as I knew, no. He spent several winters in Rome. He was well received, especially by the ladies. I did not trouble myself with the details of his social successes.

"I eschew the world—but I distinctly understood that he had formed no serious *liaison*.

"Believing that he would obey my desire in marriage, as in all else, after much reflection I selected the daughter of a Sienese family, originally Papal and Roman, but transplanted here, as we are, from Mantua, by the possession of large estates.

"The lady, though nineteen, was still following her education in a convent. Indeed, convent life exercised so deep an influence over her mind (she had shewn some disposition to take the veil) that her family resolved at once to arrange a suitable alliance."

"The love of God to be superseded by the love of man—the devil as usual getting the best of the arrangement. Eh, Anzano?"

But the Marquis received, as he always did, my feeble attempts at satire with stern and unsympathetic silence.

"Knowledge of the lady's tastes pointed her out to me as a fitting partner for Sigismund. So holy a maid would surely develop into a devoted wife and mother."

"Not at all, Anzano; there you are wrong. You could not make a greater mistake. The reasons you give are sufficient for her becoming independent and worldly. Nothing like restraint to make young women rebellious."

"That is not my experience," returned the Marquis

coldly; "in perfect good faith I arranged every detail of the marriage. Sigismund was absent, but expected to return——"

Here, as if dreading to proceed, he moved away from the chair on which he had been seated, and began vaguely to wander about the room; taking up here a tazza, there a bronze statuette; examining a coin, with apparently minute attention, then throwing it down on the table, and moving off to place himself abstractedly before one of the wall-frescoes—a battle scene, the life-sized figures rising against a lurid sunset —thence wandering off to arrange the folds of the door tapestry, gazing blankly before him all the while.

At last he settled himself against the gilt moulding of one of the mirrors, where he remained with his eyes fixed on the ground.

"What was I saying?" he asked, turning to me with a start. I believe he had forgotten, at the moment, that I was present.

"You had appointed Sigismund to meet the Sienese lady."

"Yes, yes," he answered quickly, passing his hand across his brow. "I beg your pardon, Lucius—yes— I remember. Well, conceive my indignation. Sigismund positively refused even to see her! Such audacity astonished me. I ordered him at once to visit her at Siena.

"He persisted in not going. Altogether questioned my right to interfere. High words ensued. It was our first quarrel.

"If he disobeyed me, I told him, he could not remain in my house.

"He replied that nothing should move him, for to

this house, and to this place, he was bound by a link stronger than life.

"I called upon him peremptorily to inform me what he meant. When he answered me I fell senseless to the ground."

The Marquis' hand, which he had stretched out in the eagerness of narration, fell to his side. Then coming close to me, he fixed his deep-set eyes upon me with a look of unutterable appeal.

"Will you force me to go on?" that look seemed to say.

Having made up my mind what was right to do, I avoided the appealing glance, and, after a moment, he proceeded, though in a tone so low that I had to strain my ears to catch his meaning.

"There is a member of our family you have not seen—a helpless child—a girl." Each little phrase seemed dug laboriously out of him.

"I love her tenderly. I have reared her as a daughter. I am bound to her by stronger ties than those of blood—the ties of honour. Yet our blood flows in her veins. A crime committed in this house links her—and one who has gone before—unalterably to me. To *me!*" he repeated, shouting out the words, and striking upon his breast. "Do you understand?—to *me!* Blood calls for blood! She is ever before me. She hovers in the air I breathe—impalpable but real."

He was growing incoherent. He had sunk down on a chair. His ashen face all the more ghastly from the contrast with the rich purple velvet that covered it.

Gradually his glazed eyes fixed themselves on the large mirror opposite—fixed themselves with the intensity of actual vision. Something was there he saw, or thought he saw.

Words cannot describe my alarm. I rushed to him and caught him as he leant forward.

"Speak to me—speak, Anzano!" I cried, shaking him in my earnestness. "I would never have questioned you, could I have foreseen this!"

He heard not, but sat as rigid as if turned into stone.

"Go—go!" he shrieked, raising his arm menacingly, and pointing to the mirror. "Why are you come? Why call me? Three times in the wood I heard you. I have forgotten nothing. What have I done that you should haunt me?"

The starting orbits of his eyes wandered to and fro, then again fixed themselves wildly on the glass. Every drop of blood had left his face.

"Am I to blame for Sigismund?" he asked, with frantic gesture, throwing up his arms. "The curse has fallen on me—on me—not on him! Take my life—my life—not his! Spare him! Not Sigismund's!"

"Anzano!" I shouted in his ear, "shake off this horrible nightmare!"

I placed myself before him, hiding the mirror. I chafed his hands. They were rigid.

"Forgive me—forgive me!" was all I could say.

Slowly the natural colour returned to his cheeks, and his dilated eyes resumed a more natural expression. He passed his hands over his forehead, and drew a deep sigh.

"Is she gone?" he asked, looking up at me as I leant over him.

"There is nothing, Anzano. Rouse yourself."

"What have I said?" he asked, anxiously survey-ing me, to detect in my face the effect of any revela-tion he might have made.

"Nothing," I replied soothingly, "we were speak-ing of Sigismund's marriage."

"*Only* of the marriage?" he responded, bending his sunken eyes upon me.

"Only of the marriage," I answered.

"I thought someone else had entered."

His glance swept cautiously round the saloon, darkened by the closed shutters.

"You are deceiving me, Lucius. Surely you saw her! She stood there." He pointed to the mirror. "Her long hair matted with blood—the gash in her neck open. Her blood!—it must have dropped upon the floor."

He was rising. I drew him back.

"No one has entered. We are alone."

"On your honour, Lucius?"

"On my honour."

"Did you hear no voice?"

CHAPTER XIV

As the words of denial rose to my lips, a concealed door in one of the frescoed panels flew open, a shaft of sunshine shot like an arrow across the darkened floor, and out of the sunshine emerged a slight, girlish figure, entirely in white, her long, flaxen hair moted with the sunlight.

One bound, and she was beside us.

"May I not come to you, Gonzago?" she asked, her voice ringing as clear as a young bird's. "It is not true that you have forbidden me? Say so—say it is not true! You are not angry with me?"

She had flung her arms round the Marquis before she perceived me. When her large blue eyes, following those of my friend, rested on me, she gave a startled cry, and would have rushed away.

But he detained her, holding her as she had placed herself, upon his knee.

"Lela, you should not have come," he said gently, smoothing the meshes of her abundant hair. "Did I not warn you?" pointing to me.

His voice, his manner, as he addressed her, melted with tenderness. Her eyelids dropped as she listened, the full black fringe of the lashes sweeping her delicate cheek.

Her half startled movements, her sweet timidities of attitude, and a kind of hesitating restlessness with which she clung to my friend were infinitely charming.

As I looked at her all sorts of disjointed recollections floated in my brain.

Filippo's description of the "donnina" Gigia would keep coming into my head. This was the precise type he had described.

Regarding her closely, I perceived that she had even that slight droop he had mentioned, in one of the eyelids. The flaxen hair, the black lashes and eyebrows, the graceful undulating movements, nothing was wanting.

On one fact I at once decided, it was no ghost, but Lela that Frederick had seen the night before.

"Do not tremble, my Lela!" the Marquis was saying, noticing the throbbing of her temples, and the unconscious disquiet of her little feet.

"This is my oldest friend, Mr. Anstruther. Speak to him, my love, now you are here."

She looked up, and stole a timid glance at me; then held out the smallest and whitest hand I ever saw. I hardly dared to touch it.

"Let me go, let me go, Gonzago!" I heard her whisper. "I thought you were alone—and oh! I did so long to see you. I have so much to tell you."

"To tell me, Lela?" the Marquis said, holding her still in his arms, and gazing earnestly into her face. "What have you to tell me? Nothing, I trust, that I shall not hear with pleasure."

He paused, a stern look stole over his brow, which

deepened into a frown as he vainly waited for a reply.

Lela's cheeks flushed under his steady gaze. She darted a glance at him from her speaking eyes as he bent over her, then looked down again, and a flush of colour suffused her face and arms and neck.

"Let me be with you," she pleaded softly, pressing his hands, and then carrying them to her lips. "Let me be with you, Gonzago, *always*."

"Lela, darling," replied the Marquis, trying to be peremptory, but failing utterly under the witchery of her eyes. "For some days we must part."

"Must we?" she said mournfully, arching her mobile brows. "No, no, not part with all of you!"

He shook his head.

"It must be, Lela; you know the reason."

By a sudden movement she seemed to shrink into herself. Again the restlessness of her tell-tale feet testified to the rapid coming and going, the dancing, the running of the nymph-like creature before me.

"You must not part me from—" the rest of the sentence was whispered into his ear.

He shook his head, and with a cold glance put her from him.

"It must be, Lela; it must!"

These last words were spoken in a more imperious tone than he had yet used.

This evidently alarmed her. Her fair head sank upon her hands, which she pressed against her eyes, the abundant hair falling over them.

The Marquis contemplated her in silence. For an instant she raised her head, and touched him. The contact of her hand soothed him. Again he drew her to him, and delicately raising fold after fold of her wondrous hair, lay each golden tress back on her shoulders, smoothing it lingeringly, as though the silky texture delighted him.

Lela glanced upwards and smiled, but it was not the same joyous smile as before.

"You will let me go into the ilex-wood," she whispered entreatingly. "I cannot live out of the fresh air—away from the trees. Don't shut me up, Gonzago, or I shall die."

She clasped her hands imploringly. (She had forgotten apparently that I was present, I had retired into shadow, hidden by an ebony cabinet that projected from the wall). Then, venturing to approach nearer, she twined herself about the Marquis, as a delicate tendril clings to a tall tree, her eyes, with their wonderful lights, sparkling upon him.

"No, my child, no—I dare not. But, oh, Lela!" he cried, straining her closer to him, "why have you done this? You were my light—the light of the house—the only comfort I had—and now——"

She shook her head pensively. There was the same restless hesitation, the same internal tremor, which had betrayed themselves in her movements ever since she had entered the room.

Some secret, or some thought withheld, was warring with the frankness of her nature. A something she yearned to tell, yet dared not.

"Do you think it costs me nothing to lose you?" asked the Marquis, with an unwonted trembling in his voice.

But the fairy-like creature burst into a laugh.

"Don't lose me, then, Gonzago. Keep me close—close!" and she nestled to him playfully, and toyed with his hands. "I only want to go into the woods. I must have been born there, I think, for they always seem to me like home.

"And Sigismund?" Lela whispered into his ear. "Are you afraid, Gonzago, that he will meet me in the woods?"

As Sigismund's name passed her lips, I could see that an indescribable joy shone over her.

"Shall I promise you to hide from him behind one of the statues?" This was said with a gay laugh. "Oh, the beautiful woods, with the great black ilex-trees, the sweet, damp air, and the red rocks which form seats in the shade!

"Everything loves me in the wood, and I love everything. I know the different voices of the trees as the wind sweeps through them, and they speak to me. The birds, too, know me, and flutter down when I move. Will you believe it, even the swine gather round me and look at me like friends."

The Marquis sat, dazed and confounded.

Not receiving any answer, Lela laid her hand gently on his arm, but he did not stir.

"No," she said, reassured by his silence, "I shall not be shut up in the gloomy house. Unless I whistle, Sigismund will never know where I am."

So little did Lela understand the tragic nature of Gonzago's determination to part her from her lover, that she laughed aloud at the notion of Sigismund seeking for her in vain, and with a coquettish little toss of her head, drew from the folds of her dress a golden whistle, which hung suspended from her neck.

"Shall I call him now? Where is he?"

As she was raising the whistle to her lips the Marquis grasped her hand so tightly that she uttered a frightened scream.

"Lela, beware how you trifle with me. I command you to forget Sigismund. I will hear his name no more."

"Ah, that is because you do not love him. If you loved him half as well as I do, Gonzago, you would ask for him every hour of the day. You could not help it."

"Child—this is unworthy trifling. I tell you, you must forget him as though he had never lived."

"Impossible!" she cried, throwing up her arms, from which the light dress she wore fell back, displaying their finely moulded lines. "We have lived together ever since I can remember. You might as well tell me to forget myself.

"I have always loved Sigismund; long before I knew what love meant. I understand it now. If he had not loved me, I should have gone down and hid in the ilex-trees and died. While I live it will be the same. Sigismund is like a god. I worship him."

"Lela, it is for his sake that you must part. Your love will destroy him."

"Destroy him! Oh, Gonzago, that cannot be!"

A grave look came over her bright young face, and she put back her hair, and pressed her hands to her forehead, as if to address herself to this idea.

"Sigismund is a man, and he knows his own mind.

He loves me. I have his word. He told me never to leave him. The trees heard me, by the statue of the Satyr."

"The Satyr!" shouted the Marquis, starting back with horror. "Unhappy child. Do you not know——" He stopped abruptly. Then with white and quivering lips, proceeded—"He cannot keep his word. If he did he would be ten times a traitor to every Gonzago that ever lived. He must not! He *shall not!*"

The Marquis' voice rose into a tone of menace. The look of horror deepened on his face. His hand lifted. I thought he was about to strike Lela in the fury of his rage, but with an imprecation he dashed aside.

Lela's blue eyes fell upon him. She stood unmoved.

"Sigismund will never change," she answered firmly. "Nor shall I. Where is he now? I thought I should have found him here. Have you sent him away, Gonzago?"

Before he was aware of what she was going to do, she had leant down and impressed a soft kiss on my friend's hand, her eager eyes seeking a reply.

I could see from the working of his features how much he suffered. That he felt truest and purest affection for this young girl no one could doubt who watched the softening of his glance as it rested on her, or heard the tender inflections of his voice, even when commanding her obedience.

"Sigismund is not here," he answered. "Nor will he come any more."

Lela shivered.

"Promise me, Lela, not to seek him until I give you leave—do it willingly."

Again he passed his hand over her face and head, and lifted her tiny fingers, still red with the marks of his pressure, to his lips.

"Will it be for long?" she asked anxiously, trying to call up a smile. "I can wait a day — two days perhaps—though that would be too long. I will wait one day, I cannot promise more."

Her voice—her looks were so winning that it required more than mortal firmness to resist her. Even the Marquis faltered in his purpose, as she clung to him, half crying, half laughing in her eagerness.

"If it is not too long I will try—yes indeed," she repeated, in answer to his pained look of doubt. "I will try to obey you, Gonzago, and to wait."

Her fresh young face was raised again to his. "To wait," she added, thoughtfully. Then lighting up again.

"After all, I do not believe he is gone away at all. Now I come to think of it, I am sure that he is not."

"How do you know that?" asked the Marquis sharply. There was a dumb menace in his tone that made me fear he was, after all, but playing a part with this sweet young creature.

"That is my secret," she answered archly. "Supposing you *have* told him to go, how long will he stay?"

"As long as I deem it needful," was the stern answer.

There was a terrible inflection in my friend's voice as he pronounced these words, painfully contrasting with Lela's childish gaiety, and confidence in his love.

"But if he went," she cried. "Oh, Sigismund!" Her lover's name came from her in a wail of anguish. Nothing she could say could have been so piteous as that cry.

"My brother shall not come," answered the Marquis, putting her roughly from him, the lines on his face showing those signs of gathering passion I knew too well.

"That shall be my care."

Neither of them moved, nor did Lela raise her eyes. Her silence evidently wrought up my friend to fury. The nervous working of his mouth and lips, his hard breathing and changing colour, the excited flashing of his eyes as he watched her, betrayed that, spite of the anguish her suffering caused him, there lurked an unalterable determination to separate her from her lover.

Not for an instant was that determination shaken.

He was the first to break silence.

"My poor child—my little Lela!" he said, in his softest tones. "Through all the years you have known me, have I ever given you cause to think you were not dear to me?"

Again she raised her tearful eyes to his, and again, as if obeying an irresistible impulse, she stooped and kissed his hand.

"Gonzago, I know your goodness, but——"

"Say no more, Lela, I implore you; it breaks my heart to see you suffer."

"But I must suffer," she answered, as she wiped away the tears that lay wet on her cheeks, "if I cannot see Sigismund, when I am to be his wife." Her voice was low, but her blue eyes never faltered.

Such a reply, after all he had just urged upon her, was more than he could bear. Catching at her suddenly, she staggered and fell, white and trembling, against the wall.

I was about to interpose, when the stern menace of his look and attitude arrested me.

"Speak to me no more!" he cried, his whole form quivering with passion. "You are henceforth a prisoner in your own room. Your *own* room," he repeated, in an imperious tone. "If I find you at large——" He stopped, as if afraid of what he was about to utter.

"Go!" he continued, waving her off; "go; and if you ever loved me, never see Sigismund again." Then, with a stern and formal courtesy, he led her to the door.

The shaft of sunlight still shot across the dark parquet floor.

As Lela passed into it, her whole form was transfigured.

She stood clothed as in a fiery cloud, her wonderful eyes bent upon the Marquis in a last appeal.

But whatever she might have been about to say remained unspoken.

His imperious aspect and immovable attitude silenced her.

Making me a timid little curtsey (I had followed my friend to have one more look at her), and casting a parting glance at him from under her long black lashes, she burst into a flood of tears, and vanished.

With her the sunlight vanished also.

————

CHAPTER XV.

THE sad-faced butler now made his appearance through the tapestry hangings.

"The Excellency is served," said he, with a profound bow, addressing himself to the Marquis.

The butler was retiring as noiselessly as he had entered, when the Marquis, looking up from the spot where he had remained beside the secret door through which Lela had passed, arrested him by a motion of his hand. The well-trained domestic stopped as suddenly as does a machine of which the main-spring is broken; bowing low, he awaited his master's orders, who, with nervous haste, drew him into a corner, where, with much gesticulation he addressed him, but in so low a voice I could not catch a syllable, Antonio replying with a succession of profound bows to what appeared to be most numerous and emphatic directions, frequently repeated.

Left alone, I naturally asked myself, "Who is that lovely girl? And why should she not marry Sigismund?"

Just as my friend was about to explain, she had entered. I was no wiser than before, except that I had seen her. What had that innocent creature to do with the curse of which the Marquis spoke?

Mystery! mystery! deeper and deeper; hopeless mystery.

Even while I was standing beside him, the Marquis had been under the impression that some supernatural presence had visited him. The words he had uttered betrayed to me his belief that this presence haunted him continually.

Having at length dismissed the butler, with many last urgent injunctions, all received with the same profound respect, Gonzago crossed the saloon towards me, a sickly smile, in which no particle of cheerfulness entered, on his face.

For the first time in my life I felt a certain restraint in his presence. His violence towards that helpless girl had shocked me beyond expression. I doubted too his good faith. Was he acting a part with *me*, as well as with Lela?

"You have seen Sigismund's love," he said hurriedly, his eye in the meanwhile wandering round, as if he had grown so habitually suspicious, where she was concerned that he could hardly trust himself to allude to her, even in the solitude of his own house.

"Your curiosity, Lucius, is now gratified."

I saw that while he addressed me, he was scrutinizing my face, in order to judge what impression the meeting had made upon me.

To ask a direct question was not his habit; his strange mode of life had brought him into a condition of nervous reserve upon all subjects, specially those touching the hidden springs that agitated his troubled existence.

"You complained just now of my want of confidence. Could I show you more than in admitting you to be present at that interview? You must not wound me by any further reproaches of that sort.

You ought never to have heard Lela's name—never to have seen her."

"Why not?" I asked quickly. "Why should you try to hide her?"

Thinking of the girl, so gentle, yet so courageous —my feeling got the better of me. I proceeded to address the Marquis with the freedom of one to whom he was accountable.

He stared at me in amazement; then drawing himself erect, listened in offended silence.

"How can I reconcile," I proceeded to say, "what I must call your cruelty towards her, with your professions of affection? Why should you part her from your brother? Where in the whole world would you find a worthier wife for Sigismund? I will pledge my honour she is all that she appears. Truth is written on her brow. Do you think that threats will make that brave girl give up her lover? I do not, I tell you plainly.

"Her pledge—her promise is to Sigismund, not to you; nor will your brother ever forgive you. It is an unwarrantable interference with his liberty of action."

The haughty astonishment depicted on the Marquis' countenance when I began to speak, had gradually given place to a sorrowful, puzzled look.

My reproaches, obtrusive as I felt them to be, had hit him hard. I had presented Lela's position in a new light.

I flattered myself I had made some impression. Oh, that I might be enabled to help her.

"But I do love Lela," he reiterated. "I love her as fondly as if she were my own child. If you only knew how dear her life has cost me. I cannot explain. You must take my word for it."

From this admission I was about to urge what I considered an unanswerable argument in favour of the marriage, when his rigid look arrested me.

"We will not, if you please," he said, with the frigidest politeness, "enter into that subject at present. Some other time, Lucius. Much as it grieves me to incur your censure, where my duty is concerned I must remain the sole judge of my own actions."

There was a natural dignity about my friend that in a moment put back from him all interference, with a rebuke to the interferer.

"Pray do not," he added, "mention the accident of your knowledge of Lela to your nephew, Mr. Stanley."

I thought of Fred's midnight encounter with the fair-haired spirit.

There was no doubt that it was Lela, who, by some accident, had entered the room assigned to him.

The double rooms, and the locked door, which the Marquis had not been able to open, might explain this. The gestures Frederick had interpreted into some weird lamentations must have been a passionate burst of grief at my friend's opposition.

Oh, if Anzano would only be more straightforward and unreserved, and that I could dare to tell him freely all I knew.

"I am quite willing to promise to be silent to Frederick," I answered. "What he may find out for himself—he is remarkably curious and imaginative—I cannot answer for."

At this the Marquis knit his brows—plainly showing his displeasure.

"There is one remedy, my dear friend—we can both leave."

There was a tone in my voice, a stiffness in my manner that had never appeared before. I had always given my friend credit for perfect justice, probity and honour.

Since seeing Lela I had begun to doubt how far I was justified in this opinion. Quick as lightning he detected the change.

"Lucius," he said, returning to all his old sweetness of manner, and placing his arm upon my shoulder with that familiar gesture so habitual to him.

"Lucius, I understand how much you blame me. Alas, I dare not justify myself. I can offer you no explanation. But believe me when I say that your presence here is the only satisfaction I can *now* enjoy.

"I am cut off from all human sympathy. If you leave me, you would but add a bitterer pang to what is already well-nigh unendurable."

"I will not go," I exclaimed impulsively.

"I know you will not! Do not ever allude to such a possibility. There is such comfort in the presence of a friend. Yes, yes!" he burst forth, seizing on both my hands and leading me towards the door. "But there are subjects upon which I cannot touch. My brain, yes, my brain fails me."

In the ante-room we stopped accidentally under the picture of the Cardinal. Although my friend's back was towards it, some mesmeric consciousness warned him that it was there.

With a sudden movement of disgust he rushed out upon the landing.

"One moment, Anzano," I said. "I want to ask

you a question. How can I help you if I remain
here? Pray reflect before you answer. I arrive here
at a critical moment. You yourself told me that you
almost determined to decline my visit. You are
greatly agitated at your brother's intended marriage. I
have seen the lady. She has won my heart. How can
I take any part against her?"

"She is an angel!" exclaimed the Marquis.

"And she loves you, Anzano."

"I know it—I know it," he replied, his whole soul
beaming out of his eyes. "But she can never marry.
She is ignorant of everything connected with herself.
I never had the courage to enlighten her. Sigismund
always treated her as a sister. She was dear to him
—dear to us both. A sacred charge committed to us.
Until I questioned him, I believed Sigismund's feelings
towards her resembled my own. Why should he have
chosen *her*—*her* of all others?"

My friend broke off suddenly, the wandering, distressed look rising in his eyes.

"Fate—evil fate!" he cried. "It was predestined!
Neither you nor any living man can help me. Alone
I must bear my burden. For a moment the tempta-
tion of opening my heart to you overcame me. But
she—you saw her—you heard her!"

I shook my head. I dared not contradict him.
His looks were wild. His words disjointed.

Opposite, from the still open door, gazed down the
sinister effigy of the Cardinal, a sardonic smile on his
full, red lips.

"She stood there!" he cried, pointing to the mirror
in the central panel of the saloon, just visible through
the tapestried drapery of the door.

"She rose from her grave to forbid it! Sigismund must sacrifice his passion to his duty."

"And if he does not?" I interposed.

The Marquis closed his hand convulsively upon my arm. A flash like the savage wrath of an animal shot into his eyes.

"For shame—for shame, Anzano!" I cried. "Am I come here to find my friend turned into a murderer?"

"No, not a murderer!" He spoke under his breath, the grasp of his fingers tightening painfully upon my arm. "It is justice—justice to the dead!"

That his mind was diseased—his reason shaken, who could doubt? His very virtues were turned into vices. Under this exaggerated sense of duty, this sensitive defence of principle, he was capable—No, no, I cannot write it!

"Lucius!" he said, gradually loosing the pressure of his finger from my arm. "Help me! Speak to Sigismund. Warn him. You are a man of excellent judgment. Warn him—Save him!"

Could I make the Marquis understand that nothing I could say to his brother could have the slightest effect, when I knew no facts with which to support my arguments, even if those arguments were feasible?

"May I see Lela?" I asked.

"No, no!" At her name his vehemence became excessive. "You must see her no more! That you have seen her at all is fatal."

"How fatal?"

"Because it reveals too much."

"If you desire it, I will speak with Sigismund."

He acknowledged this with a look of gratitude.

"Can the priest, Don Antonio, do nothing?"

"Nothing. Don Antonio is bound to act according to the law. Besides, I fear——" he stopped, faltering.

"Does he take Sigismund's side against you?" I asked, greatly relieved at finding some one of sufficient common sense to adopt my views of the question.

"Not wholly, but in part. Don Antonio wearies me with his antiquated notions of the impartial position of the family confessor, of his duty to the church, of the claims of nature, and the sanctity of marriage. I know what all this means. By Heaven, what has the Church—were it represented by the Holy Father himself—to do with upholding the spotless honour of our name?"

A bell sounded at this moment from without.

"That is a second summons," he said, "to warn us that breakfast is ready. Let us go, Lucius. We shall find Don Antonio below in the hall. I must introduce you. Come!"

CHAPTER XVI.

IN the hall we found Frederick, as well as Don Antonio. They did not appear to have spoken. Fred was lounging on two chairs, his heels much higher than his head. The priest was walking slowly up and down, his hands clasped behind his back, among the Roman emperors—very stern and very defiant in the half-light of the darkened casements, Caligula especially prominent, with that bestial cast in his eyes and swollen hanging lip.

Straight from the open door, shooting down the centre of the hall, came a flood of light and heat, laden with the heavy fragrance of flowers, the murmur of the fountains, and the rustle of the mid-day breeze.

Don Antonio, pacing up and down, looked less like a peasant than he had done in his tawdry robes the day before. Still shabby, with well-worn knee-breeches, worsted stockings, clumsy shoes, and a long black coat, the days of whose glory had long since departed.

So much for his appearance. In course of time I came to know more of the nature of the man who filled these homely garments.

The Marquis presented me to him emphatically as his "oldest friend."

Dear fellow! In his calmer moments how he delighted to keep that fact ever before him—"His oldest friend!" and his expressive voice always softened as he said it.

"This is not the first time I have had the pleasure of meeting Don Antonio," said I, bowing to the guest.

"Ha!" returned the Marquis, eyeing us both suspiciously. "Not the first time? How is that?"

"Yesterday was the festival of St. John. When I was coming from Siena, I met Don Antonio in the procession on the road near his church."

The Marquis' jealous inquisitiveness relaxed; he was satisfied, left us together, and moved on to where Frederick was sitting.

Frederick, who, apparently, had not, until then, observed our entrance, rose, and in so doing, contrived to knock over both the chairs on which he had been reposing. Then, giving himself a shake, something after the fashion of a water-spaniel, reluctantly placed his hand in that of his host.

"Good morning, Mr. Stanley," I heard the Marquis say; "I hope you rested well. I see you have already been exploring the ilex-woods." A glance at Fred's boots, stained with red earth, showed that the boy had not had the grace to change them.

"Yes," was Fred's laconic answer, spoken with the utmost brusqueness, "I have been looking for your brother."

"My brother is not here," answered the Marquis coldly.

"Not here? Why, I saw him, and some one else with him, early this morning, in the ilex-woods."

"No, no; impossible," replied the Marquis angrily.

"You must have mistaken some one else for Sigismund."

I stood in the doorway, listening to the dialogue. I had dreaded something of the kind when Frederick met my friend. What on earth was I to do with him? He was evidently acting out his resolve of "showing the Marquis what he thought of him." This in his own house, too! The idiot!

If I was watching Frederick and the Marquis, Don Antonio was watching me with the eager curiosity with which one surveys a new species of biped.

Probably I was the first Englishman he had ever seen; if English—Protestant; if Protestant—not Christian. I believe the good man was debating in his own mind whether his sacerdotal dignity would permit him to eat with us. As it happens, I, at least, am a good Catholic. Fred, who followed his father's religion, is a Protestant.

The Marquis decided any possible scruples by leading the way into the dining-room.

"Don't disgrace me *more* than is absolutely necessary," I whispered to Fred in the doorway.

"Don't bother me, uncle, until you hear what I have to tell," was his rejoinder.

"That cannot affect a proper consideration towards our host," I replied, in the same low tone.

"I don't know that," he answered: "a man may receive you, and be an infernal rascal all the time."

"It will be well to remember," I whispered, more enraged than I dared to express, "that the day is hot, and that if your bad manners get us turned out of the house, we shall have to walk nine miles back to

Siena. Perhaps that fact may exert some influence over your chivalric intentions."

"What are you waiting for, Lucius?" asked the Marquis, turning round. "Everything is cold already."

Under present conditions the meal was not hilarious; the Marquis, with all his tact, could not conceal that he was restless and ill at ease. He repeatedly pressed us to eat and drink, insisting on my tasting of every dish. This it was impossible for me to do, as there were many courses. Strange to say, such a trifle as my refusal fretted him. Then he turned to the priest, discoursed about the estate and the crops, specially the approaching vintage. From that, passed into an eager discussion of some particular kind of grape that would only flourish in one special soil.

In the middle of a course of roast beef he called for some of those particular grapes, and declared that Don Antonio must taste them. They grew on the rock, he said, therefore had a particular strength and flavour, admirable for mixing with other wines.

Fruit was only a vegetable, he insisted, in reply to the Padre's look of dismay. Then he appealed to me.

"The Germans eat stewed fruit with roast meat. Everyone eats vegetables, why not grapes as well as cabbages?"

I felt sure all the time my friend hardly knew what he was saying.

Don Antonio, however, accepted the insistance, as well as the grapes, in good part, all of us, save the Marquis, eating with excellent appetite. His plate lay before him empty.

Notwithstanding the little episode of the grapes,

the priest shovelled down huge pieces of beef, keeping his eyes, nevertheless, actively engaged in surveying myself and Frederick.

While the Marquis and Don Antonio conversed together, the aspect of this young gentleman kept me on tenter hooks. He nudged me under the table, and favoured me with what I may call "flying remarks," spoken into my ear.

It was in vain that I moved my chair further from him.

"Uncle, look at that fellow, the butler. I know he is administering poison; we shall never get up alive from this banquet."

A moment after, he was treading on my foot. I had carefully gathered both my feet under my chair, but his long limbs pursued them even there.

"I wonder in which dish he has put it? In the gravy do you think? Uncle" (this time so loud I was in a fever lest the Marquis should hear him), "don't take the gravy. There, look at him; the aged retainer is warning his master not to take any!"

Spite of this chaff, I was fully aware that something serious was germinating in Frederick's brain. He was unusually excited, his full, boyish face pale, his lips compressed, and a general air about him of having found out something quite incompatible with the outspoken volubility he usually brought to bear upon all subjects.

His appetite, however, was by no means affected by his pretended dread of the butler. He partook of every course with such avidity that it suggested to me absence of mind.

At last he laid down his knife and fork, leant

back in his chair, and raised his eyes to the Marquis. By his heightened colour, and a certain nervous twitching of the muscles of his face, I had an instinctive feeling that something was coming.

"Marquis Gonzago," he said, raising his voice. "I want to tell you that I *did* see your brother Sigismund in the ilex-wood this morning, under the statue of the Satyr. You contradicted me just now when I told you so, but it is quite true, I can swear to it. It was the Marquis Sigismund. He was not alone. A lady," here Frederick broke down a little, and stammered, "well, a girl, I mean, was with him. I was standing on the road outside the wall of the Thebaide." (How Frederick had mastered all these names I could not imagine.) "They were standing under the statue. To show you that I am telling you the truth, here is the young lady's sash, I picked it up when she was gone."

He fumbled a little in his pocket, then, with a triumphant air, held up a broad blue sash.

"I found this on the ground. They were both gone—your brother and the young lady, but I daresay," he added, in a tone of sulky defiance, "you know to whom it belongs. When I say a thing," continued Fred, eyeing the Marquis with that desperate kind of courage that comes to the nervously-shy when once set going, "I do not like to be doubted. If I had not been sure I should not have repeated it."

These final words were added in a more deprecatory manner; indeed, they were partly addressed to me.

("Oh, that the mountains would cover me!" was my only thought during Frederick's peroration.)

The Marquis remained perfectly still—his dark eyes riveted on my nephew—not a muscle betrayed what he felt.

The priest, not understanding English, looked from one to the other—then at the blue ribbon—quite at a loss, though evidently the sight of the ribbon discomposed him.

"Allow me to apologise to you, Mr. Frederick Stanley," said the Marquis, in his perfectly correct English—with only a slight foreign accent, "for having been guilty of the rudeness of contradicting you. I have already had opportunities of admiring your amiable frankness. It is a great quality in youth."

His sonorous voice rang out in the silent room.

"I perfectly believe," he continued in the same measured tone, "all you tell me, though I confess I did not credit the possibility of such an occurrence. Would you mind confiding to me that blue ribbon? If you attach any value to it, I will return it to you bye-and-bye."

The complete self-possession of his manner, the dignity with which he delivered himself of this apology amazed me.

Frederick, his temporary burst of indignation past, was blushing scarlet, as, with the ribbon in his hand, he rose to comply with my friend's request.

Was this effort to command himself beyond his physical strength? As the long, delicate fingers of the Marquis came in contact with the ribbon, his sallow cheeks turned deadly pale, and his hand shook so violently he had the greatest difficulty in taking it and forcing it into a side pocket, one blue end, nevertheless, still protruding.

The efforts of the sash to escape (it was a lovely blue, just the colour of Lela's eyes, and fresh and new, with only the slight wrinkles produced by the knot), came to me as typical of Lela herself—struggling to escape from the thraldom imposed on her.

Was she also to be engulphed and buried out of sight—(Sweet, pretty soul!)—like that poor ribbon? Alas, alas! How I longed to save her!

Before he rose from the table, Gonzago had shaken off that momentary tremor. He stood erect—dominating us all.

How small we were beside him! Fred—huddled together on his chair—a mere heap of clothes without a soul to animate them.

The priest, keen-featured, parched up, his small, restless eyes noting each word and action.

Myself—need I again allude to Filippo's contemptuous designation of me? I could only fold my hands in dismay and ask myself, *What* was going to happen next?

"Lucius," said the Marquis. "I am sure you will forgive me if I ask your permission to retire to my study. I have important business with Don Antonio."

The priest's quick eyes were on him in a moment. As much as such weather-beaten features as his could express anything they expressed concern—almost consternation.

"My dear friend," I replied, "nothing but absolute liberty of action ever contents me. I think I will—in your own house—extend the same liberty to you."

The Marquis called up the faintest semblance of a smile at my little speech.

"Ah, Lucius, I too joked once. Then I could give you a Roland for an Oliver—but not now—not now."

He pressed my hand with as much warmth as ever—an immense relief to me. Then, with a bow to Frederick, who, suddenly recalled to himself, struggled to his feet to return it, he opened the door resolutely, and insisting on giving the precedence to Don Antonio, who, with many gestures of expostulation, craved to be allowed to follow him, disappeared into the room.

CHAPTER XVII.

"Now I come to think of it, uncle," said Fred, rising from the table, "I am deuced sorry I gave the Marquis that blue ribbon. How do I know what use he will make of it? He looked as black as thunder when he took it. You don't know how sorry I am."

We re-entered the hall as Frederick was speaking. At this moment I was so nettled at his behaviour generally, and at his late passage of arms with my friend in particular, that I knew, if I answered him, I should not be able to keep my temper. The consequence would be a violent quarrel which I wished, if possible, to avoid.

"Do you think, uncle," he asked, quite unconscious of the volcano of wrath I was inwardly nursing, "I could get that ribbon back again?"

"You had better try. Follow the Marquis into his private room, and demand it. If he does not restore it at once, you are strong, and can force him. I presume your curriculum includes *Bargees* and *Boxing?*"

"Now, uncle, do speak for once without a sneer. There is no chaff in this. I am sorry to see from your face that you are really angry."

"Well," I replied, crossing the hall through the open doorway to the colonnade, "perhaps I am—perhaps I have reason to be. Having brought you here, I am responsible for your conduct."

"Now, don't go ahead like that, uncle. Surely, if one man puts another into a haunted room, you will allow he has a right to inform himself who the ghost is——?"

"Ghost," I ejaculated, "be hanged! Really, Frederick, I believe you to be a good lad, but if I had known how ridiculously you were going to behave, I tell you frankly I would have seen you shot before I brought you here."

"I am sorry to offend you, uncle Lucius, but nothing on earth will persuade me that what I saw last night was not a ghost. The sudden cold that struck through the room, the hazy grey colour of the figure, the way it flung about its shadowy arms—I don't like to think of it."

"Because," I continued, too angry to pay any attention to Frederick's explanation, and walking to the furthest corner of the colonnade, where there was most shade, "because you do not find here the counterpart of English life and English manners you either ridicule everything, or you take upon yourself the odious and ungentlemanly office of a spy—a spy, Frederick, upon your host and his household."

"A spy!" retorted Frederick. "No, by Jove!—not a spy. Don't say that of me!"

The march of Frederick's intellect was, on no occasion, rapid. At the present moment the rush of new ideas concerning his own conduct, as seen in the light of a spy, was too much for him; he grasped the collar of his coat with both his hands, and stared straight at the curtains.

Thus I left him to digest his reflections, while I

proceeded to settle myself in a comfortable position on a chair.

The colonnade was hung with draperies of striped cotton suspended between the open arches. It was luxuriously matted, and provided with wicker lounging-chairs and sofas, the empty spaces filled with choice plants in vases of decorated pottery, laurel-rose, waxy tuberoses, starry gardenias, and tender pink hydrangias, throwing out intoxicating perfumes.

Without, the fountains gurgled and sparkled refreshingly. The palm trees waved lazily in the sun, the cacti threw up unwieldy limbs, and the pampas grass swayed indolently in the hot breeze.

A broad wicker couch stood invitingly at hand. I moved from the chair I occupied and extended myself upon it.

To a stout man there is nothing like a good roomy couch; it is better than all the arm-chairs that were ever invented.

The stifling heat of mid-day, the stillness of the air, the buzzing of the flies, to say nothing of the substantial breakfast I had eaten, and the extreme comfort of the couch, admirably adapted to meet the requirements of a certain hollow Nature has placed very unreasonably in the curve of the spine, all combined to lull me to repose. The whole aspect of my mind changed in this epicurean atmosphere.

My anger towards Fred melted away altogether. I do not think, at that moment, I could have remembered what had caused it.

How easy it seemed to make life happy in such a paradise! If my excellent friend, the Marquis, would only divest himself of superstitious crotchets, allow

Sigismund to marry whom he pleased, and accommodate himself to sound sleep and a healthy appetite, leaving the spirits in the wood to their own devices, how exquisite a month passed here would be!

This was my last intelligible reflection. By degrees a dreamy unconsciousness stole over me.

I knew that Fred had something to tell me—I did not wish to hear it. I knew I ought to speak to Sigismund as I had promised, but it was too hot, and I was too lazy.

Just as I was dropping off into a sweet slumber, something buzzed in my ear, and roused me. At first I thought it was a bee, and put up my hand to drive the troublesome insect away, but the buzz gradually formed itself into the sound of words. Alas! it was that abominable nuisance, Frederick!

"Uncle, how can you have the heart to doze off in that way, when you know I have something most important to tell you?"

"Another time, my dear fellow, another time; leave me alone now," I muttered, struggling with the lethargy of sleep.

I was in the act of dozing off again, when Frederick laid his heavy hand upon me.

"Uncle, wake up! that foxy old Marquis has too many irons in the fire to allow us to be long alone."

"Upon my word, Fred," I am sitting up now and rubbing my eyes, "you are born to torment me! What the deuce have you got to say?"

"Lots, uncle. You remember what I told you last night?"

"I should think so," I replied, leaning back on my cushion, and stretching out my legs. "You woke me up last night when I was in bed; you wake me up to-day when I am not in bed. Go on!"

But Frederick is in a state of mind beyond banter.

"Uncle Lucius, I was up at daybreak. Not a soul was about. I passed the iron gates, and wandered up a road with walls on both sides until I came to an arched gateway with a fresco over it of the Last Supper.

"Beyond was the glimpse of as solemn an old grove as ever those ancient Greek parties wrote about as surrounding their altars. A broad road struck down the middle, and at the further end a temple or a chapel—I don't know which—something classical, with pillars, rose quite hazy in the distance. I decided that this plantation or grove, or whatever it was, must be the place called the "Thebaide," laid out by the Cardinal, Sigismund had told me about, for prayer and meditation. You remember the driver spoke of it also.

"The big black trees hung over the path so thick that I could not see the sky, and there was a drip of dew from the leaves, and patches of white moss like wool, hanging yards down from the boughs."

"Go on, Fred—enough of that! spare me the picturesque. We can go to Dr. Syntax for that, easier than you can furnish it."

It will be seen that I am recovering my good humour. I am coming, by degrees, to my friend's belief, that it is useless to combat the decrees of fate.

"Well, but it all hangs together," is his answer. "The dead leaves lay so thick on the ground and on large blocks of flat rocks, like gravestones, along the path, I could not hear my own steps. The sun had only just risen, and a damp mist lay about, particularly over some pools of water as black as pitch.

"I am sure someone was drowned in that water, and walks about at night under the trees. Well!—I see you look bored, uncle—it was all so ghastly in this cursed walled-up place I got a fit of the horrors, confound it! The trees seemed alive and going to speak to me.

"I ran along the wood as fast as I could, but the trees, and the drip, drip on the leaves followed me. The faster I ran the more they seemed to follow.

"Running with my head down, full tilt, not to see anything—(you know that ghost last night—don't be savage, uncle)—I stumbled up against a high pedestal with the statue of a monk upon it. The face was covered with a cowl. You would not believe it, uncle, but I was such an idiot I stood stock still trembling all over and holding on to a tree. I was thinking what sort of a face I should see if the monk were to lift up his cowl and look at me.

"At last I got under weigh again, and set off once more as hard as I could pelt."

"Why, Fred," I exclaimed, "I must add to your other good qualities, that you are become a perfect coward!"

"Never mind, uncle, I never was one before, and I shall not be again. It is all the effect of this confounded place. Ever since seeing that figure last night, I am as nervous as a cat. I don't deny it. As I ran, I was thinking how awfully still it was, when I heard a faint, sharp sound from below, like a distant cry.

"I turned off from the main road, in the direction of the sound, and scrambled down a gully full of red rocks, and leaves up to my waist.

"At the bottom was a boundary wall, on the other side of the wall the road by which we came last night, bad luck to it!

"I knew it by that cursed ugly statue of a Satyr. There it was grinning on the top of its high pedestal, crusted all over with moss and weeds; its sightless eyes fixed on the sky. Uncommonly gruey, I can tell you, in the grey morning.

"A second time I heard the same sound, shriller and nearer.

"I climbed over the wall, and stood looking up and down the road.

"A third time I heard it, so near now and so loud it made me jump.

"Certainly it was a whistle, but I could see nothing for the trees.

"At last, out of the turn of the road, suddenly appeared the figure of a girl, a long white veil falling to her heels, and a broad blue ribbon fastened round her waist.

"She came bounding forward like a fairy, quite light and airy, and was close upon me before I knew.

"Will you believe it, uncle, she was the living image of the 'donnina,' that the coachman described, the girl who was murdered by the Cardinal; long flaxen hair, blue eyes, black eyebrows and eyelashes, and a light-complexioned face.

"By Jingo! I did feel cold."

"Your ghost of last night, of course. How happy you must have felt to see it again. Eh, my boy?"

"No, no, not the ghost, but like it, very like it. I give you my word, uncle, uncommonly like it, but not the same. I thought so myself at first, and, I can tell you, got a confounded scare."

CHAPTER XVIII.

FRED had become very grave at this point of his narrative.

He crossed over, and seated himself beside me in the shade.   His face shewed he was in earnest, and he gave a prolonged sigh—very unusual in Fred; indeed I do not think I ever heard him sigh before.

"I assure you, Uncle Lucius, every sense I had was in my eyes.   The figure—whatever or whoever it was —passed close by where I was standing, behind the trunk of a big ilex-tree, at the edge of the grass, in front of the Satyr—close.

"Ah, now I breathed, for I could hear her light step upon the gravel.   I could see the real colour on her cheeks, and the folds of her white dress rising and falling on her breast.

"Uncle Lucius," here Fred stopped and breathed audibly, "a great weight fell from me.   This was no ghost, but a living creature—a real beauty.

"Well, I suppose I was a spy after all—though it was the last thing thought of just then.   I did not mean to be one, I declare solemnly.   But I was so taken aback that I kept staring and staring without moving.   There is no doubt I ought to have shewn myself, to have come forward and said something.

"But I was fascinated—fascinated by her beauty. I shall never forgive myself"—this Frederick repeated several times—"specially after what you have said to me about being a spy. That hit me hard, uncle."

"Well, Fred, the harm is done now, past praying for. Go on."

"All at once I thought we were going to have a sudden storm; for as soon as she appeared, the boughs began to rustle and heave in a most extraordinary way though there was a perfectly clear sky overhead, not a cloud to be seen and the rising sun shining in yellow streaks through the leaves.

"At this the little girl seemed to laugh to herself, and kissed her hand to the trees, and to the nasty old Satyr, for all the world as if they were friends, the sight of whom did her good. There was something about this girl more than beauty."

Here Fred, very shame-faced and red, backed his chair further from me, and forgetting the thread of his story, burst out into what I may call an "ungodly" digression.

"Uncle, I do love little feet. I may be awkward and I know I'm rough. Fellows often do shirk introducing me to their sisters, but I know what a pair of feet ought to be. Of course the little girl held up her petticoats to come along the rough road. Her feet were perfect. So full of life too. Would have carried her anywhere—as springy as a racer's hoof— and the little shoes—stunning!

"From her feet I looked up at her face — it matched them; altogether so different from anything I

13*

had ever seen! All the other young women of my acquaintance just coarse flesh and blood in comparison. So graceful too! So arch! So child-like standing there, and bending her little head from side to side like a—well——" (after several gurglings and gutturals, Fred got it out at last)—"like a lark singing on a roof. I have never been in love," continued Frederick, with the utmost gravity. "I always used to laugh at fellows in love — as spoons. Now, Uncle Lucius, I understand what it means. It came over me like a fit. Such a burning—such a buzzing—my blood running wild up and down—and pulses all over me beating like blazes."

I turned round and stared at him, an image of Frederick as he then appeared—his prominent eyes, and full unfinished mouth generally wide open—rose before me. How horribly ugly he must have looked! All the same, joking apart, his matter and his manner were both alike amazing.

The girl he is describing must certainly be Lela— the person of all others he ought not to have seen. Of whose very existence, indeed, the Marquis had warned me to keep him in ignorance.

Here is a complication!

"For a time," continued Fred, returning to his narrative, "she remained quite still, only her laughing eyes were roaming round and round the trees, which had not ceased rustling.

"After the first, I did feel deuced queer, I must own, looking at the little creature from behind a tree, and she thinking herself all alone. But I could no more have plucked up courage to speak to her than I could have flown. She was looking dead the other way and would have been awfully frightened. The truth is, I did not think of myself, but of her.

"Now, uncle Lucius,"—Frederick is rolling himself against a marble pillar in front of me—"don't chaff at what I am going to say. It sounds like a dream, come to me wide awake. Everything was so strange and unnatural—only it did happen just as I am going to tell."

"Laugh, my dear fellow! I am much more likely to cry than to laugh," is my response. "You have developed the most unfortunate art of seeing everything you should not see, and of doing everything you should avoid, and as the consequences fall upon me, I assure you, it causes me the very reverse of amusement."

"I cannot help that—all this came of itself."

"Yes, Frederick, but it was your own act to get up before daybreak, and go out to look—to look in fact after a ghost. The proceeding is in itself singular, and, as taken in connection with a visit to my friend——"

"I am trying to tell you exactly what I saw, uncle, when you, as usual——"

"What you thought you saw, Frederick," I interrupted, correcting him, and at the same time, smiling a little maliciously. "Remember the spectre of last night!"

Fred grew purple—he was about to make an angry rejoinder, but, with an expression of terrible earnestness on his flushed face, he checked himself, and only held up his hand, as though generally declining any discussion at that particular moment as inopportune and useless.

"By degrees, uncle, I became aware, that a strange kind of commotion was stirring all round in the wood. The dear girl, with a gesture of command, moved under the branches and about from one tree to another muttering something to each.

"She smoothed the rough bark with her fingers, twisted about the little green buds, and drew down the lower boughs to her mouth and kissed them.

"At this the trees seemed all alive; swaying and bending up and down, and rustling of their own accord—I mean the ilex-trees round the edge of the circle in front of that nasty old statue. I take my oath they did. The branches see-sawing as she went in; then rising high up to let her pass out. Further back the trees moved less, but from the moment she appeared, there was a trembling and a vibration all over the place as far up as the top of a wooded knoll.

"Even then I could see the tops of the large trees trembling against the sky. The birds, too, turned up and twittered among the boughs, and a wood-pigeon began to coo just over the pretty little head.

"When she came out into the open space, her face shone in a kind of rapture. She flung herself down on the ground, and lay her face to the earth, the Satyr grinning over her like a fiend. I could have knocked his bleary old head off for daring to squint down upon her in the way he did. Then, as if she had forgotten something, she started up, and ran her eyes eagerly up and down the only bit of the road that was visible. Nothing was there. Nothing was to be heard, only the twitter of the small birds, and the cooing of the wood-pigeons overhead. I don't reckon the noise the trees made, for that went on all the time, as if talking to her in some language she understood. I am sure she did understand what they meant, for after awhile she waved her hand impatiently, as if she had had enough, and seated herself on the marble bench we saw last night in the moonlight. You should have seen her little feet then," cried Fred, in a burst of rapture. "If I am to go on I must not think of her feet. That same bench, you remember, uncle, the driver said the 'donnina' was sitting on when that villain of a Red Cardinal first saw her.

"She pulled out something from somewhere—her pocket, I suppose, if she had a pocket, which I am sure I don't know—anyway, she pulled out from somewhere a gold whistle, and whistled.

"It was the same sound I had heard above in the Thebaide. Then she stood still, and listened, her eyes growing larger and rounder as they searched up and down the road.

"'Bring him to me—bring him to me!' she said to the trees, in a voice that just matched with her perfect little feet.

"Round and round she turned, and from side to side, her eyes up-raised, her hands spread out as if supplicating the trees.

"To which they answered back, rustling awfully,

especially one dry old chip of an ilex with little of life left about it.

"From the way its old mossy limbs cracked and swayed, and the few green leaves left at the end of its branches shook, this old tree seemed to have a great deal to tell.

"'Don't say that,' she answered, quite sharply, looking up at it. 'I forbid you; you have no right to complain. I am not ungrateful. I love your voices— I do indeed, moaning to me overhead like waves. But it *is* true that I love the sound of *his* voice better. Should this make you wroth? I have been away so many years, from the time the Marquis took me by force to live in a house with walls, instead of out of doors under the beautiful canopy of your leaves. Now I remain there because I like it, and that sort of life is best. *He* is there to make it sweet to me.' (Who the deuce is *he?* thinks I, and I got red and hot all over, uncle!) 'But I never forget you. It is very hard to reproach me, when I come down full of joy to meet him in your midst. Why I am here, you know—why don't you help me? Oh! when will he come?' she cried out in a weary tone of voice; she was getting infernally impatient, I can tell you, walking up and down on the grass.

"Of course there was a 'He!' How could it be otherwise? And even if she had not already found one, she would never have condescended to look at me. I gave it all up for lost, then and there. It was folly, sheer folly, to think of her.

"'Can you see him coming?' she asked the trees. 'Do look out, higher up the road. Is he in any of the paths leading down from the house? You are so tall; you can see ever so far overhead.'

"The answer came to her from the rotten old tree croaking and bowing about in a sort of fury. Then the other ilex joined in, backing up the old one, all doing wonderful things with their boughs, and scattering their leaves as if in a high wind.

"With a grave look on her face, and a quivering of her mouth, she began picking at the flowering grasses and the weeds which grew rank under the shadow of the Satyr. Quite absently, though, for her eyes continually turned up the road until, picking and picking, she had gathered quite a pile at her side, out of which she twisted a sort of wreath with her nimble fingers. This she placed on her head over her white veil, laughing all the time, and turning to the ilex-trees to admire her. I know *I* admired her," adds poor Fred, with a kind of groan. "I shall never see anything like her again, if I live to be a hundred.

"'See,' she said, as she threw the rest of the weeds at the trees, 'you stupid old things! No pretty flowers will grow near you. They say there is poison in your shadow, but I can make a garland out of anything. Sigismund cannot say I am not ready for him when he comes—with a crown like this!'"

"Sigismund, of course!" I interrupted. "I expected that, just because Sigismund is the last person who ought to have been there. And my poor friend believes the two do not meet. What a complication!"

Here Fred turned upon me quite savagely.

"If you stop me, uncle Lucius, with any of your observations about the Marquis, you will put me out, and I shall never get into the swing of my story again. It is deuced difficult, I can tell you.

"The ilex-trees had never ceased all this time making a hollow kind of noise, first one in the circle, then the other taking it up, until at last she sprang to her feet, and planted herself upon the grass before them.

"'Oh, do not keep pressing me so!' she cried, wringing her hands. 'I cannot—I cannot; indeed I cannot! And yet it breaks my heart to say "No!"'

"With her hands clasped together, she stepped from tree to tree.

"'It cannot be the old life again. Never—never!' Then to the old ilex-tree:—

"'I know well the care you took of me long ago when I was small. How you sheltered me and comforted me, when I had no one else. You are wise, and you are good; you have balm for every wound, because you have knowledge of many things; but oh! my brother, you cannot take from me the love for him that burns within my heart. I cannot live without him! Do you think *you* could fill his place?'

"A proud smile parted her lips as she asked this question, as if in mockery of her friend. How I wished the fanciful little beauty would have called me her brother!"—Fred sighed profoundly—"and looked up at me with those melting eyes! I should have answered her something, though I am such a rough sort of chap.

"'I know,' she went on, as if still in argument with the trees, which kept up the same rustling noise, 'I know you would nurse me and feed me well with fruits and herbs and roots. You did it when I was little; you can do it again now.'

"At this speech of hers there was a universal shindy all round. Even the mossy face of the Satyr bleared out in the rising sun quite knowingly; indeed there was such a row going on at the time, I could hardly hear her voice.

"'How you bathed me in damp, sweet smells. And what a soft bed you made for me, like a nest, with dry leaves and moss in the cave on the hill-side! I slept there warmer than the dormouse or the hare!

"'But I have learned another life now, and Sigismund and I are going away. I am to stay together with Sigismund, and he'—she added, with a merry laugh—'cannot live among the trees, so I cannot either, for I shall be with him.'

"At this, one young ilex-tree (the largest and finest thereabout) trembled and beat itself about so violently, that many of its smaller branches snapped off. She held out her hands to catch them, lifted them to her lips, then dropped them gently, one by one, upon the ground.

"After this the young ilex-tree shut itself up like a box, and never moved so much as a shoot afterwards.

"But the old ilex-tree began again to wave its stiff old boughs.

"'I cannot tell,' she answered, after a while. 'I do not know who my mother was, nor my father—nor do I care. Gonzago never told me and I never asked. I do not understand what use a mother is, nor what she does. I was born among you.

"'How odd it seems to come out of the bark of a tree. *You* ought to know who my mother was, for you took me when I was running wild with the swine. I can just remember how we all slept together on the bare ground. You always said the Satyr knew all about my mother, and how she came to leave me alone in the wood. It was for that I got used to his mossy face, just the same as long as I can remember anything—and the hollow noises he makes when the wind blows, which frighten the peasants, but seemed company to me in the long winter nights.

"'I did ask Sigismund once where I came from, but he told me never to mind, for it was better not to know, and that it was all the same to him if I were only myself.

"'So I thought no more about my mother, and as to the magic words you taught me to draw all animals round me and to understand what the birds say, I have forgotten them.

"'I am more sorry about the swine than the birds, for they are *so* fond of me, and come running down from ever so far and grunt at me for half-an-hour at a time. I wish I could still talk to the swine.'

"Again her eyes were on the road, where the shadows of the branches went and came.

"'Oh, Sigismund, how long you are!' she cried, and the gold whistle was at her lips, but she did not sound it. 'His words were—"*at daybreak*"—and then —and then—'

"Some happy thought struck her, for she caught up her dress, and ran in among the trees, kissing and hugging them, and singing little snatches of song, to which they responded, swaying down—and the wood-pigeon joined in, and flew down to a lower branch. The small birds circled round her, and a robin, bolder than the rest, settled on her shoulder.

"After this, hearing nothing, she seemed to lose heart, sat herself down on the bench and began to cry."

CHAPTER XIX.

"I could not stand that," says honest Fred, wiping his face with his handkerchief, and shifting his place from the chair to the pillar, and then back again.

"I give you my honour, it was more than I could bear. I was just coming out at all hazards, to beg her not to talk rubbish to the trees, but to let me go and look for Sigismund, or do any earthly thing she wished; when, as I was making up my mind how I should address her, I saw two men turn the angle of the road. The first I set my eyes on, was that brown-leather animal of a priest, who hangs about at the villa, in his snuffy coat, and shovel hat.

"The other was Sigismund, with a colour on his cheeks that made him look superb.

"What chance have ugly fellows like me against such a swell? Sigismund ought to be dumb or blind, or something, to make up for his good looks. I could have kicked him!" and impulsive Fred reddened at the recollection; "but I didn't, all the same, don't you know!

"As soon as the priest caught sight of the girl, which was not difficult, in her white dress, he whispered a word or two to Sigismund, who smiled back at him with his grand air, and the priest disappeared down the hill.

"Then quicker than thought she ran forward.

"'Oh, my love, my love!' was all she could say, dear little thing, in a choked kind of voice. 'How long I have waited!'

"Sigismund's arms closed round her; he covered her with kisses. By the immortal nine, I never saw a fellow so much in love before!

"What a pang of jealousy shot through me! I kept telling myself I was an infernal fool, a damned ass, and all that, but I felt as savage as a bear.

"It was all I could do, not to reach out and punch his head.

"But what excuse could I have made? I was hiding. Yes, uncle, you are right—I was a spy, and I had to suffer for it.

"At first the little girl submitted quietly enough to be hugged and kissed, but as Sigismund still went on, small blame to him, she got angry, or frightened, or both, and broke away from him, and ran under the trees, at which, a rushing, angry whish of wind hissed through the whole bank of them, as if winter had sprung up, and smitten them with its blast.

"'For shame, Sigismund,' she cried, sobbing out of the shade, holding on firmly with both arms round the trunk of the old ilex-tree, which, too stiff to move like the others, rattled over her head.

"'For shame! I will not go away with you if you hold me like that.' Here she sobbed piteously. 'I will be free to do what I like. I won't be forced to anything.' (Another sob not quite so violent.) 'While your arms are round me, my head seems on fire.'

"Again she burst into a regular fit of crying.

"You may fancy, uncle Lucius, how cursed awkward it was being where I was,

"Not even the glimpses I got of her beautiful little feet could reconcile me to it, and that's saying a good deal.

"Sigismund seemed so excited, I think he could have killed me, had he known where I was, so I kept uncommonly still. I can tell you, uncle, Sigismund has a deuced deal of soft sawder about him, in a lofty kind of way, but for all that he looked completely at a loss.

"'Lela, Lela!' I heard him say, 'what have I done that you should be afraid of me?'

"'I don't know'—she answered very low, turning crimson to the tips of her fingers.

"'What has changed you?'—he asked, edging up nearer to her, but he could not catch her eye; she wouldn't let him.

"Little by little very gently he stole his arm round her waist—(He did it very well, Master Sigismund, I must say, though I was in tortures of jealousy) His voice—you know what a deep tone it has—Really it is too bad he should have everything!—dwelling upon her name (which name, by-the-bye, I heard now for the first time).

"'Lela, my Lela—Lela, Lela!'" repeated each time more softly, as he drew her closer to him.

"There was a little struggle, but Sigismund would not let her go. By and bye, he took her hands, and joined them in one of his, while, confound him, he managed to lift her veil and to kiss her, passing his fingers over her curls, and among the leaves of her green crown.

"'Shall we go now, Lela?' he asked, very humbly,

looking fixedly in her face. "'Don Antonio is waiting, he will think it unkind to be kept so long.'

"They stood close together as he said this—his dark eyes glowing down upon her like live coals. He was fighting hard with himself, I could see, Master Sigismund, not to begin it all again. But if he had, she would have been off to the old ilex-tree again, as sure as fate.

"She made no direct reply, but her whole countenance beamed back on him with joy.

"The sun struck down over them, and a sort of vibration passed through the trees.

"The birds struck up loudly and the insects chirped out of the leaves.

"Lela listened motionless, her very soul was in her eyes.

" 'Do you hear them, Sigismund?' she said, stretching out her arms, 'since you came they are reconciled. "Go," they are all saying. Every one of them says it. Don't you hear the murmur of their different voices? And the birds, and the insects. They are all saying that if I love you, I ought to go, and Gonzago——?'

"Here she stopped suddenly.

"'Will he ever forgive me?'

"She was supporting herself with her two arms linked in one of Sigismund's as she asked this question.

"'He is your brother, Sigismund, can you make him?'

"Sigismund shook his head.

"'He thinks we do not meet; I almost promised not to see you; I meant to try to keep my word, but—'

seeing Sigismund's dark face bent down upon her, 'but you sent for me, and I am here. How false, how wicked I am!'

"'Lela, why do you think about my brother? It is my turn now. Is not my love enough for you? You know how strange he is. You must not listen to what he says. I am willing to risk his anger for your sake. He *may* forgive *you*, he will certainly curse *me*.'

"'Curse you because of me! Oh, Sigismund, what have I done that Gonzago should curse you?'

"She clasped her hands and looked up for an answer.

"'Do not ask me, Lela. This is not the time; am I not with you?'

"His grave manner seemed to startle her.

"'Yes, yes!' And she flung herself wildly at his feet. 'Not to-day! Not to-day! To-day no one but you. No one but Sigismund! To-day and all the days of the year. What is Gonzago to me compared with you? Oh! my love, my love!'

"Nothing more was said. They made peace with a look. I am not good at describing, but I shall never forget *that look*.

"All this time a devil of a row was going on all round—everything seemed alive. A buzzing as of millions of bees came from the shaking ilex-boughs; the birds chirped like mad, and flew about; the frogs croaked out of the brake, and the wood-pigeon that had been frightened into silence cooed again louder than ever.

"Once the dear little girl faced round and cast her eyes on the trees, then dropped them again, and turned away to follow Sigismund.

"Whatever he wanted she had granted. There was no mistaking the conquering air with which he led her through a break in the wall, down the rocky descent, by the same path the priest had taken.

"A few steps and her white dress caught on one of the rocks that break the soil, which brought a saucy laugh from her, and another little scuffle with Sigismund.

"Now I'll take my Bible oath, uncle, that laugh was taken up by all the wood, and sent ringing back as far as the satyr.

"I could have sworn the satyr laughed too, with a horrible kind of gurgle; but when I looked back, rather nervously, there was its toothless mouth full of earth, and gaping holes for eyes, blinking as stolid as ever in the sun.

"Sigismund got his own way in the scuffle, as he got it about everything else, lifted her bodily in his arms and carried her down hill.

"When Sigismund and Lela were out of sight," continued Fred with a most dolorous expression—(the vein of poetry which the sight of Lela had developed in him, as well as his agility in understanding what had passed, was not the least wonderful part, to me, of his most wonderful narrative).

"—I came out of my hiding-place, and looked about. I do not mind owning that what I had seen made me feel deuced queer.

"Now the little girl was gone everything was perfectly quiet; not a leaf stirred, and the birds were as still as death.

"I pinched myself to be quite sure I was awake. The more I pinched the less I doubted I had been awake all the time. To prove it, there, scattered on the ground, were the weeds she had plucked, the grass she had trodden with those adorable little feet, and lying on the earth a blue ribbon, under a tree—her sash, which must have caught, when she was running in and out in that desperate sort of way.

"I rushed upon the ribbon then and there, and bagged it. It was part of her; I would keep it for her sake! And now, like a fool, I have given it to the Marquis! It was all my abominable temper. I got so mad with him, when he contradicted me about having seen Sigismund, that I brought out the ribbon to prove my words.

"I am sure I have got that dear little girl into trouble by splitting upon her and Sigismund."

"She *is* in trouble, my boy," I answered. "All the blue ribbons in the world cannot alter that."

"Then you have seen her, uncle?"

"Yes, and I can tell you, Fred, the Marquis will crucify us, if he so much as guesses that you know of her existence."

At this point Fred's humour changed, and he became extra sulky.

"What do I care? As far as I am concerned, I shall be very glad to go, I assure you. I am tired of pottering about in this haunted hole, with no one to speak to, and nothing but ghosts to look at. Sigismund is not likely to come back, being in such good company, and if he did, that would only make matters worse. But, uncle Lucius, as you seem to have learnt a great deal, can you enlighten me as to who this young lady is? Why she talks to the trees as if they were human beings? And what she has to do with the ghost of Gigia, the 'donnina?' This Lela whom I have seen is her very ditto, only she is alive, and the other is dead. She has even that little droop in one of her eyelids that Filippo mentioned. I noticed it just at the last, when she stood with her eyes cast down, while Sigismund was pressing her to go away with him."

"I can tell you nothing more, Fred, except that the Marquis, for reasons of his own, which I am not at liberty to divulge—I am not certain that I understand them myself, so I cannot divulge them—desires to keep the existence of this girl a secret."

A new light came suddenly into Frederick's face. "Ah! I see how it is! That old villain wants to make away with her, and Sigismund is going to marry her to save her life. Bravo, Sigismund!"

"For shame, Frederick!"

"Oh, I don't care what you say, uncle. You are infatuated about that man, who is, I do believe, next cousin to a certain old party not mentioned by persons of my distinction and breeding. I was not at school with him, and I see him as he is.

"However, Sigismund has many hours' start with her, specially if the priest has the *nous* to keep a light trap handy at the edge of the wood."

"Perhaps they are not gone at all," I suggested, recalling Lela's appearance in the saloon.

"Be that as it may, uncle, fancy that crafty old curate having all this in his head while he sat at lunch with us just now, as solid as an owl. I tell you what it is," he added, suddenly seizing his coat with his two hands — his favourite action when flushed and nervous—"I really cannot run the risk of seeing that girl again with Sigismund. I can make up my mind to anything for her good, but I could not sit by and see the love-making. Nor is that all. I cannot for the life of me get over being called a spy. So deuced dishonourable, you know, and nasty, and the worst of it is, I feel that it is true.

"Shall I walk over to Siena this afternoon, and wait for you at the Hotel? It's only my vow about finding the ghost that keeps me. When a fellow makes a vow, he is bound to keep it."

"I absolve you from your vow, my boy—You have seen the ghost as I told you. It is Lela, believe me, and no other."

I should be sorry for poor Fred to realise what an immense relief this unexpected proposal of his was to me. Ever since my arrival he had been like an incubus.

In the new crisis that had arisen it would be difficult enough for me to control the indignation of my friend.

But if Fred were present, Heaven knows what difficulties his mischievous tongue and his admiration for Lela might give rise to!

Knowing, however, his inconsistent temper, I took good care not to acquiesce too readily in his idea of leaving, or he was quite capable of changing his mind.

"Think it over, my boy," I answered, secretly chuckling at the prospect of a speedy deliverance. "Think it over."

"Think it over, uncle! I never thought so much before in my life. What I want is not to think at all for the next twelvemonths."

To relieve his feelings, Fred had recourse to the solace of a very large cigar. Finding no matches in his pocket, he informed me, he was going to his own room to fetch some.

"What I may do, I don't know. Anyway, if you don't see me again, uncle, you will know where to find me, at the Hotel. I shall console myself with the landlady. I can talk English to her. Oh, Lord! Those jolly little feet!"

CHAPTER XX

No sooner had my nephew disappeared at the end of the hall, than I caught sight of the Padre's black figure stealing cautiously down under the orange trees, close by the corner of the colonnade, evidently making for the path leading to the garden wall, under which Filippo and his friend Achilles had discoursed in the morning.

If I could only catch Don Antonio, I thought I should certainly hear something definite about Sigismund.

I had promised the Marquis to remonstrate with his brother on the subject of his marriage. There was evidently no time to lose.

My own curiosity — I have never, in the whole course of this narrative, concealed the fact that I am curious — prompted me also, specially after hearing Frederick's narrative, which, even allowing for his folly and love of the marvellous, was most unaccountable, as far as Lela was concerned, and pointed to some new resolution on the part of Sigismund—an immediate marriage probably, (the Marquis had told me that "*the day was fixed*").

Had the marriage taken place already? And was this meeting between them in the ilex-wood, witnessed by Fred, a rendezvous on the part of Sigismund for that purpose?

I had no time to consider. Don Antonio was already round the corner, so I jumped up, and hurried after him.

But the outer air was hot, the sun scorching, and, worst of all, the priest thin and light, while I am obese and heavy.

I was only just in time to catch sight of the skirts of his black soutane vanishing behind the stables, and to behold his priestly shoes, with their metal buckles, carrying him swiftly down the deep descent of the road.

"Good gracious! What on earth am I to do, if I miss this man?" I asked myself, with dismay. "I can never hope to find Sigismund in this wilderness, and deliver his brother's message!"

I did not dare to call after him lest the Marquis should hear me—Heavens, how fast he goes! He is distancing me every moment!

My stride breaks into a run, yet,—devil take him! —the nimble ecclesiastic, with those long black legs of his, is still far ahead of me.

I am at the summit of the hill, he at the bottom, in the middle of a broad and dusty road—flying, it seems to me, his black skirts spreading out behind him like huge wings.

I must mention that, on this side of the house, the ilex-woods recede considerably towards the mountains, leaving open spaces planted with young olives, and filled with rows of mulberries and vines.

At the bottom I perceive a small chapel or covered

shrine, with a frescoed front, a green gate, and a path winding among rough stones and scrub towards the borders of the wood.

Don Antonio is evidently making for the green gate, and the forest.

Once among the rocks and ilex-trees my chance of catching him is gone.

What a position for a pursy old gentleman, under the fierce August sun, without even the protection of an umbrella for his head!

Surely the claims of friendship have bounds! Palpitating and breathless, I come to the conclusion that I have overstepped them all.

Half-way down the hill, when sun-stroke or apoplexy seem inevitable, I stop.

The villa is just over me. Don Antonio winding in and out among the rocks, still flying. I am certain he must be aware that I am following. That he desires to avoid me is apparent. This motive, doubtless, adds speed to his limbs.

What can I do? I must chance being heard, and I call out.

"*Reverenza!*" (I am shouting at last, driven to desperation.) "Stop!"

I have to repeat this several times before he will slacken his pace. I am sure he hears me.

"Don Antonio," calling again, very loudly. "I beg —I entreat of you to wait a few moments—only a few moments!"

At this last appeal, Don Antonio does turn half round, and stops.

When I join him his face shows plainly that he would have escaped me if he could.

"Don Antonio!" I gasp, quite overcome by my exertions. "Pardon me—only an instant, to get my breath! How wonderfully agile you are—in such broiling heat too! Don Antonio, I have a question to put to you. Most important, or I should not have exposed myself to this dangerous sun. Tell me, as you seem in a hurry, where is Sigismund?"

The frankness of my interrogation has the effect of nettling the already irritated ecclesiastic.

"Don't mention that name so near the house," is his curt rejoinder. He is moving onwards—watching his opportunity as it seems to me, to avoid answering my question by actual flight.

"Not so fast, good father," say I, managing to place myself before him. "I have not heated myself in this fashion for nothing; before you go, you must be good enough to answer me."

Still dexterously dodging me, Don Antonio glides onward to where the trees rise large and thick. I follow.

Cost what it may, he shall not go without telling me where to find Sigismund.

"Don Antonio!" (I am now speaking in a tone of grave remonstrance.)

"Allow me to observe that your conduct is utterly unreasonable."

This is in answer to an uneasy expression on his mahogany-coloured countenance, while his eyes wander off towards a clump of trees screening a ledge of red rock, to the right of the path on which we are standing.

Seeing that I am observing him, he instantly shifts his glance to the opposite side.

"Do, I beg of you," I continue, "stand still, and listen to what I am about to say."

Angry as I am, and expiring with heat, I endeavour to take things good-humouredly, and I contemplate the peripatetic ecclesiastic with a smile (I am conscious it is but a feeble one).

"I ask you again, Father, where is Sigismund?" Now I am literally hanging on to him, lest he should bolt.

Short of a complete disruption of his outer garments, I am resolved he shall not escape.

"Why do you address yourself to me?" he answers at last, in a sulky tone. "How should I know where Sigismund is?"

"I am certain you do," I answer from the folds of a handkerchief, which I am compelled to take with one hand from my pocket to mop my head and face, while with the other I hold on to the priest's long arm.

"It is by the express desire of the Marquis," I add, trying to catch his restless eye, "that I put this question."

"Doubtless, Sigismund is to be found by those who have a right to seek him," is his offensive answer, trying to extricate himself from my grasp.

"I possess that right, Don Antonio," I reply, with as little courtesy as he shows me. (I confess I am waxing very wroth at his persistent disbelief in my mission.)

"I have seen Lela, reverend Father—I am deeply

interested in her fate. My earnest desire is to reconcile the brothers, and to arrange the marriage."

"Possibly you are, Signore Anstruther, like many
others, full of good intentions!" This Don Antonio
says with a sneer, and a contemptuous drawing up of
his sharp nose.

"But it is too late; I advise you to leave the affair
alone. The brothers cannot be reconciled, and the
Marquis will never consent to the marriage."

"But surely, Sigismund cannot be as obstinate as
my friend! Something can be done with *him?* He
will make concessions, it is his duty."

The priest shakes his head impatiently—again he
tries to move forward—but again my hand is upon
him, clutching at his coat.

"Really, signore," he adds remonstratingly, "It is
useless—"

"Allow me at any rate, to try," I urge; "I have
been specially authorised to do so. Surely, Don Antonio, in your Christian office, you ought to pity this
innocent girl? Have you not consented to perform
the ceremony of her marriage?"

"If the papers of the Marquis Sigismund Gonzago
are in order, I have no choice; the law compels me."

His stolid acuteness is utterly exasperating. In
spite of all my exertions, bodily and mental, I can get
nothing out of him.

I believe him to be on the point of breaking away
from me by main force, and darting off into the mazes
of the wood, when I make a last appeal.

"You cannot mean to insult me, reverend sir," I
say, "by doubting my word, when I solemnly declare

that I am here by the express desire of the Marquis *himself?"*

I am interrupted by a stir among the lower branches of the trees behind the ledge of rock, towards which the priest's gaze has so often been directed.

———

CHAPTER XXI.

"I WILL not doubt you, Mr. Anstruther, and I will thank you for trying to help me," speaks a deep, melodious voice I instantly recognized as Sigismund's, out of the thicket of ilex-trees. "Don Antonio means well, but he is really too hard upon you. Pardon him. It is only his anxiety lest my brother should discover my presence so near the house.

"I am here in answer to his own summons; he considers himself responsible for my safety."

While he speaks, the tall figure of Sigismund uprises from the background of dark red rocks, among which he lay concealed.

He had so far condescended to disguise himself as to appear in a heavy peasant's cloak, with a hood, and a broad-brimmed felt hat, that shaded the upper part of his face. But it would have required a much more complete disguisement to conceal the grand pose of his head, his massive shoulders, his aristocratic air, and the dignified ease of every movement.

He smiled at the bewilderment his sudden appearance caused me, and at the blank dismay depicted on the priest's countenance.

"I can answer for Don Antonio's vigilance," I replied, surveying with a certain exasperation, his aspect of perfect coolness. The only evidence he gave of any consciousness of the temperature being the production of a large red pocket handkerchief, while I, purple in the face and throbbing all over, felt as if the ferment in my blood would never subside.

"Mr. Anstruther, you see in me a fugitive,"—continued Sigismund, looking so like a fairy prince in disguise, that at the moment I began to doubt the reality of the whole scene, only my sufferings from the heat were a cogent argument for painful reality.

"Condemned to exile for treason to my liege lord. But the court of Love absolves me. You too, I hope, hold me innocent?" And he turns upon me, with one of those radiant smiles that must have won the heart of any woman.

"Innocent in intention," I reply gravely. His light jesting tone jarred upon me. The thought of his brother's horror at what he was about to do, rose vividly to my mind.

From me, Sigismund glances at the priest, who is contemplating us both with cynical glances.

"Do not be alarmed, Don Antonio, I will answer for the discretion of my brother's friend. Mr. Anstruther is an Englishman — therefore a man of honour."

I bowed at this compliment to my nation, and to myself.

Don Antonio only responded by another suspicious glance, muttering something about the extreme necessity of caution in the Marquis's over-wrought state of mind.

"Before any more is said," added he, "let me beg

of you to retire further into the wood. The mid-day heat makes the air so still that voices can be heard a long way off. Certainly as far as the villa."

His deprecatory manner continued unabated. "He," it seemed to say, "had made no revelations. Come what might he had done his duty!"

His sullen countenance, and a wide spreading out of his hands and a raising of his shoulders, gazing first at me, then at Sigismund, as he led us into the shelter of the ilex-trees, expressed all this clearly.

"Now or never," I said to myself, "I must speak, and that resolutely."

"If you," I am addressing myself to Sigismund, "heard any part of the conversation between myself and his Reverence, while you were concealed behind the rock, you are aware that I have taken the liberty to approach you in the character of a mediator between your brother and yourself."

"I could wish the office in no better hands, Mr. Anstruther," replied Sigismund with a bow.

We had now, following the priest's lead, halted at the foot of a far-spreading tree, with a canopy of foliage so dense as utterly to exclude the powerful sunshine.

"I am not," I continue, "enlightened as to the special cause of your brother's opposition to your marriage, Marquis Sigismund, but I have seen the young lady accidentally, and——"

"You have seen Lela!" exclaimed Sigismund, and in a moment he was wringing my hand, with the warmth of an old and trusted friend.

"Then you understand me! Is she not exquisite?

My very soul is bound up in her. Life is short, and
love the one good it bestows. Surely you would not
counsel me to lose it?"

All this burst from him in a kind of ecstacy. Then
he paused and coloured, as if conscious of the fervour
of his words.

"Believe me, Mr. Anstruther," he continues more
calmly, "it grieves me deeply to be at variance with
Anzano. He has been more of a father than of a
brother to me. His devotion to my interests has
always far exceeded my deserts. But that therefore
he should expect me to resign at his pleasure the
being I love beyond all others in the world, and to
whom my word is plighted, to accept a wife I have
never even seen, chosen by himself with no reference
whatever to my taste or feelings, is to ask me to renounce my very manhood!

"You are his friend, but you cannot justify him in
such a demand. Indeed, having seen Lela, I feel certain you will rather justify me in my refusal. I pity
him profoundly for his hallucinations on this subject.
I will go further, and say, I can understand the shock
his imagination received from the knowledge of my
engagement. But that is all. A terrible event in our
family connects itself with the birth of my beloved
Lela. My brother conceives himself vicariously answerable for it. A confusion of the brain is the result,
perverting his judgment. For my part, I could never
understand why he should hold himself responsible
for another's act. Out of respect to him I bore pa-
tiently with his infatuation until it deepened into
tyranny. Then bitter words passed between us, words
that scorch and destroy affection. His furious and

senseless reproaches exasperated me. I spoke, I fear, too impetuously. I glory in my love for Lela. I told him so. You know the rest."

"But this devotion to your interests of which you speak, Marchese Sigismund, this self-immolation which you acknowledge characterises his treatment of you, his earnest desire to remove every possible danger from your path, and to instal you free as the head of an illustrious line—free, I mean from the bondage under which he himself has sunk, and which he fears will overwhelm you also, if you contract this marriage. —Does not all this call upon you to pause? I will not allude to threats, because your brother's sincere attachment to you would soon dissipate any anger he feels for what he styles your 'disobedience,' but I allude to the fact of your contemplated marriage. Of that I am bound to say the Marquis invariably speaks, as of an act in itself unnatural and sacrilegious."

A deep flush, followed by a sudden pallor, revealed the emotion which my words called up.

Hitherto Sigismund had placed himself frankly before me.

Now, gathering about him the folds of his peasant's cloak, he turned towards the trunk of the huge ilex that sheltered us, with the air of a man steadfastly minded to resist all argument.

"Pardon me for repeating such words," I say, approaching him with the deference I felt due to his wounded feelings. "To me, remember, the words I have repeated convey no sense. I am ignorant of the facts to which they refer, but to the Marquis they appear conclusive. He solemnly declares that he will never live to see this marriage consummated. Through me he calls upon you, for the sake of the honour of your name, and by the duty and affection you owe him, to renounce it now and for ever! The balance of my friend's mind may waver, but the strong sense remains that some hidden crime has been committed, for which he suffers 'vicariously' as you say. A crime that will be intensified tenfold, and for ever perpetuated, by the marriage you contemplate."

As I proceeded, Sigismund's countenance darkened, not, as I rejoiced to see, with displeasure towards myself, but as with the purpose of a stern resolve, which turned his perfect features into the rigid semblance of a Greek mask.

Don Antonio, who had drawn aside while we were speaking, still wearing on his face that air of general disapproval he had maintained throughout, was about to break in with what I imagined to be some fact or statement in defence of Sigismund. But the latter waved him off imperiously.

"And what do you think, Mr. Anstruther, has restrained me hitherto?" he asked, raising his grand head, and contemplating me with the full power of his lustrous eyes. "What has restrained me hitherto, but love and duty towards Gonzago?

"Until now I have obeyed him implicitly. For his sake I have sacrificed myself,—much more, I have sacrificed Lela. I have borne to see the joyous freedom of her youth curtailed. Her fair name stained by the memory of a forgotten crime. Herself a prisoner until I set her free. No one in the house was to mention her—to acknowledge her very existence, under pain of instant dismissal.

"Even the place at our table where she had sat

from a child, was taken from her, with the harsh command that she was never to appear there again! You, Mr. Anstruther, witnessed this outrage! Could I bear it?

"Temporising has only exasperated Gonzago. He has mistaken my patience for weakness, my silence for submission.

"Now the time for action has come. I have left his house. Lela shall follow me."

"Yet the Marquis loves Lela," I urged.

"Yes, as long as he believes that she implicitly obeys him. He will hate her as he hates me, when she crosses his purpose. To reason with him is impossible. He lives in delusion. Can you ask me to govern my life by such hallucinations? I believe they will drive him to madness. He has repulsed me, because I refuse to resign Lela. Now he would sacrifice Lela to his crazy prepossessions.

"Why, Mr. Anstruther, in the name of common sense, should I not marry Lela? Gonzago himself brought her into our house; she has grown up among us; I have had ample occasion to know her. How could I help loving her? She is a rare mixture of opposite qualities. The playful simplicity of the child, with the heroic determination of the woman.

"Her early life in the woods has poetised her soul. All nature to her is alive with beneficent influences. She is ignorant of the very existence of evil! Who would have the heart to break the charm of such angelic purity?

"Man never loved woman more fervently than I love Lela. I bow down to her; I worship her.

"Who she is, or what her birth is, matters not to

me. It is herself I adore. With her, I am ready to go forth into the world, disinherited and nameless.

"My brother must be made to understand this.

"If I voluntarily renounce his inheritance, he has no right to oppose me."

———

CHAPTER XXII

As he spoke Sigismund stood before me, flushed with the pride of youth and manhood. The words of passion flowed from his lips like a musical cadence.

Every feature was transfigured by the fire which burned within.

Never did I behold a human countenance so Godlike!

And the singular gift of beauty he possessed, was not more remarkable than the entire absence of vanity which accompanied it.

He must have been so accustomed to admiration from his very cradle, as to have grown indifferent to it.

I have noticed this peculiarity before, in others equally favoured. They had grown so familiar with the homage they commanded, that they accepted it as a mere necessity of their existence.

My whole soul went out to him in all he said. I had discharged my duty in remonstrating. I would press him no more.

"This is all very well, my son," broke in Don Antonio, no longer to be checked or frowned into silence, "but there is a great deal behind that you have not told this gentleman. I will not enter into particulars now; it would only needlessly occupy our time—but the fact is, as I say, your statement omits many important particulars.

"I summoned you here, Sigismund, to inform you that your brother is, at this very moment, taking measures to part you permanently from Lela. Some tragic fate is reserved for her—what, I know not; I dare not guess.

"I escaped from the house to tell you. This English gentleman overtook me, and insisted on following me. I tell you, you are wasting precious moments. The Marquis must not have time to mature his plans."

"Yes," I added. "Unfortunately my nephew, Frederick is answerable for this. Frederick saw you, Marquis Sigismund and Lela together in the ilex-wood under the statue of the Satyr. He also saw you *there*, Don Antonio, in their company, a fact I did not allude to before, because you, reverend sir, denied any knowledge of the subject."

I was glad to get this rise out of the wily priest, who, if he could blush under his bronzed skin, ought to have done so at the disclosure of the gratuitous lie he had perpetrated.

At all events his twinkling eyes did fall before mine. That was a certain amount of victory.

It will be observed that I kept a discreet silence as to Frederick's having listened to what passed between the lovers. Like Frederick, I did not dare to impart this to Sigismund. His dignity and his passion intimidated me.

"Frederick," I continued, "unfortunately picked up a blue ribbon or sash belonging to the young lady. This ribbon is now in the possession of your brother. He knows of your interview. Frederick is in such despair at the mischief he has involuntarily caused, that he intends leaving Sant' Agata immediately."

"I thought you had taken precautions to prevent all this, Don Antonio," said Sigismund. "When I went down to meet Lela at daybreak, you made yourself answerable that no one would see us. Has anything more transpired?" he added with flashing eyes.

"Not that I am aware of," answered the priest, much taken aback at Sigismund's tone of reproach. "I did all I could, but the forest baffles one. The young stranger must have been concealed behind the trees. How could I guess this? At that hour, I believed no one was about. But the point to be considered now is, not what *has* happened, but what is *about* to happen.

"The Marquis knows all. Lela has deceived him. He will show her no mercy. At this moment he is considering in what manner he will punish her. He is greatly excited. Possibly he may come to understand that it is too late to interfere. The law is with us. I have checkmated him there!"

A sardonic smile shot over his face, like a sungleam over a barren landscape. Later on, I understood the full meaning of that smile, but not then.

And Sigismund? All this time the blood had been rushing over his face, and spreading down to the muscles of his massive throat. His large eyes grew fierce and full as he listened. His nostrils quivered.

"Why did you not tell me all this at once, Don Antonio?" he cried, stamping his foot upon the ground. "You are responsible for Lela. He left her in your charge. What have you done with her?"

"I thought she left me to return to her room at the villa. But it appears she only went to leave word with Narcissus that she should conceal herself in the wood near the Satyr, until you joined her."

"I will go to her instantly. Too much time has been already lost. When Lela is safe with me, all need for concealment is past. Then I will see my brother."

Sigismund was striding away with long hasty steps, when Don Antonio rushed forward and planted himself before him.

"Sigismund, listen! If you meet your brother now, his life or yours will be the sacrifice. What a bridegroom!" he added, bitterly. "Will Lela love you the better for this violence?"

"All this is but temporising," cried Sigismund, wresting his hands from the priest's grasp.

"He is no brother of mine, who injures Lela. You, Don Antonio, are answerable for all this. But for your counsels, I should long ago have married Lela. Are the very heavens to fall because I love her? What matter to me my brother's visions, his voices, his threats of supernatural vengeance? Is my living Lela to be sacrificed to a foul past?"

"The past has its mysteries," replied the priest, solemnly, laying his hands impressively on the shoulders of Sigismund. "As a Gonzago, respect them! '*A life for a life*' are the words of the prophecy which press upon your brother's brain. How combat *that*—which is, in itself, immaterial?"

Of Sigismund's wild, impassioned words, his agitated gestures, his stinging reproaches, Don An-

tonio took no more heed than if an angry child had
been battling before him.

How little I had judged of what stuff this rustic
ecclesiastic was made, when I first saw his homely
face under the ragged canopy.

"To wipe away the stain of a foul deed which
sullies your good name—not to gratify your passion, I
have aided you. More, I will not do; nor will I join
in any violence against the Marquis.

"The hand of God is heavy upon him"—(there is
no faltering about Don Antonio—no doubt of what he
means. His voice is full of authority, his aspect as of
a judge delivering a sentence).

"Remember, Sigismund, while he lives, *the stain is
there*. You are most unjust to him. What sacrifices
would he not have made for you, but for Lela! Surely
his are the errors of a noble mind; it is not Anzano
Gonzago, but the tortured spirit within, calling upon
him to expiate the act of another, that speaks in
him."

"Expiation!" cried Sigismund, rearing himself to
his full height against the forest background. "You
speak of expiation—what expiation is there like marriage? It reconciles all! I care not for the past!
Let it vanish, with the evil shadows of these accursed
woods! Place of mystery and of ill omen, I trust
never to breathe the poisoned air again." As he spoke,
he threw up his arms with a wild gesture of universal
imprecation. Then, turning to me—

"Perhaps, you had better see my brother before I
do, Mr. Anstruther, and prepare him. Tell him, that
nothing but death can part me from Lela. We are
one—Ah!" he exclaimed, interrupting himself, "if

you could but bring him to understand that my marriage with her closes the record of the past!"

"That is my view," interrupted Don Antonio, before I could reply; "and on that view I have acted. But the feelings of the Marquis must be considered. Time must be allowed for him to recover his equilibrium. At the present moment, nothing must transpire; he is in a state of fearful excitement. Do nothing, Sigismund, do nothing *now!* I warn you!"

"And Lela?"—as he asked this question, Sigismund glanced fiercely at the priest. "My Lela? What is to become of her? Would you, in your priestly wisdom, counsel me to forsake her? *One* must suffer, you say—is it to be Lela?"

What utter scorn curled his proud lip! What fire shot from his dark eyes! How grand he looked in the ardour of his lover-like indignation!

"No, no!" I cried, carried away by my feelings, and quite forgetting myself; "not Lela!"

I had been called upon to curse, and behold, I am altogether blessing.

"You, too, my brother's friend," cried Sigismund, grasping my hand with passionate warmth. "I thank you; one, at least, feels for me, and understands me."

"This is scarcely fair to me, Sigismund," interposed the priest, the same sardonic smile flitting across his face as I had noted before. "In my office, I cannot now counsel you to forsake Lela. I am only endeavouring to prevent a catastrophe. It is somewhat out of my way to assist lovers, but I have done it; at my own risk, too; for the Marquis, in his present mood, is most dangerous to deal with.

"Before I left the Villa, I took care to let Lela

know what has passed with the nephew of this gentleman.

"Her light feet will long ago have carried her into the recesses of the woods. There she will wait for you.

"Bring her down to me at San Martino. If need be, I will see that you both reach Siena in safety this evening. But remember, Sigismund, no rash interview with the Marquis; I forbid it absolutely; in this I *will* be obeyed."

"My sweet Lela!" cried Sigismund, in an outburst of love, all the anger dying out of his face as he named her. "At this moment she is waiting for me! Only let me feel her little hand in mine—I ask no more—she shall never leave me."

Sigismund was now hurrying onward along the mountain path, but, as if suddenly remembering something, he hastily returned.

"I cannot go without asking your pardon, my father, for my hasty words. You will forgive me!"

He seized Don Antonio's sunburnt hand, and carried it to his lips.

As he bowed his head, the priest, with solemn gesture, raised his hand over him in blessing.

"Say no more, my son," was his reply in his usual curt manner. "I can make every allowance for you— only act with calmness. Beware of accumulating a load of remorse upon your head.

"Now, good-bye. I too must make all possible haste to change my clothes, and carry the blessed sacrament to a poor woman, who is waiting for me. I ought to have been there an hour ago!"

"But Don Antonio," insisted Sigismund, arresting

him as he was again launching into that rapid motion, which cost me so dear, "remember," and a stern determination replaced the humility with which he had just excused himself, "if I do not find Lela in the wood I shall discover her wherever she may be, and claim her whoever may oppose me!"

———————

CHAPTER XXIII.

WITH heavy heart I saw Sigismund depart.

No longer under the charm of his personal presence, the thought of my poor Anzano overwhelmed me. I felt I had pleaded his cause but feebly, yet to do otherwise was impossible. From the first I had felt he was in the wrong.

And now I asked myself would he ever consent to Sigismund's marriage?

If not, what would happen? To what frenzied excesses might not his distorted fancy lead him? Would blood be shed if the brothers met? And if so, whose? A terrible foreboding crept over me. Would to God I had never come!

As I walked on, mechanically, uncertain and dejected, in the direction of the villa, no longer sensible even of the heat, and careless whither my steps led me, the still voices of the wood came to me in the mid-day silence, with a dumb perception of the multiformness of the life around.

A low chattering of birds, flying rapidly round the tree tops, a buzzing and whirring of insects among the rocks, a stir of nameless vitalities surging up from the mossy bark accumulated on the ancient ilex-trees, and from time to time the shrill call of the cicala's note, ringing out like a bell into my tormented ear.

The jays called to each other, screeching hoarsely,

the pigeons cooed sadly, far away in the distant covers.

A young eagle, circling in short and angry rotations round a lofty ilex, sounded a clear loud note of defiance, and ceaseless, changeless—intermingling with all, though separate—the dumb low whisper of the vast forest, rising and falling as the hot wind passed through the deep ranks of trees.

"I had, unconsciously, for my eyes were fixed on the ground, wandered on until I had reached a green gate by the wayside chapel. On the little homely altar lay a withered nosegay of field flowers—an offering from some lonely one, who had nothing else to give!

Still walking mechanically, I began to ascend the hill, and found myself overlooking the open country to the South.

A sudden gloom obscured the sun; a pale yellow light gradually overspread the mountains. Gigantic shadows flitted across the hard surface of the purple-tinted plain, and great white clouds, storm-laden, and massive, reared themselves ominously over the double summit of Monte Amiata, revealed in all its majesty of height and breadth.

The leaves in the olive-ground and among the trellised vines trembled as if touched by unseen hands, and spite of the heat, which was still intense, chill blasts of air mixed themselves strangely in light eddies and currents came and went capriciously.

I had now almost surmounted the ascent which leads to the house, which I had descended but two short hours before, in such lively pursuit of Don Antonio, full of confidence in my own powers of argument.

Now, all hope had left me. The decrees of fate, whatever they might be, I felt must be accomplished.

It was the hour of the siesta. Not a sound of human life reached me! Above, rose the grey-stained towers of Sant' Agata, rearing themselves out of the many attendant buildings grouped around.

The sight of poor Anzano's abode inspired me with a sudden dread. The rich carvings, mouldings, and cornices of its splendid façade, the arabesques, coronets, and medallions, brought out in strong outlines by the storm-laden shadows, came to me as the gaudy embellishments of a tomb.

What might not have happened within during my absence? How should I find my friend? What account could I give to him of my interview with Sigismund?

Now, I was within the precincts of the garden.

Of all the hangers-on and servants not one was visible. Only the white statues that marked the unsymmetrical angles of the paths, rose up out of the shrubs, and saluted me with a stony glare.

What would I not have given to encounter the cheerful countenance of Narcissus, or to have feasted my eyes on the rotund charms of the comely stewardess! Not a beggar showed himself at the gate, not a dog lurked about the doors. Even the white mastiff had forsaken his post on the gravel at the factory door. All—men and animals—were alike wrapped in profound repose, that mid-day slumber which gives the Italian life.

The same languid influence was apparent in the parterre. Under the stifling heat the flowers hung their heads, the fresh green of the leaves flagged, the grass was dried up and brown.

Only the bristling cactus and the fan-shaped palms, like well-seasoned athletes, rejoiced in the hot air, and the fountains sang on, indifferent, splashing downwards upon the gold fish, placidly sleeping beneath, balanced on the surface of the water.

Every window in the sculptured front of the villa was closed. This is but the usual custom at mid-day. Now it made me shudder. It was as if death were hidden there.

I crossed one of the gravel-paths hastily and seated myself within the shelter of the portico. The heavy curtains, drawn down to exclude the heat, filled the pillared space with gloom.

In the hall beyond nothing could be distinguished. The pent-up odour of the flowering plants piled against the walls came to me so strong and pungent that I leaned back faint upon my chair. Again the thought of death pursued me. Are not strongly-scented leaves and flowers scattered to veil the presence of a corpse?

One idea struck me with a vague sensation of relief. Frederick must have acted on his resolve, and returned to Siena, else I should infallibly have encountered him. His presence would, at least, create no further embarrassment.

*　　　*　　　*　　　*　　　*

Yes, I was alone at Sant' Agata! Alone I must meet whatever was impending.

As I sat on, without the courage to enter the house, a piercing cry from the woods reached me. It was followed by no other sound. Was it the sharp note of a bird, caught in the woodman's net, which I had seen below, stretched from tree to tree? Or could it be a human voice calling for help?

Filled with a vague anxiety, I rose and I walked towards the iron gates at the entrance of the garden.

Nothing met my eye. The dark net-work of ilex-branches reared itself sadly against the leaden sky. A shaft of lurid sunshine shot downwards for a moment, then paled, turning it into the semblance of prison bars.

While I was wondering what creature could have given utterance to that piercing cry, the sound of hasty footsteps met my ear. Minute by minute they drew nearer. There was a stifled sob, then a low wail. Surely it was the voice of Lela!

How long I waited, I know not—the moments seemed hours. At last, over the rise of the hill, appeared two figures, the Marquis and Lela.

Half dragging, half carrying her, she lay within his arms. Whatever resistance she might have offered, her struggles had ceased. Her flaxen head was rudely crushed against his side, her eyelids were closed, her cheeks colourless, the thick coils of her loosened hair swept upon the ground.

Great God! Was she dead? Had Anzano murdered her?

No link in the chain of events had prepared me for such a catastrophe. All that Don Antonio had said was, that he had left my friend considering in what manner he should punish her.

* * * * *

Now he has reached me. I can hear his laboured breathing before the power of speech returned to me.

Anzano! Anzano!" I shouted, flinging myself upon him. "What have you done?"

He was quite still. He looked me full in the face, the dilated pupils of his eyes glaring upon me.

"Touch me not!" were his words, warding me off with his disengaged arm, while with the other he tightened his hold on the passive form of Lela. "Touch me not! I am on a holy mission. *A life for a life!* Where her mother fell, she must die also!"

There was a fearful calm about him terrible to behold. He had suddenly aged as if a lifetime had passed over him. Every feature in his face was set. His eyes were scarcely human.

But, to my inexpressible relief, he cowered under my steady gaze.

"Listen, Anzano!" I managed to speak in a commanding voice. How I did this, I know not—"If Lela is not dead"—(and I raised one of her cold, clammy hands in mine and pressed it to my lips. Thank God there was still the pulse of life in it)—"let us both endeavour to revive her."

I stretched out my arm to take her, but he made no answering move. Yet, although he would not give her up to me, I dominated him.

My obvious determination to rescue her did not infuriate him. Spite of his efforts to rid himself of me, I closed my hand upon his arm with a grip of iron. Presently he submitted to my sustained pressure and loosened his hold. A change passed over him; the strain on his feature relaxed, and he bent over her as she lay within his arms.

"Poor Lela! Sweet child!" he murmured in scarcely articulate accents. "How I once loved her!"

How joyfully I hailed these signs of yielding! Now he was gazing into her half-closed eyes, his hand wandering tenderly over her face and neck. Surely reason would gain the mastery! His whole being moved within him as he stood there. His breast heaved, his limbs shook violently, yet no tear came to his relief, no sound betrayed his anguish.

Little by little, he raised her upright, then placed her tenderly on the ground.

With a low moan she broke from him, then fell forward, half-conscious, on the grass. I went to her and raised her; she had only seen me during that interview with the Marquis in the darkened saloon, but she understood that I was there to help her.

"Save me! save me!" was all she could say. Then, turning her appealing eyes to mine—"Do not let me go!" she whispered, tightening her hold on me. "He wants to kill me."

"Depend on me, Lela," I replied, putting back from her brow the ruffled tresses of her golden hair. "Take heart, dear child! Where I am, you are safe."

She thanked me by a look, then lifted her eyes in mute reproach to the ilex-trees, swaying restlessly over the balustrated wall.

"I trusted to them to bring me to Sigismund! And they betrayed me! After so many years—so many——"

A sudden gust from the wood seemed to bear away her words. She started and turned round. Then, conscious that I must have heard what she said, she took my hand with a faint effort at a smile.

"I know who you are—Mr. Anstruther, the friend

of the Marquis! Don't listen to what I am saying to the trees. You will think it nonsense!"

Here the strain of terror caused by her recent escape from death suddenly overcame her. With the certainty of safety came weakness. She drew a long breath, and burst into a passionate flood of tears.

At that moment, a low moan swept through the close network of branches, and passed down to the uttermost depths of the silent, rock-bound plain. The hollow roll of distant thunder rattled from among the far-off mountains, and the ground trembled beneath our feet.

Meanwhile, the Marquis's eyes never left us.

Again the signs of that maniacal fury were gathering on his brow.

"Lucius!" he said at last, in a hushed voice. "As you value my regard, leave Lela! She has basely deceived me. She has met Sigismund. But it is for the last time. *A life for a life!* My word is passed!"

Muttering something, he was about to fling himself upon her, when bounding from me, she faced him.

"Gonzago! Hear me!" she cried, her fresh young voice sounding like the note of a bird, "You may kill me, but you shall never part me from Sigismund! He loves me! I am his—his own!"

"His! How his? His paramour? Have you sunk so low as that, vile bastard?" shouted the Marquis, roused by her boldness to a sense of what was passing about him.

At last he had spoken! The secret of his life was revealed! Nothing but madness could have torn it from him. Had any doubt remained, he had solved it.

As the hateful words passed Anzano's lips, Lela's large eyes opened upon him. A startled movement backwards and the quick motion of her hands showed that she understood his words had branded her. Even Gonzago paused in the full torrent of his wrath, with some dim consciousness of the outrage of which he had been guilty.

For an instant only. Then, with a movement of blind rage, he precipitated himself upon her, crashing through the light barrier of shrubs that divided them.

But before he could reach her, by a rapid movement backward, she had taken refuge with me.

Holding her firmly by the hand, my looks plainly showed that I would defend her against his violence.

Evidently he shrank from any attack on me. With a baffled air he turned away, and tried to reason.

"Let her go, Lucius, let her go!" he shouted. "Her life is mine. She was thought to be dead. Orders were given by"—(here an inaudible word filled up the sentence)—"to kill her. I—I—saved her! You understand. I saved her."

He stopped. A vacant look came over his face. He had lost the thread of what he was saying. Helplessly pressing his hands upon his brow, he made a vain effort to recall it.

I seized upon this lull to retreat with Lela to the rear of one of the large marble basins. Step by step, he followed us. His haggard eye never left us.

"She is of my blood!" he muttered—"of my blood." Then louder, in a tone of menace: "I—I am her natural guardian. She must be sacrificed."

"Sacrificed to whom?" I asked, suddenly turning

on him; while Lela, understanding her danger, could not repress a cry.

"To the dead!" he answered solemnly, throwing up his arms—"To the dead! I promised! I have waited too long!"

Step by step, he was following us with the dogged persistence of madness. Each moment was weighted with Lela's doom. I saw it in his merciless face, so drawn and white, in the gleam of his glassy eye, in his set teeth, and the restless tearing action of his hands.

How could I, single handed, battle with a maniac? Would Sigismund never come?

Meanwhile, a great shadow fell upon us. The clouds, which had been rapidly gathering from all quarters of the heavens, almost obscured the sun. A hot white mist arose from the plain, shutting out every distant object. Dark lines formed along the paths, gloomy circles marked the orange trees and the big tufts of pampas grass; the statues cast blackened shadows: the front of the villa gloomed into an almost undistinguishable mass. A loud clap of thunder crashed out, and a vivid flash of lightning lit up the air into momentary flames.

"The time is come," said a voice out of the gloom.

"Lucius, give Lela up to me! They are waiting for her there! There," he repeated, raising his hands above his head, and pointing to the window of the old factory.

Lela clung to me despairingly.

"Sigismund! Sigismund! Oh, my Sigismund! Where are you?" came from her lips in little cries, heard only by me. Gonzago was trying to grasp my shoulder, but I avoided him.

"Judge between Lela and me! Judge," he repeated, making a great effort to be calm. "When I came here at Cardinal Flavio's death——"

As the hated name passed his lips, he shuddered; his self-control suddenly gave way, and he opened his arms to seize Lela.

Placing her behind me, I faced him.

"I am listening," I said. "Proceed quietly. It will be impossible for me to act as umpire otherwise."

He bowed his head. The idea of an umpire seemed to please him. He proceeded.

"Lela was then a child, wandering in the woods, herding with swine. No roof to cover her, no friend but the peasants to give her a crust of bread. I saw her under a tree."

Here his voice trembled; but neither the aspect of his face, nor the murderous action of his hands varied.

"Yes, yes," repeated Lela, who had stolen to my side—speaking low, as if knitting together the threads of remembrance—"Yes; he is right! I recollect it well; it was a happy time! But you are wrong in one thing, Gonzago, I was not alone. Besides the ilex-trees, some one with a white face came to me often. I have never seen her since. She beckoned me to follow her but I was afraid, and clung to the trees. She had blue eyes, and long, light hair, that hung down her back in curls like mine.

"I never heard her voice, but I understood her without words. Something about me always made her

weep. The trees understood her and wailed over her
at sundown, under the statue of the Satyr. It was
always in the evening. She went and came without a
sound, fading away behind the trees. I saw her at
many places, but oftenest at the Satyr.

"I am not afraid of you now, Gonzago," Lela went
on, raising her head, and fixing her grave eyes, full of
some mysterious assurance, upon Anzano. "You cannot
harm me. *She* watches over my life. Until you
spoke, I had quite forgotten her. Now, it all comes
back to me! No! You dare not touch me!"

The Marquis followed every word she uttered with
a look of terror. He no longer menaced her. He was
like a man stunned.

Standing there, face to face, a sudden impulse of
affection overcame Lela. Long she gazed at him wist-
fully; then, with outspread hands, she touched him.

"Oh, Gonzago! Gonzago! Be your own dear self
again! Do not wring my heart by your cruelty! I
have done nothing wrong! I have always obeyed you
—always, till now!

"You cannot divide me from Sigismund; no one
can, it is too late!"

Then, softening before the blank suffering depicted
in his face, again her pleading grew passionate.

"Believe me, Gonzago, *we*—that is Sigismund,
grieves for your pain. Like me, he owes you a deep
debt of gratitude. Share our love, dear Gonzago. It
will make you happy. Now, you are not yourself.
By-and-bye you will forgive us."

Lela was urging her cause in tones of the most
pitiful supplication; her hands clasped, her head bent

forward—her whole attitude as though seeking to obliterate herself in the very dust.

"Dear, dear Gonzago, forgive us! Forgive your little Lela! Forgive us both—*for we are one.*"

At this moment, the dark figure of Sigismund rose up in the fading light.

CHAPTER XXIV.

"At last! At last! Oh, Sigismund!" With a happy cry, Lela rushed forward, as he pushed his way rapidly through the intervening shrubs; crashing through the palms and the orange trees in his haste.

As they met midway, a shaft of sunshine—the last expiring effort of the once glorious day—struck downwards from a bank of clouds, concentrating itself like a pale flame upon their heads.

"Yes, my Lela, I am come. It is Don Antonio's fault that I have been delayed. What has happened?" he added, in a low anxious voice, looking towards his brother, concealed by the rich foliage. "Have you told him?—does he know?"

"Oh, my love—my love!" answered Lela, clinging to him, "Be gentle with him, for my sake! I fear I have done him a great wrong——"

"Yes, Lela, I will be gentle; but he must know the truth."

Then advancing, "Gonzago! Lela is my wife! We were married this morning! I am come to take her away. Will you say no word of forgiveness to us before we go?"

At the first sight of Sigismund, the Marquis had tottered backwards to where a broad-leaved catalpa rose up like a slender pillar out of the grass. By the aid of the trunk he steadied himself, then, with a

mighty effort, stood erect and still, his ashen lips
parted, his far-off eyes vaguely resting upon Lela and
Sigismund with a vacant stare.

He essayed to speak, but no voice came. Then
he raised one tremulous hand, and pointed with a
thin, bony finger towards the front of the old factory,
over which the shifting shadows fell like a pall.

"Hush," he murmured, in a scarcely audible
whisper. "Hush! The dead! Do you not hear them?
The Cardinal—her mother—" pointing to Lela; "Sigismund, you would not surely boast of your crime in
the presence of the dead?"

Sigismund shuddered. "Great God! His reason
is utterly gone! Mr. Anstruther! Lela! has my brother
been long like this?"

Lela whispered something into his ear.

That she would conceal from him what had really
occurred, I felt certain. Again Sigismund turned, full
of grief, towards Anzano.

"Gonzago! rouse yourself! Be a man!"

As he spoke, he touched his brother gently on the
shoulder. The Marquis gathered himself together with
horror.

"She comes! She is at hand!—I know it—I feel
it! Her feet are on the stairs—her long robe sweeps
the pavement! He is there, also—the villain! Enter
that door, and you will see them, on the upper floor,
as I saw them when I first came! O God! The
horror of it lighted a fire in my brain, that burns until
it will consume me! Oh! I am sick—sick with the
long agony! She cursed me!—There, with her white
lips, flinging about her yellow hair! She cursed me
for *his* crime! The burr, as of a mill wheel, sounded

in my ears—the blackness of eternal night encompassed me! I swooned. You, Lela——"

Lela cowered, and hid her face in her hands.

"—Are her child! A curse beyond all curses rests upon your birth!"

"Brother, brother!" broke in Sigismund, endeavouring to silence him, but the torrent of his pent-up passion rushed on with uncontrollable frenzy.

"And you live! And Sigismund has made you his wife—Sigismund, for whom I have suffered!"

Then, fixing his awful eyes upon Lela—"Destroyer of my house! Vain, silly fool, that has stepped between Anzano Gonzago and the fixed decrees of fate! Hear me! None of our tainted stock shall rise up to call you mother! Take this for your portion. The name you dishonour shall die with you!"

"No—by Heaven! It shall live!" burst from Sigismund, who could contain himself no longer. "Live, and through her!"

Drawing Lela to him proudly—poor Lela, who had shrunk back, appalled at the Marquis' malediction—he raised her downcast head, and folded her fondly in his encircling arms.

"God grant, Anzano—" he spoke with solemn emphasis—"that your reason may return to you! I married Lela because I loved her; I shall love her to the end. Of fate I know nothing, nor of any doom, nor crime, however foul, that can move me to part from her. Her pure nature is as unsullied by sin as is a diamond by the mire and slime in which it lay concealed."

"Brother," he added, after a pause which marked the working of strong emotion, "let that thought comfort you. Let us part friends."

To this address the Marquis makes no sign, nor does he notice the hand which Sigismund extends towards him. I do not think he so much as saw it. Blank despair is in every line of his countenance, as the knowledge that Lela and his brother are irrevocably united, reaches his imperfect sense.

At this moment a flash of lightning, so intense that, for an instant, it lit up the woods and mountains into the semblance of a universal conflagration, struck down, followed by a continuous roar of thunder.

Sigismund seizes Lela's hand.

"Come, Lela, we must go! A terrible storm is upon us. We shall hardly have time to reach Don Antonio's house. Do not look so frightened, love," caressing her cheek, from which all colour had fled. "My brother's words are hard to bear, but believe me, at this moment he does not know what he says."

"I do not care for the storm," is Lela's answer. "I am used to storms. But I do not like to leave him. What does he mean? Tell me," and she drew herself back, as Sigismund tries to lead her onwards. "Is it all about me? I cannot understand it. He used to be so proud of me. Do you think he will ever be himself again?"

"I will tell you what I think another time, my Lela, not now. Mr. Anstruther." And he extends his hand to me. "Farewell! You will remain and take care of my brother, I trust. Our presence can only serve to madden him."

"Yes," I reply. "For the present I will remain."

Still Lela lingers, she cannot bring herself to leave Gonzago. Abundant tears are gathering in her eyes.

"It must be, darling," insists Sigismund, in that

melting voice of his, which would thrill responsive in any woman's ears. "Bear it bravely. Out of the ilex-woods you came to me, alone, and into them we will return together. Come, Lela, my beloved, you must forget all but me."

Even then, had Gonzago, by the smallest sign, shown himself conscious of her presence, I saw by her looks she would have flown to him. But there was no recognition.

*　　　*　　　*　　　*　　　*

Slowly, as those weighted with a great joy, which robs them of all utterance, and leaves them beggared of everything but a charmed silence, Sigismund and Lela passed down the garden paths, over their heads the delicate tracery of the ilex-woods, darkening each moment in the universal gloom, the pampas-grass shaking its feathery spears, and the orange-blossoms scattering white petals in the wild wind.

With one of those abrupt, but graceful movements peculiar to herself, Lela turns to me as I followed them to the entrance-gate, and presses her caressing fingers on my arm.

"Take care of him, Mr. Anstruther," she says, with a long glance at the Marquis immovable on the same spot. "I entreat you to take care of him. It goes to my very heart to leave him. He has been very strange at times, but never like this. I am so glad you are here. You are a good man, you understand him."

Then, with her head close to mine, she whispers in my ear.

"I shall always remember that you saved my life. But keep that a secret, a dead secret. I would not have *him*" (here a glance at Sigismund), know it for the world."

Then louder.

"When Gonzago recovers, try to make him forgive us. I shall never be happy without that. Then we will come back and live with him again."

Sigismund did not speak, but his eyes endorse all that Lela says, except the notion of returning to Sant' Agata. At that he shakes his head resolutely.

I cannot answer her. My heart is full. If they are happy, it is happiness bought at the price of the reason, if not of the life, of my dear friend. Spite of my warm sympathy for them, I cannot forget this.

A sudden roar of the tempest, and another flash of almost blinding lightning shortens the moment of parting.

Hastily drawing away Lela, Sigismund pushes resolutely forward, out of the iron gates, with their mediæval carving, into the avenue beyond, bordered by colossal statues.

"And so the ilex-trees were not false, after all," I hear Lela say, as she hurries down the hill on those eager feet of hers; her clear voice echoing back, spite of the wind.

"You don't know what happened in the wood while I was waiting for you, Sigismund, I will never tell, never."

A joyous laugh follows. It is abruptly checked; probably by a kiss.

"What! secrets from me already, Lela?" I hear him say.

"Yes, dear, all sorts of secrets" (laughing). "But

the trees brought you back to me at last! The dear old trees!"

A portentous peal of thunder drowns her voice, and I hear no more.

CHAPTER XXV.

SLOWLY I return.

The Marquis still stands immovable before the long, low front of that fatal building. From his white face all vestige of passion has departed. Hope, fear, menace, and that keen desire of vengeance—all gone! Only his rapt look and the position of his hand behind his ear, tells me that in the wild confusion of the blast which whistles round, he is conscious of the unseen presence that haunts him.

A sickness of the heart steals over me as I look at him. If not wholly mad, he is the slave of hallucinations too shadowy to be combated by any argument. Of what use have I been to him? Of what use can I be?

But I have promised to remain.

Happen what will, I will keep my word.

Hitherto I have felt no fear. Now, I confess he terrifies me! More than terrifies! He is actually infecting me with the insane influences of his own fantastic brain.

Is that low-roofed house before me really visited, as he imagines, by the spirits of the dead? Are those terrible scenes reproduced in that upper chamber? Has the Marquis a sense more than I? Is he the maniac? Or am I the fool? The doubt makes my brain reel.

*   *   *   *   *

I am quickly recalled to the outer world by the constantly recurring thunder. Not in one continuous roll, but flung as it were in a series of reverberations from flank to flank of the encircling mountains, now near, now distant, till it loses itself in a parting rattle, loud and distinct as a discharge of artillery.

Incessant flashes of lightning increase the horror of the scene. Each flash revealing unknown recesses of the wood, in the full glare of a white sepulchral light.

Heavy drops of rain are now falling, and the ever raging wind bursts forth with renewed fury.

There are moments when it almost lifts me from my feet.

A whirlwind has, apparently, collected its force in the mountains near; for there are frequent and violent alternations in the direction of the wind; and the exceeding density of the clouds, which hang almost upon the roof and central tower of the villa, does not prevent my perceiving the velocity with which they fly.

I force myself to approach Gonzago. I touch his cold hand.

"Come, Anzano!" I say. "Come under shelter—at once—at once!"

He permits me to lead him unresistingly towards the house. With the same mute helplessness he allows me to seat him under the colonnade. The touch of his poor stricken fingers—the desolation of his cadaverous face—recall me to my better self.

I bend over him and try to chafe his limbs into a little warmth.

But the play of incessant lightning soon renders our position perilous.

"Anzano!" (I am leaning over him. I can scarcely hear my own voice and am drenched by the driving rain.)

"Come into the house! The storm is increasing!"

I seem to be addressing a corpse.

"You here!" he says at last, in a feeble voice, gazing up at me with a glance of transient recognition. "You here! Sigismund is gone and——" He cannot bring himself to pronounce Lela's name.

"I thought you were gone also! Is it not best that I should meet my fate alone?"

"What fate, Anzano? For the love of God, dismiss these fancies. We are all under the mercy of God. Let your old friend comfort you!"

He shakes his head. A faint smile passes for an instant over his face. He presses my hand, then lets it fall, as if from henceforth every link between us is severed.

"I thank you, Lucius! As a dying man I thank you. The time is short; my earthly probation is ended. Oh, that death could come to me without the horror of that form!"

A momentary lull has permitted me to hear these words. The next instant, the storm reaches its climax. An awful clap of thunder crashes over the house. A dense cloud of dust and earth whirls in the air. A terrific clatter strikes upon the ear, as if shields of brass have fallen upon a floor of iron.

A thunderbolt has fallen. Where? I can see nothing.

But for the lightning, which plays around, we should be plunged in absolute darkness.

I spring to my feet. I rush to Anzano, and by sheer force drag him into the hall,

Again the thunder booms and rattles. Again the wind shrieks and howls, then, crashing through the trees, screams itself hoarse among the rocks, detaching loose stones and fragments, that roll down with horrific din.

A heart rending cry from the Marquis rises shrill above the roar.

"I see it! I see it! That horrid wound! Hide it —hide it! I know it! On the neck, under the falling hair! He did it! And the blood ran down over the rich dress in which he clothed you—to meet his eye —the fiend! Gaze not on me with those steely orbs! I tried to kill her! It was too late; she is Sigismund's wife! My life" (Here he raises his hands in agonised supplication) "My life for hers! I can but give my life!—"

"Anzano!" I shout into his ear, drawing him backwards—"There is nothing—nothing."

"Nothing!" he screams, tearing himself from my grasp, and pointing with raised arms into the darkened hall, fitfully visible in the quickly recurring lightning. Nothing, when she stands there—opening those long closed wounds! Nothing! Ha-ha-ha!"

It is the laughter of frenzy! As the hoarse shout dies away in long-drawn echoes, he staggers to his feet.

The next moment he lies prostrate on the floor.

Was it death—or was it a death-like swoon? I bore him into his ancestral hall, and laid him on the marble pavement. As I propped up his head against the wall, I perceived that I had accidentally placed

him under the emblazoned coat of arms of the Gonzagos. The Cardinal's red hat, buffeted by the wind,
swayed over him.

I tore at the first bell I could find. Its deep note
blended with the tempest like an articulate tongue.
(My imagination was so wrought upon that the simplest
details came to me fraught with the weight of a mystic
significance.)

From one of the sculptured doors opening into the
hall, appeared Narcissus, followed by the major-domo.
With a silent gesture, I showed them where their
master lay. The major-domo wrung his hands, Narcissus, not cheerful now, but ready-witted and active
knelt down beside him.

"What is to be done?" I asked, while the man
busied himself in unfastening his master's cravat and
shirt collar.

"Leave him to me, signore, leave him to me—I
understand his Excellency. He has swooned before."

"Is Don Antonio in the house?"

"No," answered the major-domo, coming to the
assistance of Narcissus, whose light fingers seemed
everywhere at once.

Together the two servants raised him in their
arms. I could not bear to look at his death-like face.

"We will take him to his own room, Excellency,"
said Narcissus. "It is on the ground floor."

I made a motion to follow them.

"His Excellency will excuse my saying that the
noble marquis had better be left to me alone," re-
marked Narcissus. "This is a worse swoon than usual.
It is always difficult to deal with him when he first
comes to. Whatever subject was uppermost in his

mind when he became insensible is sure to remain. I know what to do. He may pass into a deep sleep," added he, looking into his master's glassy eyes, so fixed and corpse-like. (Alas! those eyes haunt me while I write, terrible witnesses of the troubled soul within.)

"A deep sleep will be best of all," continued the undaunted Narcissus. "*I must* be alone with him, or he may do himself some injury."

"And you, Narcissus?" I asked, "have you no fear?"

"None in the world, Excellency." Here a gleam of his natural cheerfulness reappeared. "Only leave the Marquis to me; I understand him."

Something of Narcissus' hopefulness penetrated even to me. With a feeling of infinite relief, I saw my poor friend borne into his room, and placed on a couch.

"If the Marquis asks for me when he revives," I said, "call me at once. I shall not be far off."

I left the room, closing the door carefully after me. As I did so, I noticed that Narcissus opened both the sashes of the windows, raised but a few inches above the level of the garden, in order to admit the air.

*   *   *   *   *   *

The violence of the storm had abated. Abundant rain was falling, and although the thunder had not altogether ceased, it was gradually dying away, as it had come, among the depths of distant mountains. The wind too, had ceased.

The stillness of the house was appalling. Every little crack in the wood-work, the buzz of a fly, the hum of a mosquito, multiplied itself infinitely.

My ears seemed full of noises; the effect, probably, of the turmoil of the recent tornado. Still, I could have believed that there was a muttering of voices from behind the panels, and that shadowy footsteps passed upon the stairs, stopping when I stopped, and moving when I moved.

From remote parts of the house seemed to issue, indistinctly indeed, but still audibly, low wails, mixed up with the rattling of windows, and the various draughts and currents driving into that spacious mansion, blending confusedly in my brain, until I could believe that within, as well as without, that forest domain, there hung an atmosphere peculiar to itself—with no affinity to the pure air of Heaven, but which had reeked up from the blackness of those contorted trees—like a pestilent vapour.

All this time I was slowly ascending the flight of stairs that I had first mounted in company with my friend. The upper portion was lost in the shadows of the waning day.

Without explaining what actuated me, I find myself stopping on the landing of the first floor, and turning the handle of the door leading to the state rooms.

I hurry past the spot where I knew the portrait of the Cardinal was hung (everything connected with that man seemed fraught with some horrible significance), and find myself within the saloon where I had first seen Lela.

Midway, on the brilliant scagliola floor, I pause to ask myself "Why had I come?" At the same moment, my eye falls on the thick tapestry hangings of the door before which the Marquis had placed himself, forbidding me to proceed.

Putting aside those hangings, I stand in a vaulted hall of majestic proportions; a few scattered rays of reddened light penetrate through the heavy draperies of a lofty range of windows, repeating themselves upon a polished floor.

At the first glance, the walls seem to me lined with gold. Every nick and granny filled with glittering weapons—swords, daggers, sabres, shields and knives, set with inestimable jewels; Eastern ornaments in rude barbaric chasings; Venetian filigree, fine as from silken looms; Gothic drinking bowls; pokuls dazzling with sapphires and diamonds; cups of jade and chrysoprase; Indian monsters with jewelled eyes; idols from Egypt.

Pennons and banners hang suspended from the solid beams of the ceiling—some tattered and soiled with shot and smoke—others new and many-coloured; under each, emblazoned shields and coronets and mitres, ablaze with gems.

My eyes, still struggling to penetrate into the remoter recesses of the space, fall upon quaint patterns of oriental tapestry, clothing the lower walls, up to the marvellous carving of a gigantic screen, dividing a sanctum sanctorum from the lower hall. Before the screen stands a heavy panelled table—around, twelve antique chairs ranged in exact order, awaiting—as it seemed—the dignified forms of twelve richly robed councillors.

Standing there, I feel that I breathe the monumental atmosphere of the past; and that some memorial will present itself to me, to reveal for what purpose this historic chamber was designed.

My instinct does not deceive me.

Advancing cautiously along the slippery floor, my eyes gradually penetrate the dark shadows within the screen; I behold a lofty canopy of purple velvet, from which hang massive fringes and tassels of pearls and gold; the inside wrought in a gorgeous confusion of cyphers, coats of arms and arabesques, repeated in the glowing tints of many-hued needlework. An eastern carpet lies before an estrade raised on steps, and an outer railing guards the sacred space.

These are but accessories, to which I pay only passing attention. As my eyes grow more familiar with the uncertain light, they concentrate themselves on a golden chair, superbly chased, placed on the estrade.

Upon it sits a life-sized figure! Some horrible familiarity of outline and aspect, thrill through me as I gaze.

Where have I seen that florid face? Those full, black, prominent eyes? Those proud, repulsive features?

At length the truth bursts upon me. It is the effigy of Cardinal Gonzago!

A deep red collar hangs over a tunic of whitest lace; the heavy folds of the ensanguined robe drape round him like blood; on his head is a scarlet hat, and in his jewelled finger he clasps a ring!

*　　*　　*　　*　　*

I rush from that foul presence, I know not whither; my feet carry me into the open air. Under the free arch of Heaven I breathe again.

Without, all is calm. A rising mist, perfumed by the scent of herbs and flowers, floats around me. Each blade of grass, every leaf and twig—even the gravel on the path, glitters into gems. How sweetly blows the cool breeze of evening after the storm! How softly the pale blue of the heavens gilds itself into the warm glow of sunset!

I follow the broad avenue, bordered by the ilex-cut hedges and the tall statues, along which Lela and Sigismund had so lately passed, and descend into the darkening glades of the solemn ilex-woods. The funereal foliage gathers over my head—the twisted boughs close in a leafy labyrinth above. Some trees, uprooted by the storm, have fallen across the road; others thrust themselves upwards in pollarded knots, from which a number of small shoots issue, pointing as with extended fingers.

Looking at these ilex-woods thus, by daylight, there is a pathetic humanity about them, an appealing sorrow, absolutely appalling.

The black roots, like overstrained muscles, rise up, dragging the rocky soil into ridges and furrows, and great mossy stones are strewn about, turning the surface of the ground into the roughness of a graveyard.

Glad once more to feel the elasticity of my limbs, I step briskly along the terraced road, when a huge white object half embedded in the earth, arrests me.

I stoop to examine it. It is the battered head of the Satyr—the horns and shaggy hair uppermost! The gaping mouth, the blackened cavities for eyes, the lines which had once been nose and lips, grin up at me with a contorted leer.

Both the head and the severed neck are hollow.

Doubtless, during the storm, it had been wrenched from the trunk, and had fallen at the moment I noted that tremendous din.

When the thunderbolt fell, it had struck the Satyr!

Now I am within the mystic circle of the trees—the scene of Gigia's capture—of Lela's innocent incantations! It is evident that the storm has spent its utmost fury on this particular spot. The ground is strewn with rent-off branches—and many entire trees, torn up by the roots, lie encumbering the open space.

One rotten, withered ilex, twisting aloft fantastic boughs, rests across the marble fluting of the pedestal; some dry fragments have fallen from it and crumble on the earth, like bones. On the deep-red earth lies a dark, huddled-up heap. My eye travels quickly over it.

I stand riveted, in breathless horror! Great God! It is the body of Gonzago! His rigid face turned to the sky—his glazed eye meeting mine with a scowl.

Already the jaw had fallen, leaving deep hollows in the thin, white cheeks, and the prominent eyebrows add terror to the pupils of the widely distended eyes.

He lies within the folds of a dark mantle—his arms outstretched, as if death had struck him in the act of lifting them upwards.

In his hand, clutched with the grip of death, are a few threads of yellow hair. As I touch them, they shrivel and drop into a pale dust.

Had that haunting Presence decoyed him under the shadow of the Satyr to die? Or, had he wandered down alone, and been seized with another swoon, from which he had passed into death without awakening? Who can tell?

I carefully examine his body. There is no indication of violence—none, save two small purple marks (such as the pressure of two fingers might cause), low down in the throat, just over the wind-pipe.

I dare not ask myself what these marks betoken. Had he not told me of another life — that of his affianced bride, Gemma Malvoti—passing away like this, leaving behind, evidence similar, and as inexplicable? *"A life for a life,"* he had said—not Lela's, but his own.

The drops of sweat gather on my brow, as I gaze down at him. Presently, those drops pour down, like rain, over my face. I have to cling to the nearest tree, or I, too, should fall prostrate, over the dead body of my friend.

EPILOGUE.

THAT night we laid him in his last rest, where he had fallen, within the mystic circle of the ilex-trees.

No consecrated soil was permitted to receive the mortal remains of one of the noblest beings God ever created.

Don Antonio would hear of no compromise on the point of burial.

The Marquis Gonzago had died without the sacraments; that was enough for him. If his death were natural, if it were self-inflicted, or if some diabolical agency had hastened it, mattered not to the ecclesiastic.

He, whose whole misguided existence had been an heroic sacrifice for others, was condemned to the burial of a dog! While I write these words—long after the events occurred—tears blind my eyes. My poor Anzano!

It was as I surmised. Narcissus left his master for a brief space—as he supposed, in a deep and tranquil sleep.

When he returned, he was gone. He had escaped by the open window. Either his sleep had been feigned, and his troubled spirit had voluntarily driven him to seek the evil shadow of the Satyr, where he had suddenly fallen down and died, or he had been decoyed by some Satanic influence to a silent and horrible death.

Who can say?

He is gone, and I am left to mourn him.

*   *   *   *   *

Sigismund and Lela live in the Gonzago Palazzo, at Siena. An heir has been born to the ancient name, within the ancestral walls. Lela, in her fantastic gratitude, has named the child after me and my dead friend. It is fortunate that I possess a Latinised appellation to place beside so grandiose a patronymic of classic Italy. Had it been otherwise, I should never have consented to this arrangement.

Anzano, Lucius is not so bad after all.

We are still to have some play upon these names when the next little stranger appears.

Sigismund submits to all this; pulling at his silky beard with a smile. Lela will never lose the nymph-like charm which her bringing-up in the woods imparted to her. She will never alter her mind about Sigismund, who is, if possible, handsomer and certainly more majestic than ever, now that the honours of his house have fallen upon him.

I am under a solemn promise to visit them every year in the season of the "*villeggiatura*," when the grapes are ripe, and the summer heat is modified. But I do not always keep my word.

A magnificent cenotaph has been erected by Sigismund over his brother's grave. People come from far and wide to visit it. Every vestige of the ill-omened statue of the Satyr is swept away. The terraced road winds the forest as before, but that mystic circle of ilex-trees, that waved over the marble seat where the dead mother and her unknown child sat weaving garlands, has disappeared, and a funereal garden been planted in its stead.

Once a year, Sigismund and Lela visit Sant'
Agata, on the anniversary of Anzano's death, to lay
fresh flowers on his lonely tomb. On the richly carved
marble, setting forth his age and his honours, Sigismund has, at my suggestion, had graven Anzano's
favourite quotation from the Œdipus Tyrannus of
Sophocles:—

"Pronounce no mortal happy, until he has passed
the boundary of life, untouched by suffering."

No one, since Gonzago's death, inhabits the villa.
Even Lela has bid a final farewell to her friends the
ilex-trees; but she affirms that their spirit still
follows her.

I hear a voice asking after my nephew Frederick
Stanley.

"Thank you, whoever you are." Frederick was so
disgusted with his visit to Italy, that no spot is too
cold, no coast too arid, to suit his fancy. If he could
only spend his vacations at the North Pole, he would
be perfectly content.

"No infernal mysteries there, uncle Lucius," he
says. "All plain sailing and above board."

Recent explorations would suggest that plain sailing and the North Pole are hardly synonymous. But
closeness of reasoning was never a characteristic of my
impressionable nephew.

THE END.

PRINTING OFFICE OF THE PUBLISHER.